GUARDIANS

Book One of the Guardians Series

J.L. Dumais

GUARDIANS

ISBN: 978-1-77069-184-1

Printed in Canada

Word Alive Press
131 Cordite Road, Winnipeg, MB R3W 1S1
www.wordalivepress.ca

Library and Archives Canada Cataloguing in Publication

Dumais, J. L., 1978-
    Guardians / J.L. Dumais.

ISBN 978-1-77069-184-1

    I. Title.

PS8607.U4423G83 2010   C813'.6   C2010-907463-7

Russian Transliteration

Russian transliteration is used to make it possible to write Russian with a regular keyboard.

Transliterated Russian phrases used in *Guardians* and their meanings are:

"*Zdravstvuite.*"	"Hello."
"*Kak Dela?*"	"How are you?"
"*U menja dela horosho.*"	"I'm fine."
"*Moja Dorogaja.*"	"My dear."

Russian Transliteration taken with permission from the website www.russian-translation-pros.com.

DEDICATION

To my parents, who have always backed me in any endeavour and who give everything, even when it hurts. Thank you.

To my brother James and to my children, Mackenzie and John, who bless my every day. I love you all so much.

ACKNOWLEDGEMENTS

First, I would like to thank my editor and the staff of Word Alive Press for making my dream a reality and for their great service.

I would also like to thank my family and friends for their support and prayers.

Next, I would like to thank my cousin, Sheri Falconer, for her advice.

Lastly, thank you to the customer service staff from Ford for their prompt, helpful responses and to Russian Translation Pros for granting me permission to use content from their website.

INTRODUCTION

Heaven

Eighteen Billion Years Ago

DURING THE REBELLION, lightning ricocheted from the palace roof to gray clouds which were being consumed by onyx black. The Creator's city shook, vibrated, and glowed as twelve-foot Archangels threw blinding supernatural energy at each other and at smaller angels who felled massive elm trees when their spirit forms collided with nature. Heaven's surface vibrated constantly, causing the streets to tear apart and the mansions to groan. Flashes of light danced as eight- and ten-foot angels sliced broadsword blades, making a cacophony of clashing sounds which ricocheted against the pearl gates and walls. When roars and shrieks heaved the clear waters of a massive lake, glittering multi-coloured fish vanished from the tumultuous surface.

Terrified Monarch butterflies fled into the trees when rose and lily clusters were destroyed from angelic broadswords. Severed flower petals, leaves, fractured stems, and branches lay on the ground during the struggle. Doves and bluebirds perched together like lovebirds, cowering inside the leaves of the monstrous oak trees as injured angels and glowing blades lay on the golden streets. Pieces of amethyst, emerald, and pearl lay on the grass near the outside wall of Heaven. Jagged fissures marred the mansions as angels launched into their walls.

Eventually, the rebels reached the palace. An eight-foot angel stood beside God.

"My Lord, you should have had an Archangel beside you," the humble angel stated.

"I desired my most loyal angel to be here. I can destroy the rebels with a snap of my fingers. Come, Vincent," God said, walking toward the door.

The Creator's glow was blinding and the angel stalked beside him. Then God moved his finger slightly and the huge throne room doors opened. The marble portals were never closed, but when the rebellion began Archangels had sealed the doors. One million loyal Archangels surrounded God and Vincent as they sauntered up to the main palace portals. The colossal doors swung open and the tallest, handsomest, proudest, and most evil angelic creature stood outside. Lucifer's narrowed eyes were golden, his head was tilted upward, and his blond hair splayed away from his face. Defiance and anger drifted from his spirit form. Vincent trembled slightly when the huge angel looked at him.

"Traitor!" the rebellious being hissed.

A hank of blond hair dropped over Vincent's forehead. The loyal angel stared back and perceived his own golden eyes glow as he drew his broadsword. "What's wrong with you?" he yelled.

Lucifer laughed. "You want to kill me?"

Vincent launched his sword, but the Archangel spun and the blade cut through another rebel. Vincent was shocked and felt distress tormenting his spirit form from having hit a friend.

"Lucas!" he exclaimed as another Archangel fell. Instinctively, Vincent almost glided toward his friend but God used spirit energy to keep him in place. The blond angel was thankful because he knew Lucifer would have decapitated him.

Lucifer's rebels and the Creator's loyal angels fought swiftly. Vincent desperately wanted his sword, so he crouched and scooted over to Lucas' supine form, whose golden eyes glared at him.

"I'm sorry, Lucas. Why did you become a rebel angel?" Vincent asked. Tears came to his eyes and his chest hurt as he watched his friend compassionately.

"God is controlling and Lucifer promised me a high rank," Lucas answered.

"God is not controlling," Vincent protested and tried to remove his sword, but Lucas said he would do it. Suddenly an excruciating wound in his back made Vincent vault and turn.

"Pathetic angel!" Lucifer cried contemptuously, his golden eyes emitting hatred. The Archangel's broadsword was raised to Vincent's chest. "Compassion weakens you. Angels are powerful and beautiful. That is what we should be!"

Vincent regarded Lucas, who had ousted the broadsword. All at once, the fallen angel moaned and moved, sliding the sword to Vincent, who nimbly grabbed the weapon.

Vincent and Lucifer swerved, sliced, and evaded each other. Their broadswords were the only swords moving throughout Heaven. All the spirits watched when Lucifer tried to decapitate Vincent, but the shorter, quick spirit soared into the air. The rebellious angel hissed and flew up at Vincent, who spun to the left. Vincent's blond hair blew into his golden eyes as he rotated. Their blades clashed again as they flew over Heaven, spirit energy racing through their wings.

Suddenly, Lucifer sliced at Vincent's right arm. Vincent hissed, noticing golden blood contaminating his white robe. The pain burned, but he was determined to fight for the Creator. Laughing, Lucifer created ripples and vibrations through the clear lake and in the air. While the Archangel laughed, Vincent struck his enemy's shoulder. Lucifer's eyes blasted angry, radiant light and he pointed his broadsword at

Vincent's chest. All at once, a sonic boom threw the rebellious angels over the wall which formed the edge of Heaven.

As the rebellious angels reached the top of the wall, they transformed into ugly, onyx creatures with long nails, horns, scales, wings, and hairy bodies. A terrible smell drifted into the nostrils of all the loyal angels. God raised his hand and hunks of fiery stones hailed from clouds encircling the city.

Vincent landed and lay in front of God. "My Master, thank you. Praise you, God. You are Holy!"

"My loyal angel, I have good things for you," the Creator answered.

CHAPTER ONE

Smithington, Ontario, Canada

IT WAS FEBRUARY and sometime during the night. It was really dark and I heard the wind teasing the cedar trees outside our sprawling, two-and-a-half-storey home. I didn't know what time it was. Promptly, I pulled down the flannel granny nightgown that had ridden up to my thighs in the night and attempted to slide across the polar fleece sheets on my twin-sized bed.

I handled the brass knob of my door and wisped down the hall to my parents' room. Their door was open a bit, like usual. I could very easily see the large digital green numbers of their alarm clock, which blatantly signalled 3:42 a.m.

Then I looked across to my father and noted that he was sitting up.

"Dad," I whispered, wanting to talk with him. I extended my right arm to reach him, but there wasn't anything there. In fact, my father was still lying on his side, sleeping. My eyes widened as my pulse raced. Trembling, I took a deep breath and quickly walked out of the room.

Seven Years Later

It was afternoon. I had worked the nightshift at Cedarwood Retirement Lodge the night before. Now I was trying to get some sleep. As I faced the wall, I sensed potent hate at my back. *Oh no, a demon!* I shivered and all the tiny hairs on my body rose. It was interesting to sense the feelings of others, beings who I couldn't see but feel. Once in a while, I was aware of spirit disgust, but on this occasion, due to the intense hate, I felt that the spectre wanted to murder me.

What am I supposed to do now? I wondered.

"Uhh!" I groaned. I rolled over on the flowered cotton sheet but didn't see any creatures; nonetheless, I glared. The bothersome being had woken me up!

Cedarwood Retirement Lodge

In June, over supper one day, I was walking in the seniors' dining room with a gray-wheeled cart that held tea, hot water, and coffee carafes.

"Tori!" Dorothy Witzel called. Shocked, I looked at the snowy-haired woman behind me.

Oh no! I forgot to bring tea and coffee to her table.

Amelia Roeder, at the last table, clasped her cup eagerly and coughed as she waited for me to deliver her tea. Embarrassed, I jaunted over quickly while my long, thick ponytail teased my back.

"I'm sorry," I murmured.

The four residents smiled at me. Dorothy liked tea, as did Mildred Brubacher, who moved her burgundy-coloured walker so I could get near her mug. Grey-haired Thomas Elder and robust Clancy Tomkins, on the other hand, relished coffee.

"Did you just get married, or engaged maybe?" Clancy asked mischievously while Thomas adjusted his glasses.

My eyebrows rose in surprise. "No."

"You seem scatterbrained today," he declared.

"I didn't sleep enough last night," I announced as I moved the pink, plastic-wheeled cart and smiled at another table of seniors.

A full-proportioned woman caressed her multi-coloured medallion necklace and asked, "How is your mother?"

"Good."

"Did your brother finish his engineering program yet?" another woman questioned, her thin, brown-speckled fingers holding the handle of her mug. Her name was Olive.

"No, Olive," I replied. "He has one year left."

At that moment, two younger girls who worked in the kitchen quickly lowered porcelain plates with boiled potatoes, asparagus, and ribs onto the burgundy linen surface so that the residents could eat.

At eight o'clock, after I finished bathing two residents, I stood up on a chair to check Clancy Tomkins' closet for spoiled food, which he sometimes shoved onto the top shelf. On one occasion, Clancy had hidden an orange in his closet. By the time I found it, the skin was covered with soft white and green mould.

I slid my fingers carefully across the top shelf instead of blindly brushing them. Suddenly, I lost my balance. As I fell, I felt a warm pressure push me from behind, stopping me from landing on the thick blue carpet.

"Thank you," I whispered to God. I took a long breath and saw that there was a mould-encrusted peanut butter sandwich on the shelf.

I grabbed the decaying sandwich and jumped off the chair.

*   *   *   *

At 8:30, my human lifted her right arm and pulled the drapes shut in Room 130. I regarded Tori as she sat on Amelia Roeder's bed. The elderly woman's Latino Guardian Angel, Ricardo, stared at Tori and Amelia. Tori frowned at the old woman; I was surprised, as she was normally so kind with her patients.

Tori leaned closer to the plump woman. "There's crackling in your chest," she announced.

Ricardo walked closer and touched Amelia's skin. Amelia didn't sense him, but Tori looked to the right for a moment as if she did.

Tori carefully gripped the woman's hand. "I need to get Michelle."

"I'm fine. Victoria, may I have some water?" Amelia asked.

Tori studied the older woman and brushed her wrinkled wrist. "Are you okay, Amelia?"

"Yes. May I have some water?"

"Sure." Tori's supple form stood and gracefully walked into her washroom. As soon as she stepped onto the bathroom linoleum, I heard the tap running. When my compassionate human came out, she gave Amelia the plastic cup.

"You girls are so good," Amelia stated.

Tori laughed a little. "It's no problem."

Amelia stared at Tori. "You are patient."

"It doesn't take much with you."

The Creator, my Lord, was friends with humans, so I needed to be friends with them, too. The only human I wanted to reveal myself to was Tori. I wanted her friendship and desired to interact with her. I knew that loving humans romantically was forbidden. Most angels didn't even agree that it was a good idea to be friends with humans. Restlessness consumed me, because in six thousand years I had never been able to talk to one of my human charges. Continually I protected them until God said, "Step back." Tori was different, though; she was like a Guardian at work.

Abruptly, Amelia gasped and Tori regarded her ashen face. Ricardo was glowing and I saw his golden spirit energy hurl into his wings. My forehead wrinkled as I realized that Amelia was going to die even though I hadn't seen a Messenger Angel tell Ricardo to end his protection.

"Did God ask you to step back?" I asked Ricardo, shocked.

Haunting graveness spun in the golden Guardian's eyes. "Yes, Vincent," Ricardo answered.

"But I didn't see a Messenger just now. Have the rules changed? Messengers always inform us to step back."

"He was here before your human came," Ricardo said. "He told me to step back when Amelia started having trouble breathing."

Ricardo's supernatural form was trembling. He had been guarding Amelia for eighty-six years. Tori moved the cotton sheet off Amelia's legs and saw that they were swollen. She pushed on Amelia's left leg and the finger caused an indent. Amelia started coughing fiercely. As soon as Amelia coughed, Tori's jaw dropped.

"I'll get Michelle!" Tori called and ran out the doorway. I followed her while she fled to the medication room. Michelle, a pretty red-haired nurse, observed Tori running.

"No running," the nurse scolded.

"Amelia's in congestive heart failure!"

*   *   *   *

At eleven o'clock that night, I walked out into the retirement home parking lot. Suddenly I felt goose bumps on my arms. I felt the tickle of muscles and chills scooting down my back, making me stop. I was near the front porch and quickly looked around. To get to my car, I needed to walk around the kitchen area, dumpsters, and recycling containers. The evening staff usually moved their cars to the front wheelchair parking spots before dusk, but because of Amelia's emergency I had forgotten.

It was a new moon, so the sky was dark and my car was too far away. The light in the parking lot was burnt out, so I felt anxious. Suddenly, a clammy, grimy hand gripped my arm.

"Help!" I screamed.

I grappled with a warm body but was also aware of a dark shape that seemed to be observing us. *Is that a demon?* I wondered. While I was fighting my attacker, I regarded the onyx shape and sensed hate emanating from it, which made my body tremble. The man I grappled with handled a rusty dagger and desired to kill me.

I panicked. A smelly, sinewy hand attempted to clamp itself over my mouth, but I kicked the man in the knee. All at once, the parking lot was filled with light. Swearing, the man I was fighting escaped and I fell on the asphalt, feeling sharp pain as my tailbone hit the pavement.

Examining the bright light, I gasped in awe. My jaw fell, as I found myself staring at an angel.

"Go!" it commanded.

I frowned and gazed to my right side where the dark observer stood defiantly. Yellow vapours blossomed from scaly, supernatural onyx skin and twisted with orange and red sparks. Its arrogant red eyes smouldered from the darkness, causing the angel to pull his weapon, an iridescent broad sword. The black creature vacated the parking lot.

After the demon left, I stared at the monstrous luminescent being in front of me. His radiant face was human and his golden eyes communicated peace. I was awed. My lips parted, because he was so stunning. He was my Guardian, I realized, and he wanted me to give up my human fear. Kindness, well-being, and positive thoughts surrounded him like a mist.

"Are you okay, Tori?" he asked kindly. I could feel compassionate energy when he pulled me up, but I couldn't stand on my own. My teeth clacked together furiously and my body trembled.

"Help," I whispered, my body betraying me. As I regarded the angel's glowing eyes, he picked me up and carried me back toward the retirement home.

"I'm proud of you, Tori," he murmured, which caused me some confusion. I felt warm supernatural energy travel through my uniform.

When the angel brought me into Cedarwood, Kristy, the night nurse, gawked at me and the creature who was hauling me. "Is this a new boyfriend, Tori?" she asked.

"No. He saved me. There was a mugger in the parking lot."

Kristy gasped as the angel set me down.

"Thank you," I said, looking up at him. I frowned, because it wasn't a spirit but a handsome man. He had blond hair and blue eyes, and there was a cleft in his chin. My champion was the same height as my brother William and looked incredibly muscular. He smiled at me.

"Where is your flashlight?" I asked.

His left eyebrow rose. "Flashlight?"

I turned on my heel and faced Kristy. "I'll call the police," she declared. Her black hair swirled as she sauntered to the phone.

Sometime later, I called my mom and dad and told them I was staying put at Cedarwood until I talked to the police about the mugger.

The police officers arrived twenty minutes later and I told them what had happened. To be honest, I didn't tell them that there had been a black spirit with red eyes watching the assault, and I also didn't tell them that the being who'd rescued me was an angel.

At 11:30, my parents came to Cedarwood. Mom drove me home and Dad followed behind us in my blue Mustang. The angel left, which disappointed me. By 12:30, I was in my room with hot chocolate.

"Are you here?" I called into the air. "I want to talk with you. You pulled a fast one on me."

All at once, someone laughed. Naturally, I looked around my room with worry, thinking perhaps that the black creature had returned. Grinning, the angel appeared beside me and sat on my couch.

"Sorry, Tori," he said.

"Who are you?"

"What you observed in the retirement home parking lot was reality," he explained. "I am your Guardian Angel. My name is Vincent."

"But angels don't show themselves to human beings," I protested. "You were bright at first, but now you look like a man."

"We have a human form as well. It was better for you that I took human form."

I frowned. "You're in human form now, aren't you?"

"Yes. Come here, Tori."

I swallowed, then glided over and carefully slid my fingers over his shoulder. I felt butterflies in my stomach. Wow! An angel was allowing me the liberty to touch him.

"Take angel form, please," I murmured. "I want to touch your wings."

All of a sudden, an eight-foot-tall being sat on my couch with a broadsword pointed forward. Vincent's shoulder radiated heat.

"You're warm," I announced, regarding his blue eyes. "I felt heat outside when you carried me."

Vincent smiled kindly. "Both my angel form and human form radiate heat, but especially the angel form."

I was astonished and awed. His wings were iridescent and soft, but I could put my hand through them. When I did, my fingers tingled. "My fingers are tingling, but it doesn't hurt. What is that, Vincent?"

"Spirit energy," he answered calmly, observing me.

"Wow. You're amazing," I whispered. Intrigue consumed me when I looked at the broadsword sheath.

"Can I hold your sword?" I asked.

He looked at me intensely. "No. You will hurt yourself."

Disappointment twisted inside me. "Oh," I murmured. His eyes glowed.

He was a bit scary when his eyes penetrated mine. Abruptly, he took human form and I almost fell on the hardwood floor. Fortunately, he captured my right wrist.

"Careful, Tori."

"Thanks. That black shape. What was it and why was it there?" I asked.

"It was a demon, Tori, and it was encouraging the man to hurt you."

"Why?"

"Because God loves you," Vincent replied. "He loves all humans."

"How long have you been guarding me?"

"Since you were conceived."

"Have you always been with me, all the time?"

"Sometimes I have to go on missions," he answered. "Other times I go to Heaven, but when I do one of the other angels in the house watches you for me, in addition to his own responsibility."

"Responsibility?" I asked, interested.

"Humans are our responsibilities. You are delicate."

"Do angels grumble when they have to serve as Guardian Angels?"

"No. We are God's servants," Vincent answered softly.

"Vincent, do angels like guarding humans? Do you like people?"

"We don't enjoy looking after humans when we have to step back," he stated. "Because humans are alive and on earth, sometimes bad things happen that we are not able or not allowed to stop. When someone makes a wrong choice, we can't stop the consequences, but sometimes we can lessen them."

I breathed in quickly. I wanted him to stay and talk some more. I was used to sensing demons, but I had never imagined I was going to talk to my own gorgeous Guardian Angel. I was astounded that he had revealed himself when I called.

"Do you want some hot chocolate?" I queried.

Golden energy seemed to radiate through his blue eyes as he smiled. "No thanks. However, I might change my mind come autumn."

"Thank you, Vincent, for saving me. Will you show yourself again?" I asked.

"Maybe. Go to sleep, Tori. Have peace. I will guard you."

* * * *

The next morning, I sensed Vincent. I shivered nervously, moulding my cotton sheet and comforter by the wall. I had never sensed him before but I realized that Vincent had protected me the previous evening while I was in Clancy's room—when I had nearly fallen from the chair. Now, I quickly clamoured into my walk-in closet. As soon as I walked to my dresser, I sensed him again.

"Good morning," I said, turning to look into my bedroom and grasping my hairbrush. Suddenly, my hand felt warm. He didn't appear. "Vincent, I'm sensitive. I saw an angel sitting on my dad when I was fourteen, and I felt a demon last night in the parking lot. You're my Guardian Angel. Please don't tease."

I felt spirit warmth behind me. "Tori, give me your brush," Vincent said.

"Why? You want to stand behind me and brush my hair?"

"Your hair is exquisite," he whispered.

I trembled when the Guardian touched my tresses. As soon as my body vibrated, the spirit put his fingers on my back and the warmth caused me to stop. I looked into the mirror. The gorgeous being's eyes were glowing as he gently brushed my locks; he seemed mesmerized.

Vincent lifted a brunette tress with blond streaks and appeared awed. "I have never touched human hair. Did it hurt when the hairdresser put foils in your hair?"

"No," I replied. Suddenly, I sensed terseness. Vincent looked behind him and his human form began to glow. The tress fell on my shoulder as he vanished. Disappointment and anxiety twisted together inside me.

Why did he leave?

* * * *

As I held her blond and brunette strands of hair in my fingers, I sensed irritation and tense spirit energy behind me. Annoyance swirled, because I wanted to interact with my human. Then I felt my human body taking spirit form and, of course, I began to glow. Before I vanished,

I regarded the new arrival behind me. My human form disappeared when I saw who it was.

Michael, the angel assigned to protect Tori's mother Marianne, was glowering at me. "What are you doing?" Michael asked.

"She called me."

"Angels get exiled for a hundred years in Israel if they fall in love with a human," he reminded me. Chestnut-haired Michael had been the very first Guardian. Six thousand years ago, he had protected Adam. I had been the second Guardian, taking care of Eve.

"I'm not in love with her," I snapped.

Michael crossed his forearms and his left eyebrow rose sardonically. "However, you're attracted to your human."

"You don't understand."

"She's a good human, Vincent. The Creator is fond of her and she's beautiful. Moreover, you have decent taste. Unfortunately, humans are forbidden... you'll risk becoming a demon if you let this go any further. You can't show yourself to her anymore." Michael's tone was sanctimonious as spirit energy flashed and ricocheted into his open wings.

I crossed my arms and glowered at my friend, my radiance intensifying. "I'm not going to turn into a demon."

Suddenly, Michael's golden eyes leaked compassion and he disappeared.

CHAPTER TWO

IT WAS JUNE 14, my twenty-first birthday. I had stayed up until midnight the night before to see my twenty-second year begin. My girlfriends from the practical nursing program at college were coming to my party that evening with their boyfriends. I had also recently met a stunning, sable-haired guy named Kevin, and he was attending. To be honest, I wouldn't have told my friends to bring their boyfriends if I wasn't going out with Kevin, because that would have made me uncomfortable.

Kevin had a 1987 Mustang that he'd put a 351-cubic-inch motor in. He raced in Smithington. Occasionally, my brother Will raced at the track with his red muscle car, too. In fact, Kevin had beat him three weeks ago. I had been astounded when he didn't smirk at my brother; instead, they just shook hands. Later, Kevin bought us frozen yogurt.

My white-lacquered door hovered open this morning. Someone who was agile but loud was crawling across my carpet. I slid on my cotton sheet to the side of the bed and glared into my brother William's grey-blue eyes.

"Happy birthday, Tori," he said with a laugh. I tried to jump on him, but he crawled to the door and his tall muscular form fled away.

I was slumped on the floor with a sore bum when I heard Vincent laughing next to my French doors. I looked over at him. A twinge of sadness swirled through my chest at the thought of my Guardian Angel ridiculing me. Vincent hadn't appeared since brushing my hair, but I sensed him every day. He quickly walked over to me and I saw empathy in his blue eyes.

"Sorry, Tori," he whispered. He lifted me in his arms. "Happy birthday."

I smiled at him when he let my feet back down onto the carpet. "Thank you."

"Are you hurt?" Vincent asked quietly, his forehead wrinkling.

"No. Are you going to come to my birthday party in human form?"

He grinned. "I'll come."

* * * *

That evening, I strolled onto our patio and brushed my jean shorts as a delicate breeze tickled my legs. Blue LED lights decorated the property of our sprawling ninety-eight-year-old house. I adjusted my rhinestone hairband and gazed around the backyard. I didn't see any Guardians.

"Happy birthday!" my cousin Janessa said, pushing her long hair behind her ears.

Her sister Karen walked over and smiled. "Happy Birthday, Tori."

"Thanks. It's good to see you guys." I hugged my cousins. "Where are you working this summer, Karen?"

Before Karen could answer, my friends from the practical nursing program arrived.

"Happy birthday, girl!" Kristen and Cindy called. I grinned at each of them in turn.

Statuesque and African American, Cindy and my petite half-Asian friend Kristen hugged me. Kristen appeared taller tonight, so I looked down and saw her silver stiletto heels.

"I love your shoes," I said.

Slight crow's feet appeared around her attractive almond eyes. "Carlos and I bought eight and a halves for you," she whispered conspiratorially. "That's why I wore them, so I could show you ahead of time. Trying to keep your present a secret was driving me nuts."

I grinned. "Thanks!"

Elizabeth, her new boyfriend Damien, and Carlos—with his diamond stud earring—came out onto the deck

When his intelligent brown eyes observed me, Damien announced, "Happy birthday, Tori."

"Thanks. You're Damien, right?" I asked.

"Yeah."

Carlos gripped Kristen's fingers. "Happy birthday, Tori."

"Thanks for inviting Damien," Elizabeth said, adjusting one of her chandelier earrings.

"Are you warm enough?" Damien asked Elizabeth. His brown face was attentive.

Where's Kevin? I wondered.

Someone clasped my elbow and I jumped in surprise. Kevin smirked beside me.

"You're evil," I muttered.

The moment I grinned, he pulled me into his side. He had a home gym and worked out every other day, so I got the benefit of his ripped muscles. His black hair was spiked up and I touched it gently. I liked his snug black shirt with a white stripe across his broad chest.

"You're handsome," I whispered, stroking his ego.

His light blue eyes darkened. "You look hot."

Kevin wrapped a muscled arm around my waist and kissed me. After my boyfriend let me go, Amber sauntered through the French doors attired in an orange bikini top and miniskirt.

"Amber, this is not a pool party!" Kristen exclaimed.

"Oh, you mentioned something about your pool, Tori," Amber said innocently.

I knew the real reason she was dressed like that, and she was lying. "I said we were going to have the barbeque around the pool."

"She wants William to stare at her all night," Cindy announced loudly, making Amber blush.

I noticed Kevin and Carlos staring at my blond friend. I rolled my eyes. *Why do guys always ogle the slutty girl?* I was relieved when Kevin looked at the grass. Carlos' gaze shifted to Kristen, who put her hands on her hips.

"Amber, go home and put on a t-shirt," Kristen said. "This is Tori's twenty-first birthday party. Don't ruin it by making all the men stare at your bikini top."

Amber grimaced and looked down at the patio stones. "I really just wanted William to notice. Sorry, I have a t-shirt in my car."

I smiled. "It's okay, Amber."

She glided back into the house.

I glanced around our backyard and noted Vincent standing by some trees with five other very handsome young people I hadn't invited. *Who are they?* Of course a fine-looking angel was going to stand with beautiful people. I was curious if everyone at my birthday party could see Vincent. The individual beside him was a sophisticated, light-skinned man with spiky, chestnut-shaded hair and dark eyes. He was very attractive and the same height as Vincent. There was also a handsome African American man who was three inches taller. A gorgeous Hispanic woman stood next to a pretty Asian girl with golden eyes. The fifth guest was a tall, noble-looking Middle Eastern man. I gawked at the lavish-looking group.

19

To my surprise, I realized that the chestnut-haired man with dark eyes was watching me.

Warm fingers gripped my arm. "Guess what?" Quickly, I turned back to my friends. Kristen had gripped Cindy's arm, too, but she was looking at the rest of us.

"What?" I asked.

"I'm going to Africa in January!" Kristen exclaimed.

"Why?" Amber asked.

Cindy swatted Amber. "Duh, she's volunteering. She always talked about it in college." She turned to Kristen. "You're volunteering, right?"

"Yeah. I don't need the money, but I want to help people. I filled out some forms nine months ago and yesterday, one of the aide agencies called me back." Grinning, Kristen jumped up and down.

"That's awesome," I said.

Kristen squeezed my hand. "You can come work with me. You want to work in Africa too, right?"

I smiled. "I do, but I want to go back to school again and be a nurse practitioner. Then I can have my own clinic."

"Wooo! That's a long time in school, girl," Cindy announced.

"I know, but ever since I was fourteen, I wanted to have a clinic in a foreign country."

"Why didn't you stay in school then?" Elizabeth asked.

Amber tilted her head. "Or be a doctor?"

"I remember you talked about this Nurse Practitioner thing, but I thought you forgot about it. You didn't talk about it at all during our last semester," Kristen said.

"I knew Dad and Mom could only pay for a couple years of college for each of us and that I would have to make the money by myself to finish school," I said. "I didn't know what to do, but since I'm living at home and working, I've made a lot of money. I'm thinking about going to university in January... maybe."

"Wow. That's cool," Elizabeth declared.

"I want to talk to Will," Amber whispered. Then my blond friend glided over to my younger brother and rubbed her hip against his thigh. Will smirked.

"Hey, Rex arrived," Cindy shouted. Rex, her bald-headed boyfriend was approaching from across the yard.

"Happy birthday, Tori!" Rex called.

"Thanks, Rex!"

All at once, my father called out. "Thank you for attending Victoria's twenty-first birthday party."

I observed my father. He was distinguished and looked really young because Mom dyed his hair. Mom caressed his large fingers as he spoke. The wrinkles around his brown eyes emerged when his generous smile appeared.

Kevin grasped my fingers and we walked over to the pink slab cake. I wanted to devour a few icing flowers, but everyone was watching me. Then my friends and family sang Happy Birthday. Naturally, some mischievous guests were singing alternate words.

I wondered if the Guardian Angels were going to eat cake, so I gazed at Vincent. He was laughing.

My brother William lit the candles—positioned to look like a two and a one—and I attempted to blow them all out. I didn't want to spray the food, though, so two candles were still lit when I finished.

Kevin watched me mischievously. "Where's your other boyfriend?"

*   *   *   *

Later, I wanted to find Katherine Windsor, a family friend who could see spirits, and ask her if she could see Vincent, since no one had talked to him or the other people who had stood by the trees. The dignified, strawberry-blond-haired woman relaxed on the patio in a green wrought iron chair with striped cushions.

She smiled at me. "Victoria, how are you?"

"Katherine, do you see those gorgeous people by the oak trees?"

"How many?" she asked.

"Six."

Her blue eyes danced. "Yes, I do. They're angels."

I gasped. "They're all angels... really?"

"Yes."

"The blond man wearing the white t-shirt saved me from being hurt in the Cedarwood parking lot. He had a big sword and then appeared in my room later," I disclosed. "I want to know whether anyone else can see the spirits."

Katherine grinned. "Saunter over to the oak trees. If you can walk through the beings, only you and I can see them."

Slowly, I ambled around the property so the creatures wouldn't watch as I walked directly toward them. I heard Vincent laugh when I got close. He spun and stared at me. "Your guests don't see us," he confirmed.

I smiled and walked around him so that I could see the other angels.

Vincent gestured to the chestnut-haired angel. "Tori, meet Michael," he said.

"Hello, Tori," Michael said, his dark eyes appearing austere.

"Michael is your mother's Guardian Angel," Vincent finished.

One of the others, a handsome African American angel, smiled. "My name is James. We met when you were fourteen."

My hazel eyes widened and my mouth gaped excitedly. "You were sitting on my father and it was 3:42 in the morning. You protect my dad!"

"Yes, good memory," he said with a laugh.

I then regarded the gorgeous Hispanic-looking angel. "I'm Gabriella," she announced gracefully.

"She guards your brother William," Vincent told me. His supernatural energy penetrated my cold arms. I was grateful for the angel's heat.

"Tell your brother to forget about guns," Gabriella murmured.

I stared at her. "Why? He wants to be a police officer!"

The pretty Asian angel grabbed my hand. I looked over at her. "Tori, I am Huan-Yue. I enjoy guarding your older brother, Stephen."

"It's nice to meet you, Huan-Yue."

After Huan-Yue let go of my fingers, Vincent gestured at the final angel and declared, "This is Madrikh."

The noble Middle Eastern angel smiled. "I guard your friend, Katherine Windsor."

I was awestruck to have this ability to see supernatural beings.

CHAPTER THREE

THE YOUNG PEOPLE were going swimming that evening, so a few of us angels rested around the pool. The next day, Tori and the rest of the Davenport family were departing for a holiday to Britannia, Ontario.

Tori walked out of the house. Her boyfriend Kevin, with a predatory smile, had his arm around her waist. My human was wearing a black bikini, which made me tense up. Kevin made me think of my demon enemy, Odium. While they walked along the cement deck, I glowered at him. I was irritated that Tori was wearing a bikini around this man. As I clenched my fingers, I wondered why she couldn't wear something less revealing. Having that unsavoury human see her in a t-shirt and shorts was bad enough.

As jealousy bit at my supernatural form, I seized the platinum handle of my broadsword and squeezed it. The metal burned hot but did not soften from my spirit heat. I dreamed about tripping the human male or taking human form and kissing her. Dark thoughts overwhelmed me for a few seconds as I imagined decapitating him with my blade. Immediately, I stopped obsessing; I didn't want to be-come what I hated most—a demon.

Unexpectedly, Kevin lifted Tori up into the air and carried her to the diving board. As fast as I could, I pulled my blade and emerged on the end of the diving board in spirit form. I was furious! When I hissed at him, I remembered the other Guardians. Michael knew I was at-tracted to Tori, but none of the other spirits were supposed to know, so I returned to the deck.

Tori protested and fought with him. "Kevin, put me down! The water's cold!"

I wanted to force him to set her back down, but he clumsily climbed onto the diving board and tossed her into the water. She cried out before being submerged.

I felt the same forbidden feelings heighten within me and my eyes turned golden. Angel rules said I couldn't interfere. I was surprised when she didn't come to the surface. She propelled along the tiled bottom and then came up for air at the swallow end. I waited for Tori to turn and watch her boyfriend. As Kevin swaggered off the diving board and walked along the deck, he flipped over my angel form foot and did a belly flop into the water. This human definitely couldn't see spirit feet! After-ward, I grinned and observed Tori staring at me. She was astonished.

"Thanks," she mouthed, grinning.

William and Stephen were laughing and clapping. Kevin growled as he rose out of the water. His teeth were clenched and his dark hair was shrink-wrapped tight to his head. Disgust showed through his face and water rolled down his cheeks. He pushed his wet hair off his face and glared at Tori's brothers.

By the time Tori sauntered over to him, Kevin's temper had cooled off. "I guess I'm clumsy," he said and breathed out. "I'm sorry, Tori. The water is cold."

Tori grinned. I looked away from her, observing the other Guardians staring at me. They appeared shocked. Michael's dark eyes castigated me while he stood on the Davenports' widow's walk. I wasn't supposed to interfere, but demons were known to trip humans constantly.

* * * *

Later, Michael glared at me. "Demons trip humans, not Guardian Angels."

"I found out that Kevin can't see spirits," I answered innocently.

Michael's brown orbs scowled and started to glow. "You're an angel," he reminded me. "You protect her. You don't know what can happen if you get too involved."

"Michael, you're not an Archangel. We're friends. Do you need to scold me?"

"Guardian Angels have choices, and humans do, too. Why do you think one-third of our former friends turned into demons? I don't want you to become a demon. If you wanted to help Tori, you should have stopped Kevin from dumping her in the pool. You were standing on that diving board."

"But... I was only trying to protect—"

Michael crossed his arms. "You made a mistake. Tripping Kevin was about revenge, not protecting your human."

My eyes began to glow. "I'm not going to turn into a demon."

* * * *

Even though it was warm, I was wearing pink pyjamas and a velour bathrobe. A bit of overkill, perhaps, but I still felt embarrassed about the Guardian Angels seeing me in a bikini.

"Vincent!" I called. Immediately, the robust Guardian Angel appeared, smiling. "Thank you, Vincent. You surprised me by tripping Kevin."

The angel looked around my room. "You like to adjust to cold water slowly," he observed.

"Too slowly," I murmured. "Sometimes guys chuck their girl-friends into the water. It's playful."

"A human female should be treasured."

"If you were human, would you throw your girlfriend into water?"

He stared at me seriously. "If she didn't want me to, no."

"Vincent, it's unfortunate that I can't manufacture a clone of you. It would make me rich."

"Why?" His intense blue eyes watched me.

"Humans have flaws; angels don't. You're kind, you defend me, you laugh, you're handsome, and you listen." I sighed. "Anyway, I'm tired. When I wake up, will I see you?"

"Do you want to see me?"

"Yes. It will comfort me if I have a bad dream."

"My light in angel form might disturb you," he said quietly.

"Like a big night light!"

"My angel form doesn't spook you?"

"No. You startled me at Cedarwood, but I'm almost used to the glow," I answered. "It's embarrassing to think that someone watches me all the time, especially when I don't see you. But I guess I see you most of the time now."

The slight golden glow in his eyes mesmerized me. "We give our humans privacy," he said carefully.

I pulled back my cotton sheet. "Good night, Vincent."

"Good night, Tori."

I unzipped the velour robe and jumped into bed. "Please don't sit on my suitcase," I murmured. Instantly, the handsome spirit looked around and spotted my suitcase on the couch. Vincent raised his eye-brows enquiringly.

"Your heat will melt my clothes," I teased.

Smirking, he went over to the suitcase and sat on it.

I sat up. "Vincent!"

He stood, guilt twisting his face. "Sorry... good night."

"Good night," I whispered.

* * * *

The next day, my whole family brought our bags down to the living room. My brothers then picked up the luggage and carried it to the waiting silver minivan. We had leased a cabin for one week in Britannia while Dad was on holidays from the creamery where he worked.

William, Stephen, and I raced outside to avoid being stuck in the back seat of the minivan. Of course, there wasn't enough space for all three of us in the middle seats, so I was relegated to the back.

Before I could get too angry about it, I realized Vincent was beside me. The angel sat to my left. When I looked at William and Stephen, I saw Gabriella between them; Huan-Yue was resting on Stephen's lap, which made me giggle.

William turned around and looked at me. "What are you laughing at?"

"Nothing," I said.

I noticed that Michael was outside, on the right side of the van; James was on the left. Their wings were unfurled and supernatural energy ran through them. Their wings closed when the silver van backed out of the driveway. I wondered if spirit wings affected aerodynamics.

* * * *

Upon arriving at our cabin, my brothers and I were grateful to escape from the cramped minivan. I liked the looks of the two wooden lounge chairs on the porch. While my dad and brothers set our bags on the ground, Michael and James flew onto the porch and perched on those chairs.

So much for sitting on the porch, I thought.

Huan-Yue gracefully stroked the velvety pink and burgundy petunias while Gabriella examined two cedar bushes in a flowerbed beside the porch. I liked the two expansive maple trees on the front lawn.

When I looked at Vincent, he smirked at me. "Bet you I can become taller than those maple trees," he said. His eyes were full of amusement.

"I think you are doing well enough at eight feet," I answered. I liked to tease him.

His blue eyes glowed. "I can be a hundred feet if I want to," he whispered mischievously.

I laughed. "Whatever."

When I looked away, I noticed William watching me. My brother's smoky blue eyes mocked me. "Do you need to go to the white, padded room?" he asked.

I frowned.

"You were talking to yourself," he said.

I sighed but ignored Will and walked to the backyard. I didn't want to tell my family about the spirit world I could see.

Seven gargantuan pine trees grew in front of a box-style wire fence. Suddenly the backyard became bright and Vincent loomed huge over everything. He was standing behind one of those pine trees with his head poked out above the evergreen.

"Look," he said gleefully.

I rolled my eyes. "Forty feet. Good attempt, Vincent."

Without warning, my mom walked into the yard. "What was—"

Her brown eyes were huge and her jaw dropped. Apparently, Vincent had allowed my mother to see him in angel form.

The Guardian quickly shrunk and sauntered over to us. "Hello, Mrs. Davenport."

"You're an angel?" she asked.

"Yes. I'm Tori's Guardian Angel."

*　*　*　*

Around two o'clock, I lay prone on my bed and read a brand new book I had bought in Britannia's town square. Unexpectedly, I sensed my Guardian Angel. When I gazed up from my book, I saw Vincent relaxing in human form on the wooden chair under my bedroom window.

I grinned at him. "Mom told Dad that she saw you this morning."

"I know," he answered placidly.

"Is it okay that I told my parents I can see you?"

"Sure, Tori. Do you want to go outside and walk with me?"

"Okay," I replied.

I sprung up to clamber onto the hardwood floor. As I watched the smiling Guardian Angel, my breath caught.

When we went outside, the muscles in my back danced. I could feel something evil. As I regarded the nearby spruce trees, I saw small black creatures staring at Vincent and me. They had big red eyes, sharp teeth, and sulphuric odours twisted into my nostrils. Vincent became intensely bright and the little imps clambered away.

Suddenly, I saw people a quarter mile away, walking down the road. I panicked, worrying they might be seeing my shining friend.

"Vincent," I said, pointing desperately at the humans.

Right away, he stopped shining and grasped my hand. The angel pulled me carefully down a hill engulfed in small rocks, and I was happy when the rocks gave way to pebbles. It was uncomfortable walking on rocks the size of a child's palm.

"Sorry, Tori. I didn't want to be stared at."

Vincent let go of me and I walked onto the sand. The cool waves crashing onto the beach tormented the nerves in my ankles for a minute before it felt comfortable.

*　*　*　*

For six thousand years, I guarded humans in spirit form. I had never experienced cool water under the bridges of my feet. The sand felt great. Unexpectedly, Tori plunged her fingers into the sand and threw some at my leg. The sand slid down my calf and I watched it, awed. I had never played with a human before. Grinning, I forced my fingers into the deep grit and chucked it at her stomach.

"Vincent!" she squealed.

I gazed wickedly at her. She quickly wiped the sand off with her hands and then threw two more handfuls at my head. I vanished before they could hit me.

"Vincent, you're an angel and you're cheating," she announced.

As soon as she accused me, I appeared behind her and looked down at her long hair. Instantly, she spun around. This was fun! She then launched my human form into the water with a grin. I landed in six inches of water, the cool liquid a shock against my legs. I was stunned! I shook my head and stared up at my charge.

"I'm sorry, Vincent," she whispered, guilt leaking out of her eyes. I knew she was slightly afraid of me.

I stood up and ambled over to Tori, her hazel eyes watching me gravely. She anticipated retaliation, but I didn't want to hurt her. When my arms swept her up, she held her breath and I wasn't sure why she had stopped breathing. I strode into the lake, feeling the cold liquid surge up as waves crashed into my body. Tori didn't realize that I didn't harbour any human feelings of vengeance against her.

"Why aren't you walking on the water?" she asked.

"I'm not in angel form," I answered. Sunlight danced over the constantly moving water and reflected into my eyes. My human eyes were forced to narrow, making me frown as I looked down at her. Tori was scared. Her beautiful hazel eyes were humongous, her body trembled, and guilt flushed through me.

"I'm not going to hurt you," I said. We had spent time together. It was frustrating to know that my human was afraid of me, but since I had protected humans for six thousand years I understood her fear.

"I'm your Guardian. Do you know what Guardians do?" Instantly, the tension in her face departed.

Her wide, observant eyes watched me. "God told you to protect me."

"I can't hurt my human, and I don't want to, Tori."

All at once, a vicious wave hit us. The water soaked her clothes and she squealed. I was taken aback at the power of nature. Human bodies couldn't do and go wherever they wanted without consequences. That last wave had been rough and I felt an intense current pull at my legs. I frowned, not having realized there was an undertow here. I had to leave now or take angel form; I couldn't let her get hurt.

My eyes began to glow golden when I smelt sulphur. Realizing there were demons nearby who wanted to murder her, fury twisted through me. They were going to try to kill us both while I was vulnerable in human form. I had broken the rules and gotten to know my human. This attack on Tori and I was an unpleasant consequence of my disobedience. If I stayed in angel form, she wouldn't be in danger very often—unless she made stupid choices.

"Tori, I have to take angel form," I warned. "We're being attacked."

Her hazel eyes widened and I felt her shiver. My body glowed brilliantly, then grew and heated up. I felt my broadsword against my thigh. My golden eyes looked around for any sign of demons. Relief consumed me when I saw there was nobody on the public beach, demons or otherwise.

Thank goodness! The last thing I need is people watching me.

I took a deep breath before rising onto the water and walked on the surface of the lake.

*   *   *   *

Water dripped off me as Vincent carried me back to the beach. I frantically regarded the water rolling onto the empty public beach and relief engulfed me.

"Can demons kill you while you are in human form?" I asked.

His intense golden eyes watched me. "Yes, but when I sense them my body just takes spirit form. They have never killed an angel in human form because we take spirit form very quickly. However, if a Guardian is concentrating too hard on their human and doesn't take angel form fast enough, I suppose it's possible the human and angel could die."

My body wasn't shivering anymore and I took a deep breath. When Vincent sauntered onto the beach, he set my feet down on the sand. I was thankful that I wasn't wearing jeans, as they dried too slowly. Wet jeans caused large, long red areas on my thighs that didn't go away quickly.

"I'm sorry I carried you out into the lake," Vincent said when he surveyed my dampness. "Do you want me to fly you to the cottage?"

"No."

"You're wet, Tori."

My shoulders rose. "It's okay. Did you and the other angels eat any of my birthday cake?"

"No. We were in spirit form."

"There is an ice cream store I want to go to," I announced. "Can you come with me?"

"I always do."

"In human form, I mean."

My Guardian laughed. "Sure, Tori."

*   *   *   *

The next day, William, Stephen, and I were playing Chinese Checkers in the cottage's kitchen. It was so hot that the sweat was running off us—and we were hardly even doing anything. I moved a red marble into Stephen's section.

Mom and Dad walked into the hot room and said they were going to get some hamburgers from town.

"Get me ten double cheeseburgers," William laughed.

I stared at him. "What hospital are you having your bypass in?"

William glowered at me, then glanced at Mom and Dad. "Get me three double cheeseburgers and a large fries, please."

"What do you want, Tori and Stephen?" Dad asked.

I was going to give them my order when James, my father's Guardian, distracted me. The striking African American angel drew his iridescent sword and pointed it at Michael.

"Let's fence," James said, executing an *en garde* stance.

Michael regarded James seriously. "We have to guard our responsibilities," he answered.

"Killjoy," James uttered, grinning. Then he sheathed his sword and winked at me.

It would be fun to sword fight with them, but I'm human, I thought. Gabriella and Huan-Yue looked like human females, but their extreme strength, which I lacked, was invisible. Would a Guardian Angel ever let me hold their broadsword?

"Tori, what do you want?" Mom asked.

My attention had been drawn away from my angel friends. "Sorry. Can you get me a chicken burger and salad?" I asked.

"Sure, dear," Mom replied, amused.

"Thank you so much."

William yawned. "Stephen, let's play video games till Dad and Mom get back."

"Sure," Stephen answered.

They ran upstairs.

"Were you watching the angels, Tori?" my dad asked curiously.

"Yes. James wants to fence Michael."

Dad shook his head. "I envy you. I can't believe you see that incredible world so often. Whose Guardian is James?"

"Yours. Michael is Mom's."

CHAPTER FOUR

WHEN MY FAMILY got home from our holiday, Janessa, Karen, and I went for a walk in Smithington. As we walked down the street, I saw Kevin, whose broad arm was encompassing a curvy, petite woman dressed in a skanky top. My jaw fell as I stared at them.

I've only been gone a week. How long has he been seeing that woman? I wondered.

When Kevin kissed the blond girl, I almost yelled. The sting of rejection consumed me. My body trembled when I became aware of my Guardian. I couldn't see him, but I knew Vincent was there. Then I felt his large fingers tug my hand and caress it.

"Thank you, Vincent," I murmured. I was thankful he was here. After I took a deep breath, I strode across the asphalt, avoiding a blue car that ripped down the avenue. "Kevin!"

Hearing my voice, Kevin turned around. His blue eyes grew monstrous. His jaw dropped as his dark eyebrows joined his hairline. "Tori!"

"Let's break up! I don't want to share the guy I'm seeing with a blondie." With that, I strode back to my cousins with my invisible Guardian beside me.

*   *   *   *

The next day, Vincent appeared while I was watering our flower beds.

"Do you want to fly?" he asked.

I gasped. "Excuse me?"

Does my Guardian really want to take me for a ride? I wondered.

He reached his arms out. As I grabbed his hands, we rose and I started to feel the air driving past me.

An amazing rush overwhelmed me. Naturally, I gazed down and studied my rural neighbourhood. The steep hill we used for sleigh-riding in the winter looked like the size of a sand castle at the beach. Kinkaid Road was like a thin trail of syrup on a pastry, and the neighbours' houses looked like stops on a hobby railroad board. The wind forced my hair back, up, and then in my face; I had to pull strands out of my lip gloss, but I liked how it felt when the air playfully tousled my hair.

Vincent's blue eyes were observing me intently. His slightly wavy hair soared.

"Do you like it, Tori?" he asked, grinning.

I giggled. "Yes. Thank you so much, but I have one request."

"What?"

"Let me go for a moment," I pleaded.

His eyes glowed intensely. "Not a chance, Tori." He gripped my hands tighter.

"Please, I want to know what's it's like to free fall."

He groaned. "I'm already stretching things by flying with you."

"So stay with me," I answered.

Suddenly, I fell—*fast*.

Vincent actually released me!

I gazed up at him as I plummeted. For a moment, I freaked out when I realized how stupid this was. As my pulse raced, Vincent appeared beside me.

"This isn't much of a challenge for you," I yelled as the air roared around me.

"Hardly," he answered and caught me again. His eyes were golden.

"That was short," I muttered as we hovered in the air.

Angelic eyes raked over my face. "Did you enjoy it?"

"Sort of."

"Don't ask me to let you go again. I'm not supposed to age, but I think I just did."

*   *   *   *

Michael made fists as he glared up at Vincent and Tori flying. "That human is going to get Vincent to spend a hundred years in Israel in the heavy fighting!" he glowered.

He could feel spirit energy ricochet into his wings. Humans were awed by this magnificent kind of display. The other angels didn't think he had any patience for human beings. Michael hated the free will they were given, for humans weren't capable of following the Creator—and angels had weaknesses, too.

Gabriella glanced at him. "He hasn't kissed her, Michael. He's trying to make her happy."

"But—"

"Vincent hasn't done anything wrong," Madrikh stated.

Suddenly the angels saw four red eyes lurking inside the Davenports' spirea hedge. Black gargoyles chortled and drooled.

"Bye, Vincent!" one of them hissed.

*   *   *   *

Mom was at an overnight teacher's workshop, so she had made a roast for us the day before. William crinkled his nose when I pulled the meat and potatoes out of the fridge.

"I hate eating leftovers," he complained.

"The rest of us have to make sacrifices for Mom, your imperial highness," I stated with a bow. William glared at me as I darted behind the kitchen table.

"You're a brat!" he exclaimed.

Stephen rolled his eyes at us. "Sheesh! Stop acting like teens. Dad's going to be home soon." With that, he turned and left the room.

Vincent appeared in the kitchen and I tried to hide behind him, but he was in angel form. "Tori, watch what you say," Vincent scolded. He started to give off luminescence. "We are not supposed to interfere."

William's eyes widened, as though he could see something of what was going on.

I stuck my tongue out at William and then noted that Gabriella was glowering at me.

"Angels take us seriously, don't they?" I asked Vincent.

His righteous golden eyes gazed over his shoulder at me. "Yes, we are close to our humans."

I walked around my angel, approaching my brother. "Sorry, William," I repented.

"Sorry, Tori," William said. "What is that light?"

"My Guardian Angel. His name's Vincent," I replied. Will looked astonished. "You have one, too. She's glaring at me right now."

*   *   *   *

On Friday evening, Dad and Mom attended a retirement party for the principal who worked at Mom's school. William was in his room, Stephen and his fiancée Barbara had gone for a drive, and I was playing on my laptop. All at once, the cream-coloured Priscilla drapes surrounding my French doors whistled from the wind. Goose bumps appeared on my arms and I shivered.

I glanced at the pink wing chair next to my computer desk. My eyes then shifted to my door, where a severely handsome man with black eyes and sable hair was watching me. His onyx trench coat drifted in the breeze. I stared at him, mesmerized by his supernatural looks. My hands started to perspire. His terrifying eyes seized my attention, and I knew he was a spirit.

"Who are you?" I asked.

"An angel. My name is Odium." He stepped closer to me.

I narrowed my hazel eyes. "Odium?"

He leaned over me. "I think you should know, Vincent is a demon."

"Why are your eyes black?" I asked, his wickedness and hate assaulting me.

"A curse," he murmured.

I sniffed. He was giving off an odour that reeked like a chemical from my high school biology class.

Suddenly, the room brightened. I turned to see Vincent looming large in the open doorway. His blue eyes were golden now and very bright; his wings radiated majestic light. Whirling, Odium roared and grew larger. He was massive, with grotesque amethyst jewellery on his arms. His curling horns touched the ceiling. When the two monstrous beings pulled cutlasses, fragments of plaster dropped from my ceiling onto the hardwood.

Three small imps poured in through the French doors. Their wrinkled wings unfurled as they advanced on me. They chased me onto the balcony and launched themselves at me. Their cold, black hands seized my arms, scratching me with their sharp nails.

"Vincent!" I screamed.

Terrified, I swung my arms at them. The imp I hit soared backward into the side of the doorframe. The impact caused a loud bang and the other spirits warily released me. One creature scurried to the fallen imp.

"Poor Pernicious," it muttered.

The felled creature named Pernicious hissed at it. "Leave me alone, Malice. You and Enmity make sure she doesn't run into the house." Its red eyes smouldered at me from the railing. Yellow teeth rose in the creature's mouth. Anger swirled through its form and the furious creature pulled a rusty dagger, then flung itself at me. With anxiety and anger roiling around inside me, I kicked the imp. Its sword clattered to the wooden balcony floor and the heinous creature screeched in rage.

"Kill her!" the others shrieked.

My pulse raced as they tackled me, jamming me into the balcony.

Suddenly, I felt a malevolent, cold breeze against my skin. Out of the corner of my eye, I saw Vincent grappling with Odium. In the middle of their fight, the demon vanished into thin air.

In an instant, Vincent appeared next to me on the balcony, his iridescent blade drawn. The hissing imps backed off me, crouching and glaring at my Guardian. He swung his sword, but before it could connect the demons departed.

My body relaxed as his spirit energy engulfed me. Vincent then returned to his human form and gazed down at me. "Tori, are you okay?"

My hazel eyes were huge. "Those imps tried to kill me!" I gasped. My teeth were knocking together. My whole body trembled.

Vincent lifted me and gave me a hug. It felt good to be pressed against someone so much stronger than me. My adrenaline drained away.

"Vincent, I feel exhausted." I gazed up at the angel's eyes, which had lost their golden appearance. "If I had been an angel, I would have had a sword."

I hate being human!

"I'm going take angel form to keep the demons away tonight," he announced, gazing down at me.

Frustration filled me and I clenched my fists. "Thank God," I whispered. "Why did they come here?"

Vincent frowned. "Demons pick certain humans and torment them."

"But they were trying to kill me!"

CHAPTER FIVE

Hell

TWO MINUTES LATER, Enmity, Malice, and Pernicious relaxed against a blistering black wall. Their onyx fingers and spirit bodies quaked apprehensively while small, wrinkly wings opened and folded together. Their red eyes were wide.

Odium glared at the imps as yellow clouds twisted around his Strong Man form. "You didn't throw the human over the balcony!"

"Master, she's robust! The girl kicked me!" Pernicious protested, nauseating teeth rising in her mouth.

"Humans are frail!" Odium declared angrily.

Malice rubbed her scaly skin. "This one isn't."

"What?!" Odium exploded, clenching his fists. His red eyes thinned and his eight-inch horns blasted smoke. He smacked Malice, tossing the three-foot imp to the ground. With wary red eyes, the cowering imp watched his master pace.

Odium stalked forward, the amethyst embellishments on his huge arms radiating light "I used to be handsome! Vincent exposed our prince! For that, his human has to die!"

With that, he slammed his fist against the black wall of Hell.

*　*　*　*

After the attack, I ran to William's room to see if he had been hurt by any demons. I barged into his room without knocking.

"Are you okay?" I gasped.

He turned from his video game, frowning up at me. "What are you talking about?"

I groaned, realizing Will knew nothing about what had happened in my room. "I'm sorry, Will. I was worried about you."

"Why?"

I swallowed and gazed at the hardwood floor. "Believe me, I have a good reason. But forget about it." I sat down on the edge of his bed. "Dad and Mom's anniversary is getting close. I'm thinking we should take them out for supper."

My little brother grinned. "Sure. I can afford that kind of present."

Unexpectedly, someone knocked on Will's open door and I whirled. It was Stephen.

Thank goodness! I was still on edge from the demon attack. William and I fled over to him.

"Tori and I want to take Mom and Dad out for supper for their anniversary," Will said.

Stephen's intelligent brown eyes sparkled. "That's a great idea! I don't have a lot of money right now, but a good dinner is possible."

"Where should we go?" William asked.

"What do you guys think of the steakhouse in Smithington?" I asked.

"Great!" my brothers answered.

* * * *

As I lay in bed that night, I thought about the imps and trembled. If I hadn't fought the demons, I might have died. Vincent had the advantage of his sword, so I needed to know how to use an angelic broadsword. To be honest, I was scared to pick one up.

"What time is it?" I got up to look at the red numbers on my digital clock—11:00 p.m. Vincent was sitting in my wing chair, glowing, but I didn't talk to him. Instead, I grabbed my phone and dialled Kristen's cell number; she had been taking fencing lessons for ten years and knew how to handle a sword.

"Hello," Kristen greeted. I heard noise from a movie in the background.

"Kristen, it's Tori."

"Tori? What's wrong?" I heard the creak of her getting up from a recliner.

"I was attacked tonight," I disclosed.

The movie noises stopped. "What!?"

"Hang up," I heard a man's voice whisper.

"Stop it, Carlos. It's Tori," Kristen murmured. Then I heard a crackle, like when you rub the speaker part of the receiver with your hand. Soon the movie noises started up again.

"Sorry, Tori," Kristen muttered.

"No worries. I'm sorry I interrupted your time with Carlos."

"It doesn't matter. What happened?"

Oh no! I can't tell her about demons. What do I say?

I bit my bottom lip while playing with the edges of my bed sheet. I desperately glanced at Vincent, who was staring at me seriously. I looked away from him and said, "Intruders in my house tried to push me over my balcony. One had a dagger."

Kristen gasped.

"Can you teach me how to fence?" I asked, hoping my friend wouldn't ask any more questions.

Unfortunately, Kristen wanted more details. I suppressed a groan. "How did you get away?" she asked.

"A family friend scared them away."

"Thank God. Did you call the police?"

"Not yet," I said. "Can you teach me how to fence?"

"Why? You should be taking a self-defence course. People don't fight with swords anymore."

"These intruders did," I answered honestly.

"Okay. Come over on Monday and Master Jovanovich can give us a lesson," she replied amicably.

Relief and happiness flooded over me. "Thanks so much."

"No problem. See ya."

"Good night," I replied, then hung up.

*   *   *   *

I gazed at Tori, sleeping. How could she sleep when Odium had gotten so close to her? Even I was disturbed by the Strong Man's sulphuric odour, and I was a Guardian! It was my fault that Odium had even shown himself to Tori. For a moment, I regretted being a loyal angel during the rebellion. I clenched my fists tightly and stalked up to Tori's French doors. She was my friend and I couldn't let my enemies kill her.

Sensing warm supernatural energy, I whirled to see Michael watching me.

"I don't know what to do," I said, beginning to pace.

"Demons will attack her because you care," Michael said solemnly.

I glared at him, scanning his face for criticism. But instead, all I saw in his eyes was sadness.

"If you stop talking to Tori, it's possible Odium will leave her alone." Michael's glowing eyes gazed at me compassionately.

I looked back at her. She was sleeping peacefully. "I can't protect her if more demons appear! She was almost hurt tonight."

Michael smiled. "She's feisty. Not many of our charges would take on demons."

"Tori's not supposed to fight demons. I am. She's only human, Michael." I walked over to her bed as she shifted and turned over. A long strand of hair dropped over her mouth and I moved it, deliberately brushing her warm lips.

Michael's energy moved nearer. He touched my arm. "Careful, Vincent."

* * * *

On Monday evening, Kristen and I ran around her father's recreation hall doing stretches. A tall, middle-aged Russian man grinned at us when he entered and placed two hockey bags on the hardwood floor.

"Miss Petrovich," Master Jovanovich spoke with a bow. His green eyes pierced mine. "You must be Victoria Davenport."

I smiled at the self-assured, dark haired man. "I am."

"Good. I am Master Jovanovich."

"Nice to meet you, sir."

We helped him remove swords, helmets, and padded garments from the bags. He glanced at Kristen. "You don't mind just going through the basics tonight, do you?"

"No," she answered.

"Good. Come here, ladies, and stand on this line." He gestured at a black line painted across the middle of the hall. We walked to the line and stopped. "Tonight we have to work on footwork. Everything starts and ends with the *en garde* stance." Master Jovanovich demonstrated and pointed at me. "Go ahead, try it."

I tried to stand like him, but I was more awkward.

"Bring your arm closer to your body," he instructed at my bent right arm. "Now go lower." He pointed at his torso. "Pretend you are sitting on a stool." I bent my knees more. My feet were supposed to be at a ninety degree angle. "Good!"

At the end of the hour, my leg muscles ached from moving forwards and backwards in the bent-knee stance. I was grateful when Master Jovanovich and Kristen started practicing so I could sit on the hardwood floor and take a break.

CHAPTER SIX

IT WAS EARLY in the morning of July 4 and I lying in bed, exhausted. Mom and I had planned to go out for breakfast. We didn't get to spend much time together with me working days, evenings, and some nights at Cedarwood and her working during the week.

As I woke, I sensed Vincent's warm spirit energy near my bed.

"I want to sleep," I whispered, pushing my face into the pillow.

"Your alarm is ringing," he reminded me, pulling my comforter away from my face.

"Oh my goodness." I rolled onto my back. His face was leaned in so close to me, he startled me. I felt shivers running through me as I stared at him. Was I always going to want him to kiss me? The Guardian's iridescent smile could have been featured on an ad for dental whitening. His blue eyes glowed. I wondered what he was thinking.

When Vincent straightened, I thrust my arms behind me and propped myself up. "I'm so hungry ..."

I lost my balance and nearly fell off the bed. Before I could hit the floor, Vincent thrust his arm around my waist and caught me. My shoulders crashed into his chest, his spirit energy calming my nerves. Unfortunately, my attraction caused me to tremble ferociously. Vincent hugged me tight.

"You woke me up, Vincent, but—"

"Tori, I have to talk to you!" Mom called outside my door. Vincent disappeared as I went to the door and opened it.

"What's wrong, Mom?"

"You're not dressed?"

"No."

"Katherine Windsor just called. Ruffles got hit by a car last night. She's upset and I was wondering if it would be okay for her to come with us this morning?"

"Oh no! She loves her cat." I pursed my lips, then shrugged. "Sure, Mom."

I was disappointed that we wouldn't get to be alone with each other, but Katherine was a friend and it was our duty to cheer her up.

My mother smiled at me. "Thanks, Tori. I'll call Katherine and tell her we'll pick her up."

*   *   *   *

Fifteen minutes later, I was in the car with my mom. Perched in the driver's seat, I opened my jean purse and lifted out my sunglasses. While I slipped them on, Mom mischievously reached over and started the car for me

"You had a slow start this morning," she said.

"I know," I replied. "I didn't hear the alarm, so Vincent woke me up." She grinned. "I'm just teasing."

My family liked to tease each other. I heard a sound behind me and knew that Michael was there, waiting in the backseat. I wondered if

49

my mother could hear or sense her Guardian. "Mom, do you ever see your Guardian Angel, or sense him?"

"No, but I wish I could."

When we got to Katherine Windsor's three-storey apartment building in Smithington, Mom got out of the car and gracefully walked along the sidewalk to the main entrance. Before she got there, Katherine strode out the front door. Katherine was happy to see us, but she also looked sad and I felt sorry for her. Mom gave her a hug as they started back toward the car.

Madrikh, Katherine's Guardian, followed. His fingers rubbed the platinum hilt of his blade. He waved at me. I smirked, thinking it would be nice if the Creator let Madrikh guard Mom and the austere Michael guard Katherine.

I felt spirit heat on my neck and back, signifying Vincent's presence. "What are you thinking?" he asked.

"I wish Madrikh could guard Mom and Michael could shield Katherine," I answered.

"Why?"

"Madrikh is friendly."

"Believe it or not, I wish God would make Michael go to China," Vincent whispered. I snickered.

Mom and Michael sat in the back while Katherine settled into the passenger seat. I looked over at her. "I'm sorry about Ruffles. Are you okay?"

"The poor thing. It makes me sick to think of what she looked like after she got hit."

I hugged Katherine and then started the car.

Madrikh's wings spread while I drove. Golden spirit energy careened through his wings, distracting me.

"Tell Madrikh to close his wings," I told Vincent. "The glare is distracting."

"Anything for a human who can see us," Madrikh responded. Just like that, the light went out.

"Humans shouldn't converse with Guardians while they drive," Michael reprimanded. I rolled my eyes rebelliously.

"You gentlemen could take human form and eat with us," I said.

"We're Guardian Angels," Michael answered. "We don't need to eat."

"Hey, sour angel. I would love to eat with humans who can see us!" Madrikh protested.

Vincent nodded. "Let's do it."

I heard a snort and knew it had come from Michael "You're not hurting for human time, Vincent."

When we arrived at the restaurant, we got out of the car and I locked the Mustang. I felt spirit warmth on my palm. Warm human fingers collected my hand. I smiled at Vincent, whose bright blue eyes radiated specks of golden energy. I glanced over to the passenger side. Madrikh, in human form, was holding Katherine's door. Michael put his hand under my mother's arm and held our friend's vacated seat forward.

The Guardian Angels held the front doors of the restaurant for us. I wanted to be respectful, so I let Mom and Katherine walk in first. Then Vincent took my hand.

An attractive, well-endowed, olive-skinned waitress took our orders. I was shocked that when the angels ordered, they smiled at us and didn't look at the girl's top.

"Wow, you're not like human guys," I remarked. Interested angel eyes continued to watch me, as though not understanding my comment. "You didn't stare at her," I explained.

The angels frowned. "We can't stare at anyone except demons and our responsibilities," Madrikh said.

"You're not allowed?" I asked curiously.

"You don't understand the other realm," Michael said. I was confused and I think he realized it. "Shielding our responsibility is our duty, and we only care about our human." His gaze shifted to Vincent. "Apparently, we're able to be friends with any human, but our form of love, empathy, and commitment are only intended for our responsibilities." Then he added, "Lust is not to be an issue."

I shivered at the word "lust." Michael's expression compelled me to swallow.

Suddenly, Michael's grave brown eyes turned golden. "Demons," he hissed. "See, human? This is why we're not supposed to take human form. Vigilance comes first!"

Sulphur twisted into our nostrils. Then I saw Odium! The handsome creature glowered sardonically at us, then settled thirty feet away near a baby stroller. The sable-haired, onyx-eyed spirit winked at me. Terror careened through me. My teeth chattered and my arms trembled. Vincent hauled me into his broad chest and held me.

The waitress then returned, placing glasses of juice on the table. Before she walked away, she paused. "Angels!" she exclaimed. She looked at me with onyx eyes and hissed, "How pathetic."

Hate twirled around me. The sensation of abhorrence in the restaurant was excruciating. I moaned as my head rubbed against Vincent's chest.

"Get out of here, garbage!" Michael hissed at the waitress, who it turned out was a demon in disguise. Madrikh stood behind Katherine and Mom. The spirits' eyes radiated golden energy, their muscles tensed.

"Vincent," I whispered desperately. I could feel his hot fingers rubbing my cheek. *Why do I have to react this way to demons?*

"Sergeant, do you like human form?" Michael asked the demon waitress threateningly. Sergeants were a type of demon. The sergeant hissed, her rebellious onyx eyes filled with revulsion. She backed up to stand next to Odium.

Even though I was scared, Vincent's spirit energy relaxed me. When Michael turned away from the demons, he ordered, "Madrikh and Vincent, take our responsibilities outside!"

The disarming Middle Eastern angel smiled calmly and leaned over near Mom and Katherine. "Lovely women," he said, putting his light brown hands around their upper arms. "The sun is warm by Tori's car."

Mom's jaw was trembling and her brown eyes were enormous. However, Katherine was glowering at Odium and the sergeant. Frustration filled me as I pushed my brunette hair behind my ear.

I stood up, turned on my heel, and observed Vincent. "This isn't fair!"

*   *   *   *

Tori frowned and lifted her chin rebelliously. I couldn't help but grin at her. If Tori had been a spirit, she would have been a demon-whipping Guardian.

"I want to stay. I'm hungry," she disclosed.

"We can get you protein bars from Heaven." Her hazel eyes observed me, her long black eyelashes splaying away from her eyes.

Tori rested her hands on either side of her waist. "They can't hurt us in this restaurant."

I forced away my admiration for her. She needed to leave before the situation got dangerous. She wasn't a Guardian and she didn't have a sword. There was no way she could beat a sergeant. "You were trembling before. Do you really want to eat so close to dark spirits? Odium will be watching you the whole time. Who knows? That waitress could poison your food."

Tori sighed and looked down at the red floor tiles. Her hands balled into fists. I knew she was angry.

"Let's go," I said. "Don't even look at Odium."

She looked up at me. "Why?"

"He'll never forget you," I replied intensely.

"Vincent!" Michael hissed, impatient for them to leave the restaurant.

I grabbed Tori's hand. I noticed her eyes darken and glare across the room at Odium.

"No!" I exclaimed, recklessly yanking on her left arm. "I said don't look! You're human. You're no match for him." She writhed in my grip, trying to get away. I wished she wasn't human.

Odium laughed as I ushered her outside and settled her into the backseat of the Mustang.

"I'll drive," I said as I slipped into the driver's seat. In a moment, Michael stalked outside and vanished around the side of the diner. When he reappeared, he was on the car's roof, back in angel form. I sped out of the parking lot.

*   *   *   *

I pushed my hair behind my ears and stared out the window as we drove through Smithington. I was trying to avoid looking at Vincent, who watched me in the rear-view mirror. I was sure he was angry at me for not having listened to him at the diner. I had wanted to fight those demons, just like angels could.

Eventually my Guardian turned the car into a park. He drove up a long lane bordered by maple and white birch trees. We passed two tennis courts and three pavilions hosting wooden picnic tables. I didn't know why he had brought us here.

Vincent turned my Mustang off the lane and parked it on the grass. We all got out.

"Tori," Vincent called to me.

I didn't look at my Guardian Angel right away. I grimaced. I wasn't sure if he was angry. When I did look at him, his eyes were filled with compassion.

Vincent took me by the hand. I inhaled deeply. Warm air flirted with the tresses around my face. Mischievousness was visible in Vincent's face.

"We could give our humans protein bars," he said.

Suddenly, a picnic table appeared with crystal plates, tumblers, scrambled eggs, curled bacon, milk, orange juice, and rye toast with jam selections. My eyes widened. This was definitely better than eating at the diner!

"Oh my," Katherine murmured as her jaw fell open. I caressed one of the crystal plates, curious at how the sun fragmented through the Heavenly material. The dishes looked like they were made of diamonds. I looked at Vincent and saw that he was amused by our human reactions. Sunrays mingled with spirit energy inside his eyes, making his orbs look like precious stones. Gratitude overcame me and I gave him a hug.

"Thank you," I whispered.

"You're welcome."

"While you humans eat, I'm going to swing," Madrikh announced.

After we ate the food, the crystal plates and tumblers vanished.

When everything was gone, Vincent turned to me. "I'll push you on the swing."

Together my Guardian and I walked through the cropped grass toward a nearby swing set. I settled onto the seat and held the cold chains as Vincent pushed.

"Hang on," he said gently.

I closed my eyes. Vincent was so strong, even in human form, that I soared up to the crossbar.

"Not so high!" I squealed.

"Sorry." With a single tap, he made me surge ten feet ahead.

"Higher!" I called. After a very human under-doggie, my swing soared seven feet into the air. I shut my eyes, enjoying the ride. "Perfect!"

CHAPTER SEVEN

THIS EVENING, MY brothers and I were going to treat our parents to a dinner out. Their anniversary was on the following Tuesday, but they were planning to go out that night just the two of them. Stephen and Will were bringing their girlfriends, so I asked Vincent to come also—in human form, of course.

As I applied my eyeliner, I knew there was someone in the room with me. Turning, I saw my blond angel standing in front of the French doors. Vincent looked great in his short-sleeved shirt and dress pants.

"You look pretty," he said.

"Thanks. You look great, too."

"Thank you. I'm ready to meet your family."

I looked at him questioningly. "You don't mind?"

"Your mom already saw me. Besides, I really like pretending to be human."

Just then, I heard my mother calling from downstairs. "Victoria!"

"We better go," I said.

* * * *

Vincent came down the stairs, following me. Everyone was waiting for us.

"Meet Vincent," I said.

Everyone said their hellos, then I looked up at Vincent and made all the introductions, starting with my mom and dad. Then I moved on to my brothers. "This is Stephen, and his fiancée Barbara. And this is my other brother William, and his girlfriend Cassandra."

Vincent smiled, "It's good to meet you all."

We stepped outside the house. Stephen and William took Barbara and Cassandra to their cars. Huan-Yue, Gabriella, and two other angels sat in the backseats.

"Who are those other angels?" I asked Vincent.

"The female is Gloria and the male is Alexander," he said softly. Gloria was a beautiful spirit. She had blond hair and green eyes. Alexander was tall, with black hair and olive skin. I was jealous. All the female angels were so exquisite; why did Vincent want to be friends with me, a pathetic human?

Vincent tugged my hand. He walked me to the door of my car, then got into the passenger seat.

"Why are all angels so beautiful?" I asked as I got in the car.

Vincent laughed. "I never think about it. I only think about you— and sparring with demons, of course." Without warning my body trembled slightly. Just then, Mom tapped on my window, surprising me. I bumped my head on the roof.

"Can we go with you?" she asked.

"Of course. I should've suggested it before. I hope you guys don't mind the back seat?"

"We'll be fine," Dad said. He got in first, then Mom elegantly climbed in after him.

*   *   *   *

At the steakhouse, a friendly waitress in a striped blouse and dark skirt led us to our table. A large unlit stone fireplace stood at the far side of the room.

"Marianne, you and I should come here in the winter," Dad said, pulling my mom against him. "We can reserve the table by the fireplace. The fire would keep us warm."

Mom smiled up at him while the rest of us sat down. "Frederick, I don't need the fire to keep me warm."

I was surprised when Cassandra sat down next to Vincent. I rolled my eyes. She was a flirt, just like my friend Amber.

"I have to check something," I whispered to Vincent and rose.

"Be careful," he said, watching me go.

I smiled at him and walked to the desk at the front of the restaurant. I had ordered an anniversary cake through the restaurant.

The blond woman behind the desk greeted me.

"Hi, my name is Tori Davenport. Do you have the cake ready for my parents' anniversary?"

"Davenport?" she asked.

"Yes."

"I'll check." She reached below the desktop and lifted a binder onto the desk. She flipped through the pages for a few moments. Finding what she was looking for, she glanced up and smiled. "Yes, we have it."

I thanked her and quickly walked back to my family.

The first thing I noticed when I strolled into the room was that Vincent was talking to Cassandra. My brother's girlfriend was smiling and had her elbow propped on the table; her right hand was resting against her cheek. She was ogling him! I swallowed, realizing I was jealous.

All of a sudden, I felt head pain and tightness in my throat and chest. I remembered what he had said—"I only think about you... and sparring with demons, of course."

Unexpectedly, I found Vincent staring at me. His supernatural eyes seemed compassionate. Angels weren't able to view the contents of our minds, even though they were immortal... or at least, I hoped not.

*　*　*　*

After the waitress brought our drinks, Marianne Davenport asked her to take a picture of all of us. The room we were in wasn't crowded, so we walked over to the window and stood together. I stood behind Tori and took advantage of the opportunity to hold her. As I put my arms around her, I noticed Michael on the other side of the room, glaring at me.

He is way too self-righteous! Irritation filled me, but I tried to ignore it. *There's nothing wrong with me holding Tori.*

I breathed deep, trying to calm my rising energy. I smiled at the waitress who was waiting to take our picture.

It felt strange being the subject of a photograph. I had always been fascinated when my humans posed for pictures, but I didn't think I would ever be in one of them.

After the picture was taken, we returned to our table. Tori gazed up at me and whispered, "I liked when you held me, Vincent."

My human heart began to thump harder. When I realized she was attracted to me, I perceived spirit energy accumulating. All along I had thought she was just awed by me! My chest tightened as I realized our feelings were mutual. I found it difficult to breathe; after all, Tori was forbidden to me.

*　*　*　*

After dinner, I walked to the restaurant washroom. When I strolled to the sink to wash my hands, goose bumps rose on my arms and I rubbed

59

my light skin. As I removed my lip gloss, a toilet flushed behind me and a pale, black-haired waitress glided to the sink next to me.

"Are you with the couple celebrating their anniversary?" she asked. She had black eyes and her voice was soft.

I frowned. The goose bumps were still on my arms. "Yes," I replied.

She smirked. "I thought so."

"I'm their daughter."

"Tori?" she asked. Her black eyebrows lifted.

I wondered how she knew so much about me. "Yes."

"You are pretty," she announced. Suddenly, hate came streaming out of her eyes at me and I felt weak all over. She reminded me of Odium.

Just then, a being behind me grabbed my arm and hauled me back, away from the sink. I turned to see who had seized me.

"Gabriella!" I was grateful for her presence and stopped shivering.

"Tori, get out!" Gabriella commanded. She pulled me behind her protectively. "Vincent wants to see you."

When I left the washroom, I almost smacked into Vincent, who was standing outside the bathroom. His eyes were glowing.

"Are you okay, Tori?" he asked, grabbing my hand. His voice was strained. He was very serious.

"Vincent, why did Gabriella come into the washroom?"

My Guardian smiled and shrugged his shoulders, still gripping my hand. I realized the blond angel had been worried about me. "I didn't want you to miss dessert. Our waitress came to the table and I didn't know what to order for you."

"Gabriella pushed me behind her. She acted like the woman in there had tuberculosis!" I exclaimed.

Vincent sighed and glanced at the door behind me. "The woman in the washroom was a demon and she was planning to kill you."

"Why didn't you come to save me? You're supposed to be my Guardian Angel!"

"I was trying to conform to human rules," he said. I frowned at him, confused. Then he explained. "Men don't go into women's restrooms."

"So I could have been murdered because you didn't want to go into a women's washroom?" I snorted at him.

He let his breath out. "Tori, Gabriella was nearby. She sensed the demon and came to talk to me. If there had been no female angels you knew, I would have gone into the washroom to save you myself. You were only in danger for a few seconds, not minutes."

Cursing myself, I stared at the loyal angel and nibbled at my bottom lip. "Sorry," I whispered. Vincent smiled at me and I felt my lips widening into a laugh.

"Tori, I won't let anything hurt you," he said softly.

My lips parted slightly as I watched the Herculean being. I desired him to kiss me, but I knew an angel wouldn't do that, so I walked back to my family's table with him.

*   *   *   *

Ten minutes later, I noticed Gabriella saunter into the room where we ate. Had she been in a fight with the demon waitress? She was glowing slightly, but she didn't have any cuts or scratches on her.

"Vincent, how does it work?"

His kind eyes looked toward me. "What do you mean? I'm not able to read your thoughts."

"Gabriella doesn't look hurt," I said.

Vincent licked his lower lip. "It wasn't a challenge for her. The demon was not high ranking... I assume she was a sergeant, and there was only one."

"How did Gabriella kill it?"

"You have seen my broadsword," Vincent stated seriously.

"Yes."

"Well, she probably decapitated it."

My eyes widened and my jaw dropped. "But someone will go in the washroom and see the body!"

He shushed me and leaned in close. "We're spirits. Her human form would have disappeared when Gabriella beheaded her."

CHAPTER EIGHT

MY BROTHERS AND I were in the middle of making breakfast for Mom when I decided to discuss with them a flyer we had received in the mail the day before.

"Hey guys, look at this," I announced, waving the flyer at Stephen as he scrambled eggs.

"What's that?" Stephen asked, grinning.

"You know the Cedargrove church?"

Will looked up, trying to see what was on the paper. "Yeah. What about it?"

"This Saturday they're hosting a special antique tractor display and picnic. The best part is, anyone attending is supposed to drive into town on their tractor."

"We don't have a tractor," Stephen pointed out.

I started to set the dishes on the table. "True, but I was thinking about asking Mr. Roberts if he could drive us there."

"I'd go if it was a car show," William replied. "What are they eating?"

"Chilli, homemade buns, roast chicken, baked potatoes, vegetables, and pumpkin pie," I answered as I read the advertisement.

Stephen removed the frying pan from the stove. "If we go, I'll call the minister to hide the rolls when William gets there," he teased. He glanced at me. "Call Mr. Roberts. If he'll drive his tractor, I'll go."

"Good," I said. "I'll ask him if he'll take his hay wagon. Then some of our friends can come, too."

"Don't invite Amber," William whispered in my ear.

*   *   *   *

On Saturday, Mr. Roberts drove his tractor, and the hay wagon carrying our family and friends. Gabriella and Huan-Yue were ensconced on the top of the wagon frame. I felt envy wishing I could be like those female Guardians who perched like that, but a human would be stupid to try it; humans had more to lose if they fell.

Our Guardians surrounded the wagon as we travelled. Stephen and William had wanted to sit with Vincent, so I sat with Barbara and Janessa. I turned to Barbara and asked, "Are you doing one or two years of internship?" Barbara was studying to become a doctor.

"Two years," she answered. "I'd like to be a resident before I marry Stephen, but I'll still have one year to intern after we marry. So that's not going to happen."

"I wouldn't want to marry until I was done studying," I said. "I was thinking about going to university to get my BScN, and then become a nurse practitioner."

"The RN extended class is cool, but you're twenty-one," Barbara pointed out. "I think you have to work as an RN for two years to get into the Nurse Practitioner program. You would be twenty-eight or twenty-nine by then."

I slowly frowned. "That's not too old. I've wanted to have my own clinic in a foreign country ever since I was fourteen."

"You and Vincent—" she started, but then broke off.

I took a deep breath. I couldn't marry a spirit, but Barbara didn't know Vincent was a Guardian Angel. I had to make plans and move on. I wanted a husband and baby one day. Vincent was a good friend, but...

I was so irritated that I started fidgeting on the seat.

*　*　*　*

As the wagon took us to the little brick church, I looked over at Tori. Her head was lowered and she was talking to Barbara in serious tones. My blood raced and I knew my eyes were turning golden. I couldn't look at Tori for fear that her cousins and friends would see my orbs. Angel eyes and demon eyes scared humans. My eyes became golden too quickly when I worried about Tori. I breathed in deep, gripped my jean-covered knees, and squeezed. I wanted to help her, but my feelings were too human... and it hurt.

I winced as my short nails pierced my flesh. Humans had serious disadvantages in the pain area. Being a Guardian Angel held no glory for me, but I had never cared about glory. Now, though, I wanted more—but I didn't know exactly what I wanted. I thought about my human too much. To be honest, I wasn't happy unless Tori was talking to me. She was young and we had so much fun together. Her friends thought I was her boyfriend, but the thought of her aging and not being able to move about so easily caused me pain. We would always talk, but when she was forty and I stayed twenty-five looking, she wouldn't want to be seen out with me. I would have to vanish and always remain in spirit form. Our friendship would shrivel, and someday she would marry a human. Without warning, the despair became too much. It was overwhelming.

"God help me," I whispered.

*   *   *   *

Mr. Roberts parked his tractor at the back of the parking lot. As soon as we stopped, Vincent lifted me, then bounded onto the gravel. He grinned at me. I felt a shiver of pleasure run through me as I regarded his blue eyes. My family and friends unloaded and walked toward the antique tractor display.

He hung back, clutching my hand. "Do you want to meet some other angels?"

I looked up at his glowing eyes. "Sure."

We strode away from the wagon where a tall, sable-haired angel with blue eyes appeared.

"Tori, this is Everett, Mrs. Roberts' Guardian Angel," Vincent told me.

Everett grinned broadly. "I always like to meet a human who can see our realm."

I was surprised to hear that angels liked to meet humans.

An attractive, red-haired angel landed nearby, closed his wings, and walked up to us. "I'm Patrick," the newcomer announced with an Irish accent.

"Hi, Patrick. Who do you guard?" I asked.

"Karen," he said.

An African American female angel with large curls then smiled at me from the roof of a car. She bounded down and looked at me curiously. "Wow, you can see us, for real?"

"Yes," I answered, turning to look at all the glowing spirits. I was awestruck.

A beautiful Native American angel caught my attention. "I'm Chenoa," she said.

"Do you protect Janessa?" I asked.

"Yes."

"I spend a lot of time with Janessa, but I haven't seen you."

"We have to choose for human beings to see us," she explained.

"But I thought Katherine Windsor and I could see all spirits."

"No," she whispered hauntingly.

"So there are demons I don't see?" I gasped. I was panicking. Vincent caressed the top of my hand, trying to calm me.

"Not very often, but you will always feel demons," he reassured me. "You're very sensitive."

CHAPTER NINE

SUNLIGHT CREPT AROUND the edges of my room's darkener blinds and I rose from my pillow to regard the clock. It was 7:45 a.m.

"Vincent," I called. Right away, he appeared in human form. He was so comforting. *Every woman should have a Guardian Angel she can see,* I thought. "Do you want to go for a walk in Grandpa's forest?"

"Sure," he answered.

I slid off the cotton sheets and brushed my feet on my slightly rough carpet.

"Can you go out on the balcony? I want to dress."

Vincent grinned at me wickedly, then opened the French doors. When he was gone, I ran into my walk-in closet and changed. This Monday, I wore brown cotton pants and a pink t-shirt. Once dressed, I walked out of the closet.

My Guardian slipped back into my bedroom, shutting the doors behind him.

"I need to eat quickly," I said. "Then I'll meet you outside."

"Sounds good," he answered, vanishing.

I walked downstairs.

It was warm at 8:15, so I knew it was going to be humid later. Vincent appeared when I walked onto the crushed stone driveway. He was wearing a blue t-shirt, jeans, and running shoes. Squinting, I opened the driver's door and Vincent sat on the passenger side. The sunlight caused a glare to shoot into my eyes from the car.

I drove to Grandpa and Grandma's house.

When Vincent and I arrived, my grandpa was mowing the lawn. Grandma had obviously just finished using her washing machine, because she was hanging clothing and towels on her clothesline.

"Hello, Grandma!" I called.

Grandpa turned the blade off on his lawn tractor and chased me until I jumped onto the porch. He liked to tease me. Whenever we went out for supper and I ordered fries, he would try to steal one from me. His hand would steal over the tabletop to my fries, a mischievous glint in his eyes, but if I offered him one he would pull his hand back and refuse. He was on a low salt diet, so he couldn't order them for himself. But he still enjoyed my reaction.

When he disembarked from the lawn mower I hugged him tightly. "I love you, Grandpa."

"I love you, too."

"Vincent and I want to walk in the bush. Is that all right?"

"Of course, Tori. No one's shooting in the bush today."

"Good." I strode to Grandma. "Grandpa said no one's hunting today, so Vincent and I are going for a walk in the bush."

"Have fun, Tori," she said.

"I love you, Grandma." I hugged her while her cotton-robed shoulder caressed my cheek.

"I love you, too, child."

"Come on, Vincent," I called, gesturing to him. My grandparents thought he was a good boyfriend... or did they know he was an angel? Grandpa and Vincent both smiled at me.

After Vincent and I left my grandparents' lawn, we walked through the fields to a creek which twisted through the woods. The running water sounded like it was laughing as it splashed over stones and branches. Long brown and green grasses grew high around the creek and a small wooden slat bridge without rails arched over the water. There were cedar trees around the edge of the east side of the bush where we were. The only wildlife sounds we heard were the soft calls of a blue jay and some crows.

Abruptly, Vincent pulled me backward against his chest. "Shhh," he uttered. I felt the warmth of his spirit energy flow into my back. My breathing slowed down as I looked down at his muscled arms. I knew he must have had a reason for quieting me, so I glanced up and searched the woods. After a moment, a magnificent buck gingerly strode into the fallow field.

"Oh my goodness," I murmured.

The animal lifted its majestic head and twelve-point rack as it sniffed the air and searched the field. When it noticed Vincent and me, it stood motionless for at least a minute. I was worried it would lift its white tail and run. As I held my breath, it lowered its head and commenced feeding.

"Did you know that deer shed their antlers?" Vincent whispered, his mouth close to my ear.

"I've heard that, but it doesn't make sense to me. Doesn't it take a long time to grow a rack like that?"

"No, they dump their rack every year after they mate."

A fawn with faint white spots and a sleek female hesitantly stepped into the open field. The doe sniffed the air and froze. Unlike the buck, the newcomers stayed at the edge of the field, watching Vincent and me.

"We better go," Vincent whispered. I groaned softly but followed the angel.

Vincent and I avoided the herbivores and traversed into the spread of maples, walnuts, and pine.

"Grandpa has quicksand in here," I announced, glancing upward. Vincent's blue eyes widened and he seized my arm. He didn't harm me, but his hand was firm. He never caused pain to my human body, but he was obviously capable of killing me in a second or two.

"Vincent, it's not right here. Besides, you can best quicksand, angel."

His firm fingers relinquished my arm and I tugged on his hand. I stared up at his glowing eyes and tight jaw. *He's been my Guardian Angel for my entire life. Why is he panicking about quicksand now? We're nowhere near it!*

We walked near the edge of the woods, bypassing rotting logs or stepping over them and pushing the branches of young trees and other foliage aside. The west side of the bush had been allowed to spread south for three or four hundred feet longer than the rest of the bush.

"The quicksand's over there," I said, gesturing at a ninety degree angle where the rest of the bush was cut off.

Vincent smiled. "I wasn't thinking. I remember everything from your past, but I was worried about you."

I smiled up at him as happiness overwhelmed me. Vincent didn't know how much he pleased me. However, I grimaced when I realized I had nothing new to tell him. "I can't tell you anything from the past, because you know everything."

"I like to talk with you, Tori. Tell me anything."

I gazed upward into his sun-tinted blue eyes. My body felt rebelliously weak, and I didn't understand why I couldn't control it. I liked being strong, not trembling and flaccid.

"Mom always made us stay away from the swamp," I spoke.

Dampness swept through my skin from the bush and its twisting creek. My body shivered. Even though I normally hated dampness, today I enjoyed it. Pungent skunk cabbage sprouted near the water.

Foliage from last autumn still remained on the ground. Vincent and I saw plastic water bottles and rusty aluminum cans at the base of a walnut tree that my brothers and I had shot at three years ago with a pellet gun.

"My brothers and I should have cleaned up those cans. We were going to shoot at them again, but Stephen's pellet gun stopped working and we forgot."

He produced a brown bag. Together, we gathered the refuse.

"You're amazing," I said, gesturing at the bag.

Vincent laughed. It sounded peaceful.

"What do you hear when God laughs?" I asked.

"God's laughing voice is the most exquisite music. I always have a sense of well-being when he's happy. I hear mercy and peace."

"You miss God," I said quietly.

"Of course. Heaven is so... sorry, Tori, there isn't a human word appropriate enough. Especially not in English."

I loved him. My hazel eyes settled on the peaceful and kind spirit. As my chest tightened, I turned and watched the creek. Vincent rubbed my shoulder.

"Tori, do you want to walk some more?" His compassionate eyes watched me. "Are you okay?"

I frowned and bit my lip. "Vincent, I was thinking about something sad."

Vincent seized my hand and rubbed it with his thumb. It felt so comforting when he touched my skin. I looked up at him and saw that his eyes were golden. Why were his eyes glowing?

"Come on, Vincent, we have to look at my grandpa's old maple syrup shanty. And you just watch; I'm going to be the only human who doesn't sink in quicksand."

His jaw dropped. "You can't walk on quicksand, and you won't go over there!"

"You can fly, so we can walk in the swamp," I explained.

Vincent rolled his eyes and raised his shoulders resignedly. "If you want, human…"

I laughed. "It's so nice to have you around, Vincent."

We walked through the field to the corner where the west boundary of the bush ran south. Vincent pushed the wire fence down and I stepped over it carefully. There was a small hill on the other side covered with moist leaves. Then the ground became mucky. Suddenly, my right leg sank down and I began to panic.

"Vincent!" I cried.

Vincent grasped my wrist. Soon I was standing on the muck instead of being in it.

"Did you want me to fly you home?" he asked.

I bit my lip and gazed at the swamp. "I was having fun."

He stroked my hand. "I can always get what I need from Heaven."

"Excuse me?"

"I can get you a clean pair of pants," he explained, grinning.

"Really?!" I gasped.

He smiled. "Sure. You need them."

All at once, he had a clean pair of pants in his hands and I grinned.

"Thank you. Turn around please," I said.

"If I do here, you're going to sink again."

I grasped his arm as he picked me up and flew us to solid ground. I thanked him and sped to a large walnut tree. "Now turn around."

My right leg was cold, but the new jeans felt good. Pretty soon, I was fully dressed again.

"Vincent, let's play hide and seek," I said as I came back around the tree. "Come find me, but count for sixty seconds."

The angel frowned, his eyes glowing. "Demons and quicksand," he reminded me gravely. "I can't leave you alone!"

My hazel eyes widened as my pulse quickened. "Do you sense them?" If Vincent sensed demons, there was no way I was even going to stay in this bush!

"No," he admitted and sighed. "All right, I'll count. But be careful."

As he began to count, I ran through the bush, vaulting over logs. "Oww," I complained when a prickly branch lashed me. Small wounds marred my right forearm, but I soon found the perfect hiding place behind some massive green weeds.

*   *   *   *

I could have appeared beside Tori right away, but I needed to dawdle and pretend I was human. My feet walked slowly across the fallen foliage. Suddenly, I heard a hiss, causing me to worry about Tori. My eyes turned golden as I felt myself taking spirit form. I quickly vanished and appeared closer to Tori, in front of some weeds. A pink hair elastic lay on the ground and I became certain the demons had captured her. Frowning, I felt my wings turn fiery.

"Demons!" I cried.

All at once, I sensed Odium and remembered the quicksand. Straight away, I flew back to the swamp. Odium, in spirit form, was standing on the mud with his right arm raised in the air. His onyx claws gripped Tori's left arm and she was dangling.

"Let her go!" I roared.

Odium's demonic red eyes gazed over at me. "Really? Right here?" he mocked. A swirling yellow cloud that reeked like sulphur spun through the swamp toward me.

When Tori saw me, she writhed and kicked at Odium, but he just laughed. "Stupid human." He shook his raised arm viciously. Tori's body swayed. She was terrified.

"Kill her, Odium!" Pernicious screamed, jumping and hissing. Cruelly, another creature, Fear, dug his claws into my calves and I felt a burning sensation. I pulled my five-foot blade and cut through Fear. His feral red eyes widened and yellow teeth bared as the imp vanished, his nauseating demon gore remaining on my sword. As I plunged my glowing broadsword into the ground, Tori screamed. I desperately swung to look over at the terrified girl and wished that Tori was safe.

"Vincent," she whispered. Odium had set her down on the quicksand, but he kept her wrist captive.

"Let's fight, Guardian," Odium hissed.

I raised my blade and Odium released her. Rapidly, her feet and legs began to sink and I felt my spirit energy race up into my fiery wings.

"Lay down, spread eagle!" I ordered Tori. She complied quickly.

Odium shook his black head and pulled a cutlass. We fought. Our blades crashed as he tried to break my sword. I soared up and attempted to decapitate him, but he twisted backward. I flew, revolving at the level of his abdomen, but his cutlass blocked me and I passed through a few trees from the impact. As I stumbled up, I saw that Tori was lying on her back; Pernicious was gleefully jumping on her stomach. She was sinking! My teeth clenched... there was nothing I could do while I fought the Strong Man. If I died, so would Tori.

"Help!" she screamed.

Ignoring Odium, I rushed to Tori and threw her onto a pile of leaves that I asked the Creator for so that she wouldn't die. She stared at me, shocked.

Pernicious hissed, stamping her scaly legs, and then she was gone.

Odium growled and appeared beside me. "She can die later, after I kill you," he uttered, his voice low. Enraged, I clenched my hand around the hilt of the blade. *Tori's never going to die,* I vowed to myself.

I plunged my blade into the demon. Odium's shocked red eyes bulged. He shrieked furiously, gripping his severed skin, and then vanished.

Once he was gone, Tori stood beside me, awed. "Thank you, Vincent," she whispered.

*   *   *   *

Vincent set me down on the grass outside my house, his glowing eyes piercing me. I needed to get cleaned up, so I squeezed his hand, trying to get his attention. I had his attention in one sense, but he seemed in another world even as we maintained eye contact with each other.

"Vincent, I'm getting cold," I murmured, shivering.

"Poor human. I'm sorry you're stuck in our world," he muttered huskily as he gripped my waist. He pulled me close. I stopped shivering as his heat penetrated my damp clothes. "I'll get you to your room."

He was about to fly me to my room when I heard the patio door open. I turned my head to find my brothers and mother staring at me.

Will ran toward Vincent and I with a furrowed brow. "Tori what happened to you?" he gasped.

"Remember Grandpa's quicksand?" I asked wryly.

CHAPTER TEN

THE NEXT MORNING, while out on the balcony, I felt supernatural heat near me. I smiled to myself, knowing my Guardian Angel was nearby. When I gazed at Vincent, he asked, "Are you okay this morning?"

I rubbed my abdomen. "Yes. My stomach's a little sore," I confessed.

My Guardian Angel's beautiful eyes were filled with guilt. "I'm sorry," he spoke.

"It's not your fault. It's my fault," I declared, wanting to comfort him. "I'm the one who wanted to play hide and seek,"

He blew his breath out. "My breaking the rules is not helping your safety."

I noticed his jaw tighten. Vincent stared at the wooden floor. Confusion filled me.

"What are you talking about?" I asked.

Vincent's head rose and his glowing eyes pierced me. "It's not really breaking the rules... being your friend, but because we're friends and you can see demons, you're their target." He gazed down at the wooden floor once again. I felt my pulse speed up as panic filled me. The last thing I wanted was to lose his friendship.

"What are you going to do, Vincent?" My voice quivered.

His shoulders rose, then he spoke determinedly. "I'm going to continue to be your friend."

*　*　*　*

In the evening, I walked outside and Vincent appeared, taking human form. I was grateful to see him, as I hadn't seen him since we sat on my balcony earlier that morning.

"Do you want to walk with me?" I asked.

"Sure, Tori."

The air was cool, but as I walked beside Vincent, he made wearing a jacket unnecessary. We walked along the gravel shoulder of the country road. I noticed he deliberately walked on the outside and I walked nearest the ditch. I smiled, realizing Vincent always wanted to protect me.

"Who was the first Guardian Angel?" I asked.

"Michael. He was Adam's Guardian, and I was the second Guardian, protecting Eve. I have been a Guardian for six thousand years." Vincent took a deep breath, then launched into the story:

Back in the Garden of Eden, Michael wanted to throttle the new humans after they sinned. His brown eyes glowed as he clasped the platinum hilt of his five-foot blade. Adam and Eve couldn't see us, but I wondered if they could sense our tension as they tried to make leafy clothes with which to cover themselves.

Michael growled as he paced, saying, "When the Creator says, 'No,' I understand! Do those pathetic humans speak some other language?" He threw up his hands in frustration."

"They were tempted," I muttered. I was angry at the disobedient humans, but I also felt compassionate.

"They tossed away friendship with the Creator," Michael hissed. "We are servants. They were supposed to be his friends!"

Michael made fists with his hands. I noticed his spirit energy hurtle into his expansive wings. Then he punched a large oak tree, which careened through the air. The oak smashed to the ground near Eve. She fearfully stared at the tree as she trembled.

When Eve saw Michael, it was pretty obvious. The poor woman's dark eyes grew huge and she screamed.

Without warning, I felt my own eyes glow. My eyes hadn't done that since the rebellion, so I scanned Eden. Several pairs of narrowed red eyes were watching us. Imps screeched from all around the garden. I knew they were here to mock Michael and me, because we had failed to keep God's creation clear of sin. Michael ignored the demons, though, and flew straight at Eve. When he did this, she threw herself behind a red rose bush. Michael was furious, so I emerged in front of the plant, gripping my sword to protect my charge.

"Human creatures, what a crazy idea!" he said.

"You are criticizing the Creator," I firmly reminded him.

"They sin as soon as they are created. Lucifer didn't sin for two billion years!"

Then Michael vanished.

"Wow," I whispered when he had finished telling the story.

"I understand God's joy to talk with humans and share," Vincent said. "Being a Guardian Angel was not as fulfilling before I started talking with you. There were moments when I wanted to be part of the conversation. I desired to share my spiritual knowledge with you. When you were upset, I wanted to cheer you up. I wanted to interfere when you were going to be harmed or make the wrong choice. I'm a spirit, but six thousand years of guarding humans has seemed so long; when I had to show my spirit side to scare away the man at Cedarwood, I took advantage of the opportunity and used it to get to know you personally."

"You didn't have to reveal yourself when I called in my room that night," I replied. "It would have been like the time I saw James sitting on my dad, or when my father saw James in angel form outside a tall window in their farmhouse when he was twenty."

"Your father saw James?" Vincent asked.

"Yes. When he was a young man, he looked out the window and saw an angel there. What are Guardian Angels really supposed to do, Vincent?"

He sighed and grasped my hand firmly. "Keep you safe from demons. That's why I have a sword. We also protect our humans from accidents, like falling down the stairs or car wrecks. We can keep our charges from being hurt as badly as they could have been, but we can't interfere in the consequences of the choices people make. But sometimes we can lessen those consequences. When someone wants to commit suicide, that's up to the Creator; it's a human choice and we usually can't stop people from killing themselves. You see, the Creator intended for humans to make choices."

He's seen so many things in six thousand years, so many things he couldn't stop, I thought.

I caressed his hand. "I'm sorry."

His eyes glowed at me. "You need to bless people who hurt you... except demons."

After grimacing, I said, "Ouch. Why?"

Vincent rubbed my hand carefully. "Because the Creator wants it that way."

"It doesn't make sense. It's unreasonable."

"Demons butchered the Creator's son when he took human form," he declared.

I wished I hadn't been human, because I wanted to see things the way Vincent and God saw them. I was frustrated at my pathetic mind-sets. I didn't want to hold grudges, even though humans did that all the time. I wanted to forgive. Being human was... debilitating.

Vincent gripped my fingers. His supernatural warmth penetrated my hand. I usually enjoyed his heat. "Guardians struggle, too. If someone murdered you, I don't know if I could—" Swiftly, he turned his gaze to the fields next to the house and swallowed. "My humans have been murdered from time to time. It feels like a demon cutlass in your stomach. As Guardians, we can never forget the deaths of our humans, because we really care about you. After our humans die, all we want is peace, so the Creator lets us have a holiday for three months in which we don't have to fight demons or protect humans. We can go to a rainforest or some mountain or wherever. Overwhelming peace consumes any created being when they rest in nature."

"What about demons?" I asked.

His solemn eyes stared at me. "Demons never have peace. I think they resent not being able to enjoy earth and Heaven like people and angels do."

*   *   *   *

After six thousand arduous years of protecting and losing humans, I felt at peace. My Lord's enemies never stopped. At least when Tori was awake, I could talk to her. When she was asleep, I could think of new things to teach her while I talked to God. Time was different for angels than it was for humans, but no matter what I said to Tori, time was long for me. The more time I spent on earth with my human, the more I felt human and experienced life like them. I was used to demons sticking their daggers at me, used to imps and Strong Men assailing my humans, but I didn't want them to hurt Tori. I was close to her now and I loved her. I was not afraid of being annihilated.

*   *   *   *

After a strenuous evening shift at Cedarwood on Thursday, I plopped onto the middle of my couch. Suddenly, Vincent appeared in human form.

"My feet are sore," I groaned.

He listened and then said, "Move over." He sat down on the tapestry at the other side of the couch and lifted my feet. Then he removed my socks and started to massage one foot.

My mouth opened. "Vincent, I didn't know angels rubbed human feet."

He smiled. "We generally don't, but I wanted to make you feel better."

I closed my eyes. His heat, coupled with his hands on my feet, relaxed me until I felt completely relaxed.

Vincent massaged my feet for ten minutes, then took my left hand. "Stand up, Tori. You have to go to sleep."

I obeyed him, but said, "Vincent, now let me rub your feet."

The blond angel was shocked. His blue eyes were wide. "I'm not mortal. I don't need you to do that... I'm a servant."

"But it feels good," I announced and sat down.

"I'm an angel—" he protested.

"—in human form," I reminded him. "Now, give me your feet."

The tall angel sat, raised his feet off the carpet, and rested them in my lap. Vincent's feet had perfect arches. They were probably size twelve or thirteen. I touched the soles, and he didn't squirm like my dad always did when my brothers and I tried to tickle them. I heard Vincent sigh as I caressed his feet.

"Do you like this?"

Vincent grinned. He was quite relaxed. "Yes. Thank you, Tori. I have never felt relaxed on earth, but I did for a few moments just now."

"You always have to watch out for your humans," I said softly, feeling sorry for the angel.

"There are many dangers... too many." He sounded exhausted.

"Thank you, Vincent." When I glanced at his face, compelling eyes watched me. I swallowed as my stomach hosted butterflies.

"I would do anything I could for you, Tori."

*   *   *   *

My mind shunned sleep as I faced the wall by my bed. When I felt supernatural energy, I knew Vincent was in the room with me. I wanted to ask him to talk to me, but I didn't call him. Slowly, I rolled and faced the rest of the room.

Suddenly, I realized my mistake; it wasn't Vincent, after all. Odium appeared next to my bed, his black trench coat undulating as though there was a light wind. His onyx eyes stared darkly at me and I felt chest pain. I sensed his demonic hatred.

Before I could utter a word, the spirit vaulted onto the end of my bed. His hands and nails gripped the sheets. He penned my feet.

"Go away, Odium!" I commanded as my body trembled.

He started laughing. "Human, you don't understand. I am a Strong Man; I have a high rank under the prince. I used to be an Archangel. Do you imagine I would listen to a pathetic human being? I can do what I want." Vile sulphur blew from him into my nostrils, and I glowered.

Where is Vincent?

"Vincent isn't here," he taunted, his heinous eyes raking over me. My pulse raced as I gazed around the room and shivered. *How can I distract him?*

"What was your Archangel name?" I asked, looking up into black eyes.

Gazing down at me, he hissed, "Lucas."

How do I scare a demon away?

I quickly bent and raised my legs, launching them at the demon. The onyx-clothed being flew backward off my bed and fell to the floor, cursing and hissing in a feral voice.

A powerful radiance suddenly filled my room and I could see Vincent in angel form. As I watched, a yellow sulphur cloud spread and drifted along the baseboards and rose. Odium was laughing.

"Vincent, let me murder her and you won't be a despicable enemy to us anymore," Odium growled. My Guardian's massive iridescent blade responded to the Strong Man.

*   *   *   *

The following morning, the phone rang in my room while I was dusting.

"Hello," I said.

"Hi, Tori," Kristen's voice said over the line. "Tell me you can sleep over on Friday."

"Sure."

"I'll come over and get you at six o'clock."

"Great! Is Amber or Cindy coming?"

"No."

"Bring a party dress with you," she added. "My dad's having a party on Friday. I know how you love to dress up."

"Yes," I answered. "That will be great."

After I hung up, I walked to Dad and Mom's room. My mom was looking for any pants in my dad's side of the closet that needed to be washed. He didn't like to cause more work for Mom and I don't believe he was quite as aware as she was how much dirt and mud was on his pants.

"Kristen asked me to stay over on Friday night," I announced.

"That's okay," Mom answered. Three pairs of pants lay on the bed.

"I'll put those in the wash," I said and gathered my father's laundry.

"Thanks, Tori," she answered.

CHAPTER ELEVEN

ON FRIDAY EVENING, a vehicle drove over the crushed stone gravel in our driveway as it raced up the lane. Excitement careened through me when I thought of the coming party. I grabbed my garment bag and scrambled downstairs to hug Mom and my brothers goodbye. When the doorbell chimed, I pulled the green door inward.

"Hi, Kristen," I said excitedly.

"Tori!" Kristen exclaimed.

"I bought a dress in Smithington this week."

"Awesome."

"Bye, everyone!" I yelled.

We strolled outside, where her red convertible was waiting.

"Dad's getting me another car for my twenty-first birthday," she announced.

"Sheesh," I said, smiling. "This is a nice car. You should give it to me for an extremely belated birthday present."

She sighed. "I adore it. Of course, my other friends are jealous. You like my stuff, but you don't *long* for it. Amber does. In fact, all my other friends lust for my stuff. But you don't."

"Don't put me in another class. I like my life, but once in a while, I wish I could be like Kristen Petrovich," I confessed.

Her intelligent black eyes searched mine. "We'll always be friends."

"I hope so."

*   *   *   *

The Georgian manor Kristen lived in looked like the White House. There was a mammoth, slightly garish steel fence around the lawn, and a cedar hedge grew just inside it. No part of the lawn was visible beyond the hedge.

When the sports car stopped inside the garage, Kristen turned to regard me. "My cousin Nikolai needs an escort tonight."

When she mentioned her cousin, I felt confused. The thought of spending time with a well-bred, probably handsome man was exciting, but I had feelings for my Guardian Angel. However, Vincent was an angel and I couldn't marry him. My hands perspired and I brushed them on my jeans. I felt heat in my cheeks. Oh man, I was blushing. Unfortunately, Kristen was watching me.

"You and Kevin broke up," she reminded me.

I frowned, dwelling on my intensely handsome Guardian. Vincent wasn't dating me because he was a spirit. He wouldn't care if I spent time with Nikolai. My shoulders rose, and I said, "Okay."

We strolled to the garage door, which opened for us automatically. It must have had a sensor.

"Good evening, Miss Kristen and Miss Smiley," her butler greeted. The well-groomed, grey-haired man wore a navy suit.

"Adam, don't you usually attend the front door?" Kristen asked.

Wrinkles formed around his mischievous green eyes. "I heard your convertible flying up the driveway and decided to give you a thrill, Miss, by opening the garage door." He turned to look at me. "Miss Smiley, my favourite of Miss Kristen's friends."

Adam called me Smiley because I always smiled at the servants.

"Your father wants you to know he is glad you invited Miss Victoria instead of Miss Amber," Adam said, wrinkling his nose. "That girl is not dignified."

"Well, Adam, I didn't invite Amber because she would flirt with every man tonight." Adam laughed. "Are Uncle Mikhail and Aunt Tatiana here?"

"No, Miss. Their flight from Russia was delayed. They arrived at the airport twenty-five minutes ago."

We walked into the marble-floored foyer, which was nearly a thousand square feet. A massive brass staircase led up to the second floor, and next to it was a white-panelled elevator.

Cherie, Kristen's maid, was reading a novel when we opened the mahogany-panelled double door to her bedroom. "Miss Kristen, Miss Tori," she said with a smile. She stood up after putting her book in the magazine rack.

"Cherie can do your nails," Kristen said. I surreptitiously glanced at my friend's spotless French manicure. I laid my black garment bag on her queen-size canopy bed and put my red sports bag down on the hardwood floor.

"A golden hairbrush?" I asked, perching near her dresser.

Kristen grinned. "You could have one, if you want."

My eyebrows lifted. "I'm not a golden hairbrush type of girl."

"Nikolai's very magnanimous with the girls he sees," she announced.

I grimaced slightly. "I'm not that type of girl, either."

"But he—"

"I'm not blond," I said.

"You have the streaks," she pointed out with a smile. She grinned wickedly and rested her index finger against her lips. "He gave one girl an Italian sports car."

My lips parted in awe. "Oh my goodness. Who *are* you people?"

"Nikolai says you're hot."

"How does he know what I look like?" I asked.

"I e-mailed him your picture," she said. "You know, my father married a Chinese woman and she wasn't a model."

"Your mom was very attractive," I protested.

"So are you. Mom was from a small town. Not every man wants a supermodel. Besides, it would be fun if we were cousins—except Nikolai would take you to Russia... probably." She frowned. "What colour is your dress?"

"Royal blue," I responded, but I neglected to say it was seventy-five percent off.

She smiled. "Mine is red."

"How tall is Nikolai?"

"6'2. His dad is my father's younger brother. He's Russian and very good-looking."

A half-hour later, Kristen and I were ready. She was attired in a long red, halter style dress. Her black hair was collected from the sides and pinned at the back of her head with a diamond clip. She also wore diamond earrings. I wore a long, sleeveless blue gown and silver chandelier earrings. Cherie styled my brown hair into a French twist.

Butterflies relentlessly tormented my stomach as we got ready to go downstairs.

*　*　*　*

When Kristen's door swung inward, I saw Tori gingerly stride into the hall. I stared at her, as she was incredibly striking. Spirit energy raced through my form, tingling my wings, and I desperately hoped my spirit body wasn't glowing. Had I been in human form, I wouldn't have been able to contain my excitement at seeing her.

Tori and Kristen began to descend the stairs. Waiting at the bottom of the staircase, I observed a brown-haired rogue, slightly shorter than my human height. He was ogling Tori predatorily as she descended. My eyes turned golden and I actually wanted to swear, which horrified me. I worried the Creator would be angry. The rogue stalked up to Tori.

"Nikolai, this is Tori—I mean, Victoria Davenport," Kristen introduced.

"Hello, Victoria," Nikolai murmured. He lifted Tori's hand to kiss it, then stared at her. My rebellious hand clasped the handle of my blade and I growled. I needed to look at the wall, knowing that my angel form was going to turn golden if Tori didn't get away from Nikolai—and soon. If that happened, the humans would be able to see me. But I was her Guardian, so I watched and tried not to break the platinum handle of my sword. Jealousy gripped me and my spirit form wanted to explode.

"Tori, this is my cousin, Nikolai Petrovich."

"*Zdravstvuite*, Nikolai. *Kak Dela?*" Tori asked.

Nikolai's eyebrows flew into his brown hair and I almost laughed.

"*U menja dela horosho*," Nikolai said. "Wow, you speak Russian?"

Tori bit her bottom lip. "No, just greetings, farewells, and thank you." I could tell she was nervous.

Nikolai laughed. "Well, I'll make you say thank you tonight," he murmured, observing Tori like a carnivore. She blushed. My body vibrated from my rage and I drew my sword. My wings were already turning fiery.

"I'm going to find Carlos," Kristen said.

The three young people then walked into the large formal living room. At least they hadn't seen me! I inhaled and sheathed my sword, feeling too many emotions.

When Michael appeared, I was glowering inside the doorway to the living room. He startled me. I vaulted and expediently captured my platinum-handled blade with my right hand. But I didn't pull the weapon.

"For pity's sake," I growled. "You caught me by surprise."

Michael crossed his arms. "You shouldn't have been surprised. You must be distracted."

"Go away," I hissed.

"You're concentrating on Tori too much."

My hand pointed toward my human and the rogue. "Look," I said. Jealousy expanded in my chest and abdomen, making me feel uncomfortable.

"That's what humans do, Vincent. Tori's human."

Why do you have to be so self-righteous? I wanted to say.

"You have to stop what's going on here," my friend said gravely. I frowned at him in confusion. "That human is no good." Michael was referring to Nikolai.

"I can't stop them," I growled, my supernatural energy coursing through my wings.

"You're her Guardian. He will harm Tori."

"What are your orders? Do I lock her in a room?" I asked sarcastically.

Michael smirked. "You could put her in a closet and hold the knob."

"She has free will. I can't kidnap her."

"You also have to keep her away from Nikolai."

I took a deep breath. "But you believe in sticking to all the rules. It's free will, Michael."

"Tori doesn't know he's bad. Besides, you're her friend and you already broke the rules."

"Okay," I growled. I spun on my heel and moved toward the living room. Before stepping inside, I turned back to Michael with an idea. "You get Tori. Take human form and steal her away."

Straight away, my friend's eyes started to glow. "She's not my responsibility!"

"But Michael, Tori is the only human here who knows who you are. I can explain everything to her once we're all safely outside."

*   *   *   *

Mr. Petrovich glided over to Nikolai and me as we strode into the living room. "Good evening," he announced. "You look beautiful, Victoria."

"Thank you, sir," I responded. The austere man clasped my fingers and kissed the top of my hand. "Thank you for permitting Kristen to invite me."

"I am glad she didn't invite Amber. You improve a celebration."

"Thank you, Mr. Petrovich."

"Have fun." With that, the dignified man glanced at Nikolai.

Okay, what does that mean?

Before I could figure it out, Master Jovanovich walked toward us with a beautiful black-haired woman.

"*Zdravstvuite*," he said to Nikolai.

"*Zdravstvuite*," Nikolai answered.

Jovanovich smiled at me. "Aw, my student. How are you?"

"*U menja dela horosho*," I replied, grinning.

His jaw dropped and he took a backward step, astonished. "Excuse me? I did not teach you that!"

"Learning a little Russian is a hobby for me," I explained.

"Very good," he said, then glanced at the beautiful middle-aged woman accompanying him. "*Moja Dorogaja*, this is Victoria Davenport, a very talented student." I was shocked at the compliment. I had only started fencing. "Victoria, this is my wife, Anastasia."

"I am pleased to meet Dmitri's student," she announced, exuding friendliness.

I smiled. "I'm pleased to meet you, too."

*　*　*　*

While I was dancing with Nikolai fifteen minutes later, my body start-ed to shiver. I looked carefully around the room and didn't see any imps or demons in human form with their dark eyes. That's when I gazed up at Nikolai and saw that his blue eyes were glowing. I frowned.

"You don't like my eyes, Victoria?" Nikolai asked.

"They glow."

He smirked. "Be glad they're not black."

I frowned deeper, my chest tightening. The pull from his smile was almost as strong as Vincent's.

"That gown is alluring," he murmured.

"Thank you. That tuxedo is magnificent." I grinned mischievously at the handsome man.

Nikolai laughed and gazed admiringly at me. "Wicked woman," he whispered, bending down. He obviously realized I was teasing him. "Do you want some vodka?" All at once, Nikolai turned his head to the side.

"I'd love to cut in," a voice said.

I recognized Michael's voice. I groaned, sighing as I gazed up at the Guardian Angel's brown eyes.

My date growled. "There are other hot women here. She is my es-cort for the night."

"Share and share alike," Michael answered, amused.

Nikolai growled and raised his hands like a preacher. "My father—"

"Are you warning me?" Michael seized my left hand. Nicolai glared at him brutally and then stalked off to join his mother, Tatiana.

Michael gazed down at me and pulled me into his chest. "Mi-chael!" I scolded softly.

"You're Vincent's human. I'm guarding you."

I frowned at Michael. I knew he disliked me.

"Smile, Tori. If you don't, Nikolai will come back."

"That's okay," I answered defiantly.

Michael just stared at me. "Did his eyes glow?" he queried, amused.

"Yes." I was shocked that the angel knew about Nikolai's eyes. "Is he a spirit?"

"No," Michael answered gravely, "but he's possessed."

"I shivered while we were dancing, but I didn't see any imps or humans with black eyes." Suddenly, I shivered again. "Where's Vincent?" My skin was starting to sweat and my breathing quickened. "Michael, I'm afraid."

I felt spirit compassion coming from Michael, and for once his brown eyes weren't shooting criticism. Moreover, his warm spirit energy travelled through my skin, consoling me. Michael didn't detest me, I realized.

"Thank you. I feel safe around Guardians."

"Vincent is waiting outside on the lawn," Michel disclosed. "He didn't want Kristen or Nikolai to see him, because he likes to take human form and be your friend. If there's a problem involving me tonight, it won't matter because I don't intend to take human form again. But Vincent will."

Concern twisted in my abdomen as I gazed up at the Guardian. "Kristen is going to be angry," I said, biting my bottom lip.

"She won't be angry at you," Michael comforted.

"Really?"

"I'm the one monopolizing you and scaring the Russian away."

"Thank you... by the way, I like that suit, Michael."

"Thanks, Tori. You're very beautiful." He smiled warmly, then scanned the bar. "Your possessed escort is talking to his mother." But I didn't want to even look at Nikolai. "Do you want to go back to Vincent?"

"Sure."

Of course, I was upset to learn that Nikolai was possessed; it was nice to have a gorgeous man act like he had, but I loved Vincent. Michael seized my fingers and we quickly strolled out into the rear yard.

When he speedily grasped my waist and lifted me, I gasped. We flew to the west side of the house.

I felt calm spirit energy before we landed. Michael set me down near the outside wall. Not surprisingly, Vincent was nearby. The two of us stared at each other.

"Vincent!" I exclaimed as I leaned in to hug my Guardian.

"Tori," Vincent whispered. His muscled arms pressed tight around me. I closed my eyes, leaned on the spirit's shoulder, and hugged him until my body had relaxed. Most guys would have killed to have a ripped body like his.

I sensed Michael's spirit energy dissipate and knew he had left. Knowing we were alone, I started to panic. "Is Michael going to stay around Kristen's mansion?"

"Yes," Vincent answered.

I breathed out in relief. "I'll have to go back inside with him. After all, I'm supposed to sleep overnight."

I noticed that Vincent was staring at me admiringly. He looked mesmerized. My breathing slowed. *Does he love me?* I wondered, sighing softly. *I hope he didn't notice that sound.*

"Are you okay?" he asked.

I rested my fingers on Vincent's solid chest. "Michael said Nikolai is possessed."

His glowing blue eyes watched me intensely. "Are you upset?" he asked huskily.

"Nikolai is high calibre and I was enjoying his attention," I replied, looking down.

"You're beautiful," Vincent whispered.

I gazed upward and saw his golden eyes. They turned golden whenever there were demons, nearby so I frowned. My body trembled.

"Are there demons around?" I asked.

His eyes widened and his blond eyebrows rose. He looked surprised and I didn't know why.

"A few," he admitted, "but they are inside and won't hurt you. They're occupied." He didn't look back at the mansion.

"Then why are your eyes golden?"

He groaned. "It happens when I'm experiencing strong emotions."

I pursed my lips. "You were worried about me because Nikolai is possessed?"

"Of course." His voice wavered.

All at once, I sensed Michael's return. I turned around and saw him watching us. "You need to pretend you're sick so you can go home," Michael said, holding out his hand.

CHAPTER TWELVE

THE NEXT NIGHT, I drove with my brothers and their girlfriends to get ice cream in Smithington. When we got out of the car at a seasonal ice cream store, Vincent appeared to be ambling around the side of the shop.

"Vincent!" I exclaimed. The angel grinned at me.

"Hey, Tori. I love ice cream, too," he said.

I regarded our Guardians. Huan-Yue and Gabriella sat on a wide cement flower planter. Alexander stood adjacent a red public mailbox near the plaza driveway, gripping his broadsword handle while Gloria lounged by William's red muscle car.

"Do the other Guardians want ice cream?" I asked, gazing at the golden specks dancing in his blue eyes.

"No," he answered. "They don't want to take human form, and they would have to if they wanted to eat."

I nudged the bumpy pavement with my sandal. Anxiety filled me; I didn't want Vincent to take spirit form like his obedient Guardian

Angel friends. Even though he had already reassured me he would continue to be my friend and keep appearing in human form, I was terrified of him staying in angel form for the rest of my life.

Vincent stroked my hand. "Are you okay?"

"Can you keep taking human form?" I asked, anxiously staring up at him.

"Of course," he murmured seriously.

Then, his eyes started to glow, making me nervous. "Are there demons in the plaza?"

"No. Tori," he replied patiently.

I sighed, wondering how I was going to survive the rest of my life with all the emotions and fears my Guardian stirred up. Someday I'm probably going to die from a heart attack thinking there are demons around when Vincent's eyes start to glow. But I'd rather die of fright than have him vanish.

Once I had settled down, I asked, "What flavour of ice cream are you getting?"

He looked down at me mischievously, "I don't know. Probably every flavour."

"That's not even possible. How many scoops are you planning on getting?"

He looked at me seriously. "Don't worry, no more than twenty."

"But you're in human form with a human tummy," I reminded, patting his stomach.

"But I'm really not human."

Vincent began walking toward the ice cream shop, too fast for a human. He liked to tease as much as I did!

"Hurry, human!" he called, grinning. I ran after him.

*   *   *   *

Five minutes later, Tori and I sat on a bench by ourselves. Her brothers and their girlfriends occupied one of the plastic tables. Their Guardians stood behind them and I grinned, realizing that when I took human form there was no one watching us. I frowned, remembering that I had to keep very alert or both Tori and I would be in danger. I was the one who was supposed to watch her back, but I wasn't human, so there was no one to watch my back. It was imperative for me to be attentive for demons!

Catching me off guard, Tori took my bowl filled with ten scoops. I had decided not to get twenty. She had been right; when I was in human form, I had human limitations.

"Do you mind if I try that double chocolate flavour?" she asked.

I smiled, "Go ahead."

"Thanks."

She scooped up the concoction and ate it. I looked at her small container of sherbet and wondered why she had bothered to get something low fat when she really wanted the flavours I had.

She licked her full lips. I stared at her mouth and was filled with human desires. I knew she hadn't intended to bring my attention to her lips, but I promised myself I would kiss her someday, no matter what. While I struggled to think of something else, I tried to get my spoon back from her.

"Hey, human, that's my spoon."

She tickled my hand, though, and kept the spoon. "I'm not going to eat it all," she reassured me, going for the double chocolate again.

*　*　*　*

The next morning, after I watered the flowerbeds, I sat on the ground and pulled the weeds out of the earth with my hands. The ground was soft and I enjoyed the feel of the earth as I dug through it. I was happy my mane was in a ponytail or else my face would be dirty from me constantly pushing my hair away. In May, Mom had given me money and sent me to a nearby greenhouse to choose the flowers for our flowerbed. Now that it was July, the flowers had progressed well and I hunted for dead flower heads to pull off. As I worked, I noticed white running shoes appear near my legs.

"Hello, Tori."

I grinned up at Vincent. "Do you want to help me, angel?"

"Sure, I've never helped with chores."

"This isn't a chore. I volunteered to do it," I said as a long legged spider traversed my hand, its pin-like legs tickling my skin. Vincent squatted and pulled weeds out of the earth.

"I've never felt soil on my hands," he said, studying his fingers.

"And embedded in your fingernails," I added.

As Vincent started to pull weeds again, small black ants clambered off the plants and dirt in Vincent's hand and down his wrist, which made him grimace.

"They feel strange," he said. He watched the insects with fascination.

I laughed softly at him. "Do you remember when I raised Monarch caterpillars to butterflies last year?"

"Sure. I was really fascinated. It was the first time I really paid any attention to insects."

"You know how Monarch caterpillars feed on milkweed? Well, I've checked the milkweed around our house, and even some in Smithington, but I haven't found any caterpillars this year," I announced sadly.

Vincent stared at me compassionately. "Let's walk. We can check the milkweed by the side of the road."

* * * *

Tori and I walked along Kinkaid Road searching for milkweed plants. After we had walked a while, we turned off onto a side road where I noticed wild Queen Anne's lace in the ditch. They looked like snow-flake patterns. Brazen grasshoppers clung to our shirts and then jumped through the fences surrounding the nearby fields.

We searched the numerous milkweed leaves and stalks along this road, too. When Tori looked up at me with disappointment, my chest felt tight.

"I guess all the farmers around here have sprayed their crops," she said with huge hazel eyes.

"We could drive to Smithington," I suggested.

She pursed her lips. "No. I want to keep checking, right here."

"Do want to swim later?"

Tori smiled warmly at me. "Yes, Vincent."

God, I need some Monarch caterpillars, I told the Creator in my head after we had strolled beside the field for another half-hour. Suddenly, as Tori squatted beside the milkweed, she grinned.

"Vincent! I found an egg." She pulled a leaf off the milkweed stalk and put it in my hand. A tiny yellow egg was stuck to the underside of the plucked leaf. Happiness engulfed me. Tori continued searching the plants and found three striped caterpillars. One creature was massive. "I think this one will make a chrysalis tonight."

"Do you want more?" I asked.

Her hazel eyes sparkled. "But of course, Vincent." We searched milkweed for another hour and found five more striped caterpillars. I had never examined the Creator's work like this. Being a human was so different, I thought. The more I took human form, the more I felt like a human. Unexpectedly, I felt a prick on my leg at the ankle.

"Vincent, you have burs on you!" Tori exclaimed. She squatted and pulled two nickel-sized, porcupine-looking balls off my sock and three off the back of my shorts at the hem. She grimaced when a thin piece of bur embedded in her flesh. She pulled it out and gazed back at the milkweed stalks.

We stopped along the road just as a black muscle car turned onto our road and tore toward us. I shivered violently and felt my eyes start to glow. A scaly, onyx arm reached out the window and I saw red eyes through the tinted front windshield. I knew there was a demon in that car, along with humans! One human was holding a bottle of booze through the window on the passenger side. Tori was ignoring the car and I stood near her as she collected a few more milkweed leaves to feed to her caterpillars. My human form heart was slamming and I really wanted to pull my angelic broadsword. Unfortunately, I needed to stay in human form so that I could spend time with her. I couldn't afford to have any human see me in angel form while I was with Tori.

As the car passed, someone inside threw the bottle at her. I forgot my intention to stay in human form. I took angel form, seized her, and pulled her away. The bottle smashed onto the gravel beside the asphalt and Tori screamed. I sheltered her with my arms.

"Shhh," I whispered while she trembled. I felt her energy relax, then released her. She was angry.

"Were there demons in that car?" she asked with narrowed eyes.

"One."

"This is not normal. Demons keep attacking me!"

"I hate it, too," I whispered intently. The energy consuming my body charged into my wings. "I'll take you home."

I picked her up and we flew back to Tori's house.

CHAPTER THIRTEEN

UNPLEASANT MEMORIES WERE disturbing me. I stalked onto my balcony and complained, "Life is torture!"

Vincent looked down at me with a frown.

"There are so many memories," I explained. "Life is full of memories."

The angel smiled gently. "Don't you think angels have memories? I remember everything that that has happened for the last twenty billion years."

"But most of those memories are in Heaven!" I protested.

Vincent watched me seriously. "I remember the Great War."

"World War One?"

"No. Heaven was happy for the first two billion years of my life. Then Lucifer, my friend, decided to get rid of God." Vincent looked down at the floor, feeling conflicted.

"You were friends with the devil!" I exclaimed.

His blue eyes looked at me sadly. "He told me to come to a meeting in his room. There were fifty high-ranking Archangels present. Because

Archangels are twelve feet tall, massive, and beautiful, I felt inadequate around them."

Empathy consumed me and I gripped Vincent's fingers. He knew what it was like to have pathetic human feelings, after all.

"Even though I served God personally, on certain occasions when Archangels entered God's presence they raised their eyebrows at me and smirked. My high position was desirable and I guess they didn't think an eight-foot angel should have it. That day, Lucifer told us that we would rule Heaven.

"So Lucifer called another meeting. I didn't want to go, but I did, so that I could help God. The second meeting entailed takeover plans. He told us that a third of the angels would back him. Furious, I went to God and told him about what was happening. God said, 'I know already.' I was upset because I thought another angel had told my Lord. I had hoped the Creator would be pleased with me. However, God *was* pleased, and then he said, 'My loyal, humble angel. I know everything. You will receive a reward for your loyalty. I will grant one request. Whatever it is, you can have it.' But I told him there was nothing I wanted.

"Lucifer and the angels who agreed to help him approached the palace. They lifted their swords and shouted at the Creator. God sat on his throne at first, but then walked out to encounter the rebel angels with a million loyal Archangels and me. Of course, the angels for God fought the evil angels. A lot of angels were injured during the spirit battle, on both sides. Lucifer glared at me, we fenced, and then he tried to behead me. But God raised his right hand and Lucifer fell over the wall of Heaven, becoming ugly instantaneously. All the rebellious angels turned black, and some of them shrunk and grew horns. Then a strong force threw them over the wall of Heaven. They all fell into a big hole that had fire blazing in it.

Vincent paused. I was mesmerized by his story.

"I can also recall God creating the earth," he added. "Moreover, I remember the birth and death of all my humans."

"What memory do you enjoy the most?" I asked quietly, leaning into him.

He smiled and laughed. "The evening I saved you in the Cedarwood parking lot and you saw for the first time that angels are real."

"Why? I'm only human. There are so many more significant things."

"I like being your friend, Tori. You humans are insignificant in the fact that you are so small." He stretched his arms wide. "But to God, you are incredibly significant."

* * * *

The wind had been blowing powerfully for four hours across the grey sky. The spirea shrubs around the property swayed like belly dancers. Tiny flower petals lay like confetti on the short grass. The grass was a duller shade of green than normal, I noticed when I walked out onto my balcony. Lightning bounced in the atmosphere. I liked thunderstorms.

Suddenly, Vincent landed next to me. "Where were you?" I asked.

"I was on the roof watching the clouds accumulate."

"I wish I could be an angel."

He frowned. "Be glad you're human."

"But I can't fly," I protested.

"Would you rather spend your existence fighting demons?" The thunder reverberated all around us.

"You don't have to sleep," I pointed out. "You don't feel pain."

Vincent laughed softly. "Humans like to sleep, and I do experience pain... often. While fighting demons."

I was shocked. "Do you fight everyday?" I asked.

"Almost."

"But you are strong. Your angel form scares them easily."

"True, but they never attack an angel alone. They always attack in groups of three or more. I am not God, Tori. I can be killed."

"Easily?" I asked.

"No..." He paused. "The Cherubim are the lucky ones. They stay in heaven and praise God. They don't experience pain or fighting. The Messengers don't feel pain, either. The Legion angels and the Warrior angels fight demons who try to stop the Messengers. Most angels want to be human at one point or another."

"Excuse me?!" I exclaimed.

"It's true."

"But in a storm like this, say, if you're struck by lightning, you won't die."

"Living forever is not something you would want to do," he stated.

"Why?" I asked. I couldn't understand him.

"Sometimes I get tired, Tori. One day, you will rest and go to Heaven and I will guard another human. I wish I could reap the rewards of a human who serves God. The power doesn't compensate for that."

"Do you miss your humans when they die?" I asked softly.

"Yes." He stopped watching me and turned to watch the storm with gorgeous blue eyes. When I saw a tear at his eye, my chest hurt; I wanted to carry his pain, but I was only a human.

I walked over to the balcony railing and sat on it. As I watched the storm, Vincent stepped closer to me. Lightning played in the grey clouds, revealing their formations. Suddenly, it started to rain hard.

I shrieked and tried to get off the railing, but I lost my balance and my arms flew back. Before I could fall, Vincent grabbed my waist and set my feet back on the balcony floor. His palms remained around my waist. He frowned down at me, his blue eyes taking on a golden glow.

"Please don't sit on that railing. I couldn't be an angel anymore if you died before God wanted you to."

CHAPTER FOURTEEN

THE PLEASANT SMELL of barbecued hamburgers filled our home the night of July 17, Will's nineteenth birthday. My brother had invited Chris Lowery and Derek Heimpel, two friends of his who enjoyed working on their cars together. Recently I had heard Chris telling William that he wanted to install a nitrous oxide system in his car, otherwise known as "NOS." Apparently Chris wanted to try out his new system at the Smithington track, and I hoped to be there when he did.

The sound of squealing tires told me that either Chris or Derek had arrived. When I opened my French doors to see who had thundered in, I saw Derek Heimpel in his old beater of a car trying to fix potholes with burnt rubber. I laughed and finished dressing.

I hurried downstairs and out the front door just as Chris Lowery's impressive white car rolled over the gray gravel in our driveway. The wide-bodied import had blue neon ground effects on the frame. The taillights had a yellow film on them and Chris had purchased a stylish urethane body kit so that his car sat only an inch above the gravel driveway.

"Lookin' good, honey," Derek remarked as I walked up to Chris' souped-up import.

I said hello. I didn't want to be rude, but I wasn't interested in him.

As we examined Chris' car, an exotic orange European sports car turned from the road onto the paved entrance of our driveway. My eyes widened as Nikolai stepped out.

What is he doing here?

"Happy birthday, William Davenport!" Nikolai said in a pronounced Russian accent. "Do you want to race?"

I felt tense spirit energy trickling through the cotton threads of my t-shirt; I knew Vincent was close. I turned to see if he was in human form. He was. I grabbed my cell phone to call Kristen while Chris, Derek, and William gawked at the four hundred thousand dollar car.

"Hello," Kristen answered. "Is that you, Tori?"

"Yes. Your cousin is over here with his sports car. He wants to race."

She gasped. "Seriously!?"

"Come over," I pleaded. "And bring your birthday car."

"Okay, see ya' soon."

While Derek caressed the car's expensive silver rims, I walked over to Nikolai.

His hooded blue eyes looked back at me. "Victoria, do you want a ride?"

"Not right now Nikolai. You're car's amazing, but why do you want to race my brother and his friends? Their cars aren't in the same league as yours."

He shrugged. "I just wanted to. I don't mind racing against rice rockets or souped-up domestics."

"How about another expensive sports car?" I asked, crossing my arms.

"Sure," he answered, giving my ponytail a slight tug. He stepped back to admire my legs. "You're gorgeous in shorts."

Nikolai's lips smiled and I felt self-conscious. I didn't want some possessed guy to give me compliments, even Nikolai.

"Tori!" William called. My ponytail bounced as I turned to gaze at my brother standing by Chris' vehicle.

"See ya," I said, and walked over to Chris' car. I was grateful for an excuse to part ways with Nikolai.

Sensing spirit energy, I whirled around to look up at Vincent. Golden rays danced in his penetrating blue orbs and a straw-tinted hank of hair dropped, shading his left eye. He was grinning, his eyes communicating compassion, friendship, and affection for me. I felt butterflies in my stomach.

"I've got NOS. We can race the Russian prick," Chris suggested, deviously.

Derek snorted. "You don't have NOS."

Chris caressed his car's engine and ignored Derek. "Hey Will, you're trying to be a police officer one day. Where do the cops park on the way to Smithington?"

William cleared his throat. "The Mountaindale Community Center. It's just two kilometres up Kinkaid Road. They also have speed traps at the Smithington Mennonite Church. You know where that is?"

I stared at my younger brother. He and his friends were actually going to have a street race!

Chris smiled. "Can you get your mom and dad to go out for the evening? They probably won't let us race if they know what we're doing."

Slowly, William lifted his shoulders. He seemed hesitant. "Okay."

I smiled, grateful that it bothered William to deceive someone. "Guys, I don't think you should do this. Go to the track, that's fun."

"I don't want to beat that guy at the track. I want to beat him on the road," Chris declared, gesturing at Nikolai.

"I don't want you guys to get in trouble," I said.

William shrugged. "Thanks, Tori, but it's my birthday and we're out in the country. Don't tell Dad or Mom, please."

"Fine." I didn't like the idea of this street race. If they got into trouble, I knew the Guardians wouldn't be able to interfere.

Suddenly, Kristen's gorgeous car turned into our driveway and parked behind Nikolai. As soon as she opened the door, she stalked to Nikolai and spoke to him in Russian. He grinned.

"Wow!" Derek exclaimed.

Chris whistled. "I want *that* car."

Kristen waved at me. "Hey, Tori!"

I ran over to her and said hello. From the way Nikolai was looking at me, I hoped he wasn't going to ask me to ride in his car again.

* * * *

Three hours later, I sat on my Mustang's hood with Vincent right beside me. Mom and Dad had gone to Smithington to have coffee with Katherine Windsor and her husband.

The driveway was starting to fill up with more people. Kristen had called some of our college friends, and they had come over with their boyfriends. Everyone was standing around Kristen and Nikolai's cars, admiring them.

Suddenly, the driver of a black sports coupe attempted to drift into our driveway, but instead he sprayed crushed stone at everyone. The people closest had to flee up the driveway, their Guardians shielding them from flying debris. No stones came near me.

I was surprised when Amber and a tall, muscular guy with light brown hair got out and walked toward us.

"Jackass," Derek mumbled under his breath.

Amber introduced her friend, Jack, while Chris examined several new depressions in the side of his passenger door. He was furious and

109

cursed loudly. I felt sorry for him. He had obviously spent a lot of time and money on his car.

I glanced over at Derek's rusty old car just as he started his engine. Ragged flames jumped ten feet out the tail pipe.

"Cool," I murmured. Derek rolled down all his windows and turned his radio up as loud as his new speakers would allow.

Cassandra stood nearby, stroking the red hood of William's car. She grinned and gazed up at him. He kissed her. She leaned back, her blond hair splaying over the hood's racing stripes.

Kristen, Nikolai, William, Damien, Chris, and Jack were getting ready to race

"Someone's gonna report us," Stephen cautioned.

Chris smirked. "We have license plate covers."

"Stephen's right," Will said. "We should forget about racing to Smithington and just head straight up Kinkaid Road to Mountaindale. If we don't drive to Smithington, we won't have to worry about cops."

"How far is Mountaindale?" Derek asked.

Will thought about it for a moment. "Two kilometres."

"Just make it a kilometre race," I suggested. "If you drive up to Mountaindale, someone will call the cops. You don't want trouble."

Nikolai's eyes glowed. "Tori's right."

"What do you guys think?" Will asked, looking at Damien and Jack. They agreed. "Good. We'll write down our names into two teams and flip a coin. Heads gets the west lane and tails gets the east lane. After everyone races once, the champions of the first and second races go against each other, and then that winner races the third race winner."

"What does the winner get?" Chris asked.

"Just bragging rights," Will answered. His grey-blue eyes overflowed with mischief. "Unless Kristen and Nikolai want to donate their sports cars."

"Of course not," Nikolai growled.

Stephen took a two-way radio and drove his car a kilometre up Kinkaid Road, to the finish line.

I turned to Vincent. "I want to see Chris use his NOS."

Suddenly, he took my hand and pulled me off the hood of my car. He led me around the side of the house, out of view from the others.

"If you want, I can fly you nearer the race, so you get a better view," he whispered. His eyes glowed.

I grinned. "I love flying! It'll be even better than riding in Nikolai's car." Vincent frowned down at me and I bit my bottom lip.

Stupid me! Why did I say that?

"What I mean is, I don't *want* to ride with Nikolai. I just like his car."

"It's okay," he assured me.

Then Vincent put his hands around my waist and soared upward. As we rose into the air, I felt nothing but perfect safety in his arms.

"If you glow, people will think you're a UFO," I said.

He laughed and I turned my head to get a good look at him. "I'm not going to glow," he murmured. Golden light danced in his eyes as he flew over to the halfway point in the race.

"This is perfect!" I uttered excitedly. Vincent laughed.

*   *   *   *

Gabriella clenched her fists as Will stood by his car. The race was about to start.

"Why does he deliberately put himself in danger!" she muttered.

Will grinned at his flirtatious girlfriend and she jumped up into his arms. Gabriella rolled her eyes. *Slut!* The Guardian whirled and turned her back to Will as he kissed Cassandra. Pain filled her chest, but she tried to relax.

Gabriella noticed the arrogant Russian smirk at Will. Then Nikolai's eyes turned up the driveway, where Tori was following Vincent around the back of the house. Nikolai glared and cursed under his breath.

"Come on, boys, let's get going!" Cassandra yelled, jumping up and down. Her short skirt waved around her thighs. Gabriella hurried to Will and gripped his muscular arm.

"Don't race, Will."

*   *   *   *

It was evening by this time. I usually felt cold at sunset, but Vincent's supernatural heat kept me warm as we hovered in the air. Screeching and revving noises came together down below and the smell of burning rubber assaulted me. The races had started.

Nikolai and Chris were the first to go. Squealing, Nikolai's car shot forward. Chris was almost two seconds in the rear. Together they burned toward Mountaindale, Chris surging forward in the east lane. The blue ground effect lights glowed in the dark.

Chris almost caught up, but just before the finish line, Nikolai squeaked ahead.

I felt Vincent's hands gripping my waist tighter, and it hurt. "Vincent, you're hurting me."

"I'm sorry," he whispered, loosening his grip.

I wondered who would be racing next. Abruptly, William's red muscle car and Damien's orange import flew by below us.

"No!" Vincent suddenly exclaimed.

I tensed up, not understanding what was wrong. Fear filled me and I tried to see Vincent's face, but it was too dark to get a good look.

"What's wrong?"

"Deer," he said darkly. "They're running toward the road."

All I could think about was my brother colliding at racing speed with several deer. I squirmed in Vincent's grip, not even thinking about how high up in the air I was. "You have to do something!"

"There's not enough time," he muttered.

"But you're an angel!" I wailed.

"I have to protect you."

"Please, save him!"

"If I disappear and go help him, you'll drop."

*   *   *   *

Gabriella was upset that she couldn't stop Will from racing.

Being a Guardian Angel is infuriating! she thought.

Ideas swept through her mind. Maybe she could take human form, like Vincent had. Maybe her beauty would draw Will and he would listen to her. Maybe he'd kiss her like he did Cassandra.

No! I'm a Guardian. I don't really want to kiss a human! As she touched his arm, he looked toward her. Gabriella knew Will could sense her but that he couldn't see her. She raised her hand and caressed his handsome face.

"Be careful. I love you."

A few minutes later, as Will and Damien tore up the country road, Gabriella hovered over the roof of Will's car. She loved speed—at least, she when it was her flying, and not when the human she loved raced at dangerous speeds. She hated being powerless to stop her responsibility from making bad decisions. The wind swept through her, drawing her hair back. She struggled not to grip the car and pull it backward. This was William's choice, and he had human free will.

The sound of hoofs caught her attention from up ahead. A pair of deer were dashing toward the road.

"No!"

Her body tensed, realizing that Will couldn't see them. She anxiously glanced at the Guardian flying over top of Damien's car. He, too, had just noticed the animals.

"We have to slow them down!" Gabriella yelled. The other Guardian nodded his head in agreement.

Gabriella suddenly appeared inside William's car, not letting him see her. "Slow down!" she yelled. "Stop!"

But he didn't hear her. Full of anxiety, she threw herself in front of his car and pushed backward with all her might.

* * * *

Will's car slowed and he pressed on the accelerator furiously.

"What's going on?" he gasped as his car stopped. He looked up ahead at the darkened road, convinced Damien had beaten him. To his surprise, he saw that the other car had stopped as well. As he tried to figure out what was going on, a pair of deer stormed in front of both vehicles.

His jaw dropped in surprise. Then, blinded by the light of headlights, he looked up just in time to see a car speeding toward him in the east lane. He braced himself.

* * * *

Gabriella felt fear surge into her wings. She shoved William's car off the road before the oncoming vehicle could hit it. She got him out of the way just in time.

His car jumped the nearby ditch and ploughed through a farmer's fence. Gabriella was shocked at her own strength and hoped Will was okay. She raced to the wrecked car and looked through the front windshield. Will's head was resting on the steering wheel.

"Will!" she screamed. She jumped over the hood and landed by the driver's door. His head was bleeding. Tears ran down her face. "Will, wake up!" She was about to open the door when Vincent spoke behind her.

"Don't do it."

She spun to face the golden-haired angel and his charge, Tori.

Tori ran over and tried to open the door, but it was jammed. She banged on the window.

"William! William!" She started to cry when her brother didn't respond. Tori's eyes shot up at Gabriella. "Open the door, please!"

Vincent hung his head. "She can't."

*　*　*　*

I ogled Vincent.

What does he mean, she can't open the door? Gabriella's an angel!

Vincent looked down at me compassionately as his hands rose to my shoulders. His golden eyes glowed, but his wings and broadsword had vanished. I frowned. If Vincent had been in angel form, he could have done something to save Will.

"But my brother's hurt, Vincent!" Anguish filled me and I shook my head.

"It was his decision to race," he reminded me.

I clenched my fists and stared at the ground. I should have stopped him from racing, even if he had thought I was ruining his birthday.

"Damien's coming," Gabriella told us. Vincent released me and I whirled to face the handsome African American man. His forehead was furrowed but Damien was unharmed. He rushed over to the driver's side door and gasped. As Damien stared at my brother, he announced, "I called 911."

"Thank God." I hoped Damien wouldn't ask me how I got here.

Just then Damien turned his head. "How did you get here?" I felt as if his intelligent eyes stabbed me in the darkness. I shivered, not wanting to lie. Then I heard grass crunch behind me and felt Vincent's warmth.

"I brought her here," my Guardian spoke.

Damien looked by me to Vincent and then glanced toward the

road. My Mustang was parked by the side of the road behind Damien's car! I breathed out. *Okay, who parked my car there?*

Damien looked back at us, grinning. "I see."

A fire truck roared and we all glanced toward Mountaindale as lights flashed a kilometre away. Peace filled me because I knew Will was going to be okay. "They're here!" I cried and ran to his damaged car, but horror overwhelmed me when I noticed his head was bleeding.

CHAPTER FIFTEEN

THE SMITHINGTON MEMORIAL Hospital waiting room was too cold. I shivered, wishing Vincent was sitting beside me. Dad and Mom were beside themselves that we had been having a car race. Michael watched Stephen and me critically. Mom and Dad's angst was enough; I didn't need the angel's glowing brown eyes glaring at me. James actually appeared compassionate toward Stephen and me.

"Why didn't you tell us there was going to be a race?" Mom questioned.

My chest hurt as I looked at my parents. "I'm sorry. I tried to get the boys to race at the track, but Chris didn't want to and Will pleaded for me not to tell you." I looked down at the tile and knew that was a pathetic answer. My brothers, myself, and our friends had all been caught up in the excitement of the race. Mom and Dad had been more mature at our age. I knew we all had to grow up.

"I'm sorry I let it happen," Stephen uttered and I noticed Huan-Yue rub his shoulders. I missed Vincent. I wished he was in human form and sitting beside me.

Dad looked at us, very resigned. "Your brother made a choice. Just pray that William will be okay," he said. That's when I felt Vincent's warmth on my back.

While my dad spoke, I saw a doctor in blue scrubs walk toward us.

"Mr. and Mrs. Davenport?" the doctor said, pushing his glasses up on his nose. The rest of my family looked up at him. "Your son is going to be okay. The CT scan was normal and the bleeding from his head was very minor, but he has a concussion. We're going to keep him overnight."

"Thank God! Thank you, doctor," my dad said. He shook the doctor's hand.

"We're glad William's fine," the doctor answered, smiling. "He's so young."

When the doctor left, I turned my head and noticed two police officers talking to a nurse who pointed at us.

No! There are too many things I can't explain.

*   *   *   *

Barbara, Cassandra, and I went shopping in a department store on Wednesday to pick up a wedding present for my cousin Brad and his fiancée Maggie. My family had just received an invitation for the August wedding the day of Will's accident. I was grateful for the reprieve to get my mind off our problems. It had been hard talking to the police at the hospital. Vincent had walked through the door to the waiting room when the police began to question us, so he answered the difficult questions as to how I had gotten to the scene. The police had warned William that they could charge him with dangerous driving or street racing, which were criminal offences. Instead they slapped him with a lesser charge which wouldn't give him a criminal record. I'm not sure why they decided to favour him, but he still had a fine, a license suspension, and he had to help the farmer fix his fence.

Will had been so serious when he got home from the hospital. He wouldn't play his video games or watch television. I tried to get him to go for a long walk with me, but he just sat on his bed and refused. Dad and Mom were so disappointed with all of us.

As I pushed the shopping cart, static electricity pricked my fingers. Getting shocks was odd for me and I wondered what was going on.

"Tori!" Barbara called.

I turned my head and looked at her. "What?"

"I was trying to ask you, what colour is Brad and Maggie's bedroom?"

I pursed my lips. "I'm sorry, I was just distracted."

The two women gazed at me compassionately. "Were you thinking about Will?" Cassandra questioned.

"Not now. It was something else." I shook my head and looked at the girls seriously. "Brad and Maggie's bedroom is blue."

"What were you thinking about?" Barbara asked.

"Oh nothing."

Eventually we reached the linen section.

"I have to get these," Cassandra announced, picking up sheets with blue and green lips on them. I grinned at her.

"Get those if you want." Suddenly, sparks rose off the cart. "Ow!"

The two blonds gazed at me. My pulse raced as I gazed down at the cart again. Demons bodies sparked. Were there demons on this cart? I frowned. I couldn't sense any demons nearby.

I glanced back up at my friends. They needed an explanation. "I keep getting shocked by this cart."

"You're very electric, Tori. I think we could plug a hair dryer into you, but maybe that's too high voltage. Maybe a toaster," Cassandra rambled.

Barbara grabbed the cart and pushed it away. "Don't touch it any-more. There's something wrong with it."

* * * *

When I walked into my room after shopping with Barbara and Cas-sandra, Vincent took human form.

"Do you know what was going on with the shopping cart?" I asked. "Why was it sparking and giving me so many shocks? Were there demons on the cart?"

Vincent regarded me seriously and put my shopping bag on the couch. My pulse sped up again. *He's too serious. It must have been demons!*

"I didn't see any demons on the cart," Vincent finally said. "I think you must have some spirit energy."

My eyes widened. "Excuse me?"

"Some humans have special abilities from God, or maybe some of my energy transferred to you when I've touched you."

I anxiously wondered if it was against spirit rules for a human to possess that kind of energy. Was he going to disappear and not see me anymore if I had supernatural abilities or possessed some of his super-natural energy? Thoughts of losing his friendship kept tormenting me. *Oh why do I have to feel this way?*

I frowned. "What does that mean?"

"I don't know, Tori, but nothing's going to change. I'm still going to keep being your friend," he reassured me.

* * * *

Gabriella paced on the roof of the Davenport house. She wouldn't leave William very long, but just standing in his room at night made her feel so guilty. He had lost his licence because she had pushed him into that farmer's field. She had pleaded with the Guardians of the police officers to soften those officers toward Will. If only she had gently pushed Will's car behind Damien's instead of into the field. Her chest hurt and she started to cry when she remembered him slumped over in his car. She loved Will, but as a Guardian she wasn't supposed to have those feelings.

"It's my fault," she muttered as she looked toward the lights of Smithington. Warm supernatural energy increased behind her and Gabriella hoped Michael wasn't there. Michael was already angry with Vincent for falling in love with Tori. Gabriella didn't want a lecture from him.

"What's bothering you?" Vincent questioned and Gabriella turned to look at him.

Relief swept through her. "Vincent, what are you doing away from Tori?"

Vincent was compassionate and knew how she felt. The golden-haired Guardian smiled gently.

"Tori's sleeping and I won't leave her long. I sensed you were having problems."

Gabriella sat down on the roof and Vincent sat near her.

"It's my fault Will lost his license and injured himself. He really liked his car and he loves to be independent. I took that away."

Vincent snorted. His eyes were serious and his voice was low. "Gabriella, you kept Will alive and saved him and the family in that other car from a head-on crash. He needed to learn a lesson, but you did what Guardians are supposed to do."

"I don't want to be a Guardian anymore," she murmured as her chest tightened.

"We don't have a choice," Vincent whispered hoarsely. "But I don't want you to feel guilty about the accident. You did your job."

*   *   *   *

On Friday, after I dressed, I stood on my balcony and looked down. My eyes widened and I jumped back when I saw angels standing around the outside of our house. *What's going on? I've never seen so many angels before.* They seemed to be ten- and twelve-feet and their fiery wings rose about five feet above their heads. The burning wings on the twelve-foot angels were a foot above my balcony floor. Even though I had touched Vincent and seen other Guardians, I was too intimidated to touch the burning spirit matter. The beings grasped massive platinum-handled blades that were taller than me.

Suddenly, Vincent stood beside me.

"Why are all these angels here?" I asked.

"They are Warrior Angels," he answered.

This was the first time I had seen Warriors. They were scarier than Guardians. My heart thudded in my chest from anxiety. These supernatural beings wouldn't be barricading my home unless there were demons coming.

I gasped and my body trembled. "Are demons coming?"

"Yes," he answered in a low voice.

When he said this, my body shivered violently and my teeth started to chatter. Was I sensing them? When I looked up at Vincent, I noticed his serious blue eyes turning golden. His human form glowed.

"Tori, it's okay," he said compassionately. Vincent walked over and hugged me. As his supernatural warmth consumed me, my body stopped shivering. This was wonderful! My teeth stopped chattering and my heart stopped pounding as I rested peacefully in his arms.

"Squeeze tighter," I whispered into his white t-shirt.

His muscular arms tightened around me. "I don't want to hurt you," he murmured.

"This feels good."

When his body temperature increased and started to burn my skin, I had to pull away.

"Go lie down, Tori, or play on your laptop," he instructed.

I knew he wanted to distract me, so I walked into my bedroom. But I didn't want to do anything except go back on my balcony with Vincent.

I turned my laptop on but I didn't like waiting, so I walked back outside and noticed hundreds of imps grappling with our spirea hedge. Our house was built on a hill and even more imps pooled at the bottom, climbing the rise. Vincent's entire spirit form radiated light as he drew his five-foot blade. In a moment, his wings ignited and blazed four feet over his head.

"Tori, you should go inside," he spoke urgently, all the while watching the imps.

"But what if Odium and Pernicious appear in my room?" I asked.

"Scream," he answered.

When a sulphur cloud appeared on the wooden balcony, goose bumps rose on my arms. Imps shrieked and hissed below us. Of course, I wished I had an angelic broadsword—or any sword, for that matter. I wanted to fight. Once again, I walked over the threshold of my room, but this time I closed the French doors, resigned.

All at once, my muscles shivered ferociously and I felt hate behind me. I turned around slowly and took a deep breathe. Odium grinned, appearing amused.

"What do you want?" I asked.

"The answer would be an exhaustive list, human. Neither of us have time for that."

I crossed my arms. "Vincent said to scream if you appeared."

"If you don't scream, the Guardian won't come," Odium answered, mockingly.

I felt a presence behind my back and knew that Pernicious was there. I spun to look behind me, but the scaly imp was nowhere to be seen. However, a black archer was—and he had a black arrow with slime on it pointed at me. My body trembled violently; I could feel the hate from that arrow. That slime had to be demon blood! Sulphuric vapours twisted and writhed to my ceiling. The slime bubbled and sparked. How was it possible for blood to spark? I was mesmerized by it.

"Tori, if you scream sixty pounds of pressure will hit you right in the chest. Not to mention that the black junk on the end of the arrow is demon blood, and it will make you hate both God and Vincent. Imagine for a few seconds hating God so intensely that you go to Hell! Or the archer can shoot your leg or arm, and you can hate all things good for decades. You can be like a demon." He slowly circled me. "Would you like that?"

I glared at him, but when I made a whimper he grinned maliciously.

"Did you notice all my imps?" he asked.

I stood defiantly. "Did you see all the Warrior Angels?"

"I can send sergeants and commanders as well," he announced proudly.

When Vincent had let me see him, something had changed. I was now part of the spirit world. However, I was the easiest target in it, and instead of me being a blind human who could sense spirits and was attacked subtly most of the time, these demons were now trying to brutally execute me.

CHAPTER SIXTEEN

EVEN THOUGH I had told my human to stay inside, I'd thought Tori would come out anyway. She was stubborn and valiant for a human. Suddenly, I felt Fear grab my foot. When I swung my shining blade down at the imp, it released me and growled. Slinking backward, it remained on the balcony. I frowned when I realized Fear needed a more powerful demon to get it inside the Davenport house while the Warrior Angels surrounded the home. Only a demon who had the power to take human form could appear in the house or on the balcony; the Warriors' spirit power stopped unaided demons from entering.

"Odium!" I hissed. I wanted to yell, but instead exercised self-control and stalked to the French doors, opening them. Tori gaped at me. Odium was standing next to her. His black eyes were huge when I entered but a mocking expression surfaced on his visage.

"Vincent!" Tori exclaimed.

"Why didn't you scream?" I asked.

All at once, I became aware of the black demon holding a bow with demon gore on the poised arrow. I vanished and reappeared by the demon archer, gripping the hilt of my angelic broadsword.

"Go away, Vincent," Odium commanded. "Poison's first action will be to shoot Tori if you don't appear elsewhere on the property."

Glowering at Odium's helper, Poison, my spirit energy raced into my wings and I drew my blade. A demon archer wasn't faster than me! I narrowed my glowing eyes, desiring to intimidate Poison. He growled at me with his yellow fangs clenched.

"Imagine Tori as hateful as an imp or instantly in Hell. It'll happen if you don't leave," Odium warned. His narrow black eyes glared at me. As soon as the Strong Man spoke, I gazed at him and walked backward, but I didn't go out onto the balcony.

"Guardian..." Odium's low voice hissed.

I watched the human I loved. Her body was shivering violently. I could appear in front of her and Poison would shoot me. Then God would throw me in Hell. If I was shot with the demon blood, I would never see my human again, and if she was shot, it would be the same.

All at once, Michael and Gabriella appeared. Relief overwhelmed me. Odium was shocked, but then took demon form. Gabriella pushed Tori into the closet and I swiftly beheaded Poison. The female angel and I grinned and strode up to Michael and Odium, who fenced until the demon was aware there were three Guardians to kill him.

Odium vanished.

When I pulled Tori out of the closet, she gazed at all three of us gratefully.

"Thank you so much!" she exclaimed.

* * * *

A call bell buzzed the next evening at Cedarwood. I was annoyed at the interruption, but realized that the residents had to come first. It was nine o'clock and I ran up the hall. There was no one else there or I would have contained myself; we weren't supposed to run in the halls. The metal handle on the resident's front door was slightly cool to the touch when I opened the door.

"Hi, Tori," Agnes greeted softly. She was a very pleasant Christian woman. "I'm having trouble breathing."

I wasn't the nurse on duty, so I needed to pass this concern on. "I'll get the nurse," I said.

Since she wasn't gasping, I walked over to her instead of alerting the charge nurse right away. Because of her religion, I felt comfortable asking her if she wanted prayer. Most of my residents, when they are struggling, were receptive to this. "Do you want me to pray for you Agnes?" I asked quietly, my concerned eyes observing her. *If you seem in distress, I can get Kristy right away,* I thought.

Her blue eyes gazed at me with a little smile. "Sure," she answered.

I squatted in front of her blue reclining chair and prayed, clutching the elderly woman's hands. While I listened for her breathing and prayed, my own hands felt hot. Holding her hand was like holding Vincent's while he was in angel form! I opened my eyes.

"I feel better, Tori," she said.

I grinned. "Really?"

"Yes, child."

I gazed over at her bookshelves behind me. Vincent, glowing in angel form, stood observing us, smiling. I didn't think Agnes saw him.

I rubbed her thin-skinned hands and rose quickly. "I'll get Kristy."

The gentle grey-haired woman gripped my fingers before I moved them away. Deeper wrinkles decorated the edges of her kindly grey-blue eyes. "Thank you, child. I felt numbness in my body while you prayed, but now I feel better." She smiled.

I was confused as I walked out of the room. What had happened? I had only prayed. Her body had been numb... and why had my hands gotten so hot? As I stared at Agnes' closed door, Vincent sauntered through the wall and grabbed my hands. His intense blue eyes appeared happy. His perfect teeth shone and grinned.

"Wow," he said.

"What happened?" I asked.

"God put energy in your hands," he answered.

I was stunned, and my eyebrows rose. "Excuse me?"

"The Creator gave you supernatural healing energy. When you pray, you connect with him and God gives you the ability to heal other people."

"But I'm human!" I protested.

"There are a few humans who have supernatural abilities. Tori, you're blessed. Not even I can heal people. The only power I have is to fight demons and guard you."

*   *   *   *

Hate-consumed black eyes regarded Agnes and Tori darkly. Tori was kneeling in front of the woman, praying. Tori Davenport, why couldn't she be shallow?

Praying! Odium thought. *What are her human prayers going to do? She doesn't have healing energy.*

A disgusted hiss slithered through his teeth while he rolled his black eyes. When Tori looked up, the excited older woman smiled and gripped her hands.

"What?!" Odium exclaimed, his eyes widening. The woman had said she felt numb, but now she was better. Vincent's human had supernatural powers? Odium narrowed his black eyes. Tori was more dangerous now. The Creator's son had inspired humans to imagine they could heal. Most humans couldn't, but demons had to form doubt. If a special human didn't believe they could heal, God's power wouldn't work.

Vincent looked proud of Tori and Odium clenched his fists. He glowered at the human as she rose. Odium had planned ways to destroy her since she had realized that his world was more real than hers. He hated humans who could pray well, people who changed things. Demons liked to stay away from those people, because sometimes they had extra angels guarding them.

Odium loved to trip a human, especially when they cursed. He always laughed when a human's frail body floated up into the air, then smacked the ground as their pathetic brain registered pain. He had been flabbergasted when the Creator had chosen to make a creature so deficient. Did God imagine that a frail creature would love him more loyally than his angels? That the humans would need him because they were pathetic? Humans sinned faster than the rebellious angels! He laughed. The Creator had made humans like himself, but without supernatural powers—and they could sin. Why wasn't God intelligent enough to make a creature he could order about? His creation in angels had also somewhat failed, but the Creator never thought of angels as his children; they were servants. This human girl was a child of God, he thought bitterly.

When he saw his image in the elderly woman's window, he growled and clenched both fists. When he had been an Archangel, his hair had been blond and his eyes green. Now his hair and eyes were both black—but at least he could still appear in human form. His pride made the Strong Man form detestable, and even though he was a demon he stayed out of Hell as much as he could. Odium missed the beauty of Heaven, so he had been ecstatic when earth was created.

When he had first discovered that his Strong Man form contained enough energy to exist in human form, it was the next best thing to living in Heaven—but when he noticed his eyes were black, he had been furious. God's curse was always with him, so he tried to not look at himself too often. Tori's eyes were hazel, but he really envied Vincent. The perfect angel could always be handsome—without black eyes.

Once in a while, he regretted pushing Vincent's sword over to him on that fateful day eighteen billion years ago, because he was sure he had lost four feet of his spirit form as a consequence. He hissed.

Suddenly, Odium arched his back and laughed spitefully into the dusk sky. Vincent was disobeying the Creator by loving his human. If he could fan those emotions and get the Guardian to sin, Vincent would become a demon!

*   *   *   *

On July 25, Vincent and I travelled to a lake up north. My grandparents had rented a cottage for six weeks.

At three o'clock in the afternoon, Vincent and I paddled a canoe into the middle of the large lake, which had once been home to an old mine. Trees had actually been dumped into the mine, and a few trunks still stuck up through the water; others you could see submerged when you swam or boated by, which was fascinating but dangerous when you thought of accidentally diving or jumping onto hidden branches.

The cottages took up most of the water frontage and they all had boathouses. Some cottages were very plain while others were huge with large slanted windows, big decks, and landscaped gardens. Numerous docks stretched into the water, held up by log legs; others were several feet from shore and anchored with weights.

We canoed up a river which ran from the large lake to a smaller natural habitat lake. The line of cottages continued along the sides of the river, but the second lake had no dwellings on it. Cedar trees grew around this second lake and large stumps spouted out of the dark water. The uneven lake bottom was beautiful, mucky, and had seaweed growing from it. We noticed a boat submerged under the surface and it was covered with moss.

"There's a fish," I noted as it swam near the top of the dark water.

"I really like being in human form," Vincent said. "We don't get to do these activities when we're in angel form." Vincent leaned over to see the fish, but the canoe rocked.

"Vincent, don't do that. You're making me nervous."

"Sorry, but human form is limiting," he answered as water rippled around the canoe. The fish's green scales vanished into a dark section of the water and I sighed.

"Thank you for coming with me."

*   *   *   *

While the blue canoe travelled into the habitat lake, two imps sat on the ground behind the cedar trees.

"Calamity," Pernicious said, pointing toward the water. "Tori and Vincent are in that blue canoe."

"That's not an angel. Those are two humans," argued Calamity.

Pernicious' red eyes narrowed. "Vincent takes human form to spend time with Tori," she growled.

"That's stupid!" the other demon exclaimed, but then it grinned maliciously. Yellow plaque-covered teeth rose in its mouth. "If Vincent loves Tori, he will be exiled to Israel for one hundred years."

Pernicious laughed. "Yup, exiled." She hissed maliciously while drool bubbled in her mouth. "But if Tori dies, that will be even worse for him."

Both demons laughed, their bodies writhing gleefully.

"We're going into the lake," Pernicious announced knowingly.

Calamity's demonic eyes widened. "No!" she snapped, crossing her scaly arms.

"We get to kill Tori," Pernicious said, her eyes slanting. She smiled and her yellow teeth sparkled. "And then we'll get an amethyst bracelet."

Calamity gazed at her onyx-hued arm moodily. "Finally! I've wanted one for billions of years."

"A Strong Man is going to fight Vincent."

"What's going to happen to Tori?"

"We get to drown her," Pernicious answered cruelly.

Calamity giggled. "Cool!"

Pernicious' narrow red eyes watched the other demon jump up and down on the ground excitedly. "Shut up, Calamity!" she hissed.

*　*　*　*

Abruptly, our blue canoe flipped. Vincent and I fell into the water and I shrieked as the water's coolness encompassed me. We submerged and I could feel my hair rise over my head. I opened my eyes and studied the mucky bottom around me, then swam upward. When I emerged at the surface, I cried, "Vincent!"

Vincent's anxious, glowing eyes gazed at me as he pulled me close and turned the canoe upright.

"Are you okay?" he asked, his warm breath drying my cheek. I could feel his body growing hotter, and I knew he was worried about demons. "Can you tread water for a minute?"

Our eyes met. "Yes. Go get the canoe."

We're not in a river; this is *a quiet lake,* I thought as Vincent hastened after the canoe and I treaded water. When I gazed around, I noticed a stump sprouting out of the murky water. Right away, I swam to it.

Suddenly, two scaly imps appeared on top of the stump. I noticed their long toenails piercing the damp wood. My jaw dropped and I felt an adrenaline rush. I started to swim away, but the grotesque imps jumped on me and cruelly forced me under the water. My heart was crashing in my chest as I fought with them and tried to get to the surface for air.

While underwater, I smacked Pernicious and the she rose out of the lake, swearing. The other unearthly creature scratched my right arm, ripping my flesh. She seized my neck with rough black hands and sharp nails. I struggled to keep my mouth closed, even though I wanted to scream.

Panic overwhelmed me. I knew pushing down on the mucky bottom would imprison me, so I tried not to do it. I needed air! Thrashing, I rose up to the surface. A lone evil spirit couldn't push me under altogether, but I couldn't get her hands off my throat, even though I scratched and yanked on her scaly fingers. When I pried a few fingers off my skin, her other black fingernails pierced my flesh. I cried out.

Unfortunately, I was not able to take a deep breath with her hands besetting my throat. Pernicious giggled nearby and I frantically looked around for the imp. Then, water splashed my face!

"Like water, human?" Pernicious hissed by my head.

Both imps jumped onto my head.

No!

I was submerged again. Water engulfed my nose and it burned as panic blocked my throat. I was unable to hold my breath any longer. I foolishly attempted to touch the bottom and push up, but my feet penetrated the mucky bottom and I began to sink. I tried to push up again, but my lower legs sluiced into the muck. I was so scared.

Vincent, where are you?

When I looked up, I noticed that the unearthly creatures were gone. Radiance shone down to me and I saw my air bubbles rise toward the surface. I was exhausted and my chest hurt so badly. A white and black checkerboard-like pattern appeared in my eyes and then I blacked out.

CHAPTER SEVENTEEN

AT LAST, I jerked the canoe and stopped it from floating away. I felt triumphant! I turned the canoe and gazed at Tori just as two imps jumped on her. As they forced her underwater, terror and surprise consumed me. My eyes narrowed and I took angel form. Spirit energy raced into my wings and I started to fly.

A monstrous onyx Strong Man then emerged in front of me.

"Go, demon!" I commanded and pulled my blade. Heinously, the Strong Man grinned and his red eyes narrowed as sulphur consumed the air and water near him.

"Nice try. I'm a Strong Man, not an imp or sergeant!" he hissed.

I hated the oppressive sulphur odour of his body. The Strong Man's horns were ten inches tall, curled, and they let out puffs of smoke. The demon had ten amethyst bracelets; he was obviously high ranking. He drew a cutlass.

"What's your name?" I asked.

"Scurrilous. When I was in Heaven, I was known as Peter," the unearthly creature answered.

I glared at him. Eighteen billion years ago, I had been friends with a red-haired angel named Peter. He had been a six-foot angel who, like me, had desired to be twelve-feet, like the radiant Archangels. He had felt inadequate. Because his broadsword was smaller than mine, he complained about the Creator. Obviously, Lucifer had rewarded Peter. My fingers clenched and I felt the hilt of my broadsword heating in my hand. I was wasting too much time! Tori needed to be rescued.

We fenced. Scurrilous blocked when I sliced at him. He stamped the water and a wave pounded into me. As the water cleared from my vision, frustration and fear tormented my stomach. I couldn't see him, but I needed to end this fight; my human couldn't hold her breath much longer. When the wave faded, Scurrilous lunged and I flew up, my wings expanding. He levitated north and I feinted decisively so that the evil spirit would be deceived. For once, I was grateful for all the sword fighting I had been forced to learn as a Guardian Angel.

I quickly decapitated Scurrilous and threw my contaminated, glowing broadsword into the water. Turning my attention back to the lake, I flew to the stump and dove down to rescue Tori, fear accumulating inside me.

She was lying on her back on the mucky bottom, her lower legs, feet, and part of her torso entrenched in the mud. Her long brown hair swirled up, imitating the motion of the underwater plants. She was obviously dead.

My anger was so strong that I wanted to explode, but spirits couldn't do that. I had lost my human and hadn't heard the Death Angel or Messenger tell me to step back. I knew it wasn't the Creator's will, but her spirit was gone and I couldn't talk to her anymore. A mere holiday in the rainforest wasn't going to cure the emotions I was feeling. I had lost Tori!

Denial, confusion, and fury overcame me. I felt anger building up inside. I wished I had been there when she died... I yelled under the water, releasing my supernatural energy into rippling currents that uprooted seaweed, tore up the mucky lakebed, and sent the canoe and nearby stumps soaring.

I freed her, carrying her body back onto the cedar-covered land. My spirit form kneeled, my wings closed, and I felt her long neck for a pulse. I couldn't find any sign of life... I desperately needed to find life!

"God, please help me!" I screamed. Tears fell down my spirit face. My body felt so warm, and I didn't know where the heat was coming from. I gazed upward to find supernatural energy surrounding me like rays of sunshine.

It was God!

"My faithful angel, how do humans bring other humans back?" God asked.

I bent over and placed my mouth over hers, pushing healing spirit air into Tori. My hands compressed her chest, pumping repeatedly. After a few moments, she threw up and I pulled her onto her side.

When I wiped her mouth off, Tori's large hazel eyes stared up at me. She seized my fingers.

"Thank you, God!" I cried. "Are you okay?"

"I died and God let me see him... God's glow revealed my Grandpa Davenport... I was five when he died, and he hugged me... and there was beautiful music, butterflies, and so many lovely flowers. But Vincent, I missed you."

When Tori spoke, I changed into human form and the supernatural rays disappeared.

*   *   *   *

Pernicious and Calamity relaxed on the hot stone beneath them but didn't rest their backs against the rock escarpment. Their scaly skin, and billions of years getting used to the heat, had enabled them to tolerate Hell, but it didn't feel good.

"Tori's dead! We get amethyst bracelets!" Calamity chanted, glee widening her red eyes.

"And higher rank," Pernicious added. She rubbed her thin, scaly arms. She wanted Odium to love her. If she became a sergeant, he might just do it. After all, if she was a sergeant, she would be able to take human form. Pernicious knew Odium detested the demon form.

"When do we get those amethyst bracelets?" Calamity asked.

"When Scurrilous returns to Hell and confirms what happened to the human."

Calamity laughed and clasped her black knees. "Her legs got stuck in the mud!"

"I like when I can give a human a terrible death," Pernicious declared wickedly. Yellow saliva bubbled out of her mouth. "And Vincent will be upset! Maybe he'll even turn into a demon."

"Traitor!" Calamity growled. Her huge red eyes narrowed into thin, straight lines.

"If he turns into a demon, our Master will make him an imp so we can torment him," Pernicious growled. Her scrawny fingers fisted.

*   *   *   *

From nearby, Odium listened to the two imps. He hissed, his sharp claws cutting into his palms. If Tori really had died, those imps would not receive amethyst bracelets. Without delay, he disappeared. Those grotesque imps, and the rest of Hell, infuriated him. He enjoyed tormenting and murdering humans, but he hadn't been happy for six thousand years. He had been waiting for Vincent to desire some object so that he could steal it, but trouncing Tori and Vincent had been a challenge. The human girl's decreasing terror and boldness around imps made her less pathetic and with her supernatural energy, she had become something like a Guardian herself now. Vincent wouldn't love another of his responsibilities ever again.

Swift memories now encompassed him. Long again, he had entered the scaled, forked-tongued, blood-shot-eyed creature to entice Eve so that Vincent would fail at his mission to protect her. He laughed at the memory.

All at once, graveness overcame him. When humans gave in to sin, tempting them lost its pleasure; it was too easy. One night, he had stalked a Wall Street trader. He'd watched the man as he sat in his brown leather chair chitchatting on his cell phone...

Odium smirked as the thin, blond-haired man shivered.

"Hey, human!" he called.

The man vaulted out of his chair and fell on the floor. His blue eyes were huge and his hair turned gray at the roots. Odium laughed while the human shook his head and trembled.

"Go away!" the trader exclaimed. He rose, trying to sit back on his chair, but the chair wheeled backward and smashed into a glass cabinet. He collapsed again, broken glass shattering across the carpet. Odium placed his invisible face near the human.

"I'll give you money!" the man screamed.

Odium then emerged in human form.

The man shrieked in terror, perspiration running down his cheeks, hands, and neck. Sweat was trickling from his shirt and his hair had gone totally gray. He once again tried to stand, but his calves and thighs trembled and he fell onto his striped couch, squishing the cushions.

"I don't want human money," Odium gloated.

He took spirit form and the trader's eyes exploded... shrieking... convulsing. His gray hair began to fall out. Finally, the man splayed prone on the carpet.

Odium grimaced at the memory and flew into the second lake, submerging himself. There were stumps and logs at the edge of the lake as well as mounds of muck and seaweed. Eventually, the demon saw two shallow depressions where the human's legs had been—but there was no seaweed and obviously Vincent's energy had destroyed the bottom of the lake. In fact, the Strong Man could still feel the Guardian's grief-created energy. He hissed, realizing that the human girl obviously had died—just like Pernicious and Calamity had said.

He rose slowly from the water, sensing Vincent nearby.

He followed the river back to the first lake. Vincent's Guardian energy was palpable around a white cottage with a multi-layered deck. Odium was aware that the Guardian Angels there would sense him. When he flew to the second floor, he looked through a small window and saw Tori lying on a bed, staring at Vincent.

She was alive!

He smiled and then disappeared, returning to the dark world of Hell right in the midst of Pernicious and Calamity, who were still busy celebrating their great success.

The imps stopped cold and stared at the Strong Man, who crossed his muscled onyx arms.

"What do demons get when they murder a human?" Odium asked maliciously.

"An amethyst bracelet! And sometimes higher ranking!" Calamity announced.

"You want to get bracelets?" Odium asked.

Calamity raised onyx fists. "Yes! We killed Tori!"

"Wow!" he started. "I thought Vincent—"

"Scurrilous helped us," Calamity acknowledged.

Odium's black eyebrows rose. "Why didn't you ask a former Archangel?" he asked scornfully. "Fools! Imps don't receive amethyst bracelets. Tori is alive. Never ask some pathetic, low-ranking angel to help you again."

He laughed, which made him bend over and swat his thighs.

"But we did kill her," Calamity insisted.

Odium straightened up and glowered. "You think you know better than me? She's alive. But that's okay... we're not going to try to kill Tori anymore." Calamity and Pernicious shrieked at the revelation. "Instead we are going to torture them."

"But I want an amethyst bracelet," Pernicious protested. "I want to be made a sergeant!" Her onyx fists plunged down to her sides.

Odium was outraged. "We keep attacking them, but we never let them die. Tori has the power to heal. She is more of a threat. She is not pathetic anymore. If she goes to Heaven, she will be free and happy. Vincent will suffer, but if both of them are alive and separated, well... what could be better?"

"But—" Pernicious protested.

"Feel free to cause them both pain," Odium declared, narrowing his red eyes. "Eventually, Vincent will be sent to Israel and Tori will never find a human she can be happy with."

Odium vanished from Hell, growling to himself. If the imps had succeeded in annihilating Tori, he would have murdered them. He ambled onto a cliff and jumped down near the rented cottage Tori's family was staying at, his human form falling. He then took spirit form and laughed.

He stalked into the water by the lake, his yellow sulphur cloud twisting into vacationers' nostrils. Two water skiers accidentally smacked into each other. Yelling at each other, humans all around him scraped their knees and legs as they hastened onto the docks. Teens screamed and jumped out of the water and a personal watercraft careened into submerged stumps and tipped. The male driver of that watercraft lay prone on the branches and water.

"Guardians, you're not protecting your humans!" Odium cackled.

* * * *

After Odium left, Pernicious stamped her small black foot as her wings unfurled from her rage. Hissing, she poked at Calamity's chest. "I won't listen to Odium. I will get no glory and higher rank if I don't murder Tori. I want my amethyst bracelet!"

Calamity smiled. "We killed Tori once. Let's do it again."

Yellow fangs rose in Pernicious' mouth. "And I will make sure Vincent goes to Hell!"

* * * *

In August, Vincent and I attended my cousin's wedding. I drove my Mustang, with him in the passenger seat. I was shocked when he didn't ask me to let him to drive, because my brothers Stephen and William would have.

Before the afternoon wedding began, we sat outside in mahogany chairs. It was very hot. This year had been strange. It had been cool and wet in July, but this August our weather was hot and humid, like that of the southern United States.

Even though water was provided for the guests, every person was sweating.

Since we attended early, we were seated in the fourth row. Janessa came and sat beside me. After saying hello, she said, "Karen and I are having a costume party at the end of the summer." She handed me an envelope. "Here's your invitation."

"Thanks, Janessa. That'll be fun. I'll have to make sure I'm not working," I said and opened the envelope.

"It's on the twenty-ninth and you have to wear a mask."

I smiled at my cousin. "I don't work that weekend."

Just then, my cell phone vibrated. I pulled it out and noticed I had a new text message. *"Looking good, Tori,"* the text said.

I frowned. Who had sent that? I didn't type anything back. A moment later, another text appeared: *"Do you know what you need with that dress?"*

"What?" I typed.

The reply: *"Black irises."*

"Flowers or eyes?"

My body shivered when I got the response: *"Eyes like mine."*

Needing Vincent's reassurance, I gazed up at him and noticed he was watching me intently.

"What's wrong?" he murmured.

I whispered, "Text message." As the Guardian Angel observed the screen, his eyes turned golden and his jaw tightened. I could feel his tension as he took the phone.

"Please, may everyone stand for the bride," the minister announced.

Anxiously, I watched Vincent grip the phone. I hoped I wasn't going to have to buy another one, but he shut it off and gave it back to me. Swiftly we stood and gazed at my cousin's bride. Maggie had her platinum blond hair in a chignon and was wearing a long tulle veil with rhinestones in it and a small tiara. Her full-skirted gown was lacy and she carried a spectacular rose bouquet.

Because Maggie's father was deceased, she walked down the aisle by herself. My cousin Brad walked up to her and clasped her tanned hand. Then Maggie surrendered her bouquet to her maid of honour, clad in a dark gown, and the wedding started.

As Vincent caressed my hand, I closed my eyelids and breathed in. Everyone thought he was human except my family. I was twenty-one... I couldn't keep going to weddings and formal occasions with an angel. His human form was going to stay looking twenty-five for billions of years. I wanted to marry, but the only creature I loved was a spirit.

He actually hurt me the first time he showed himself to me in the parking lot at Cedarwood, I thought, biting my lip.

"What's wrong, Tori?" Vincent whispered. His warm breath brushed against the hairs around my ears. He couldn't read my mind, but he had watched and protected me for twenty-one years, so he knew my feelings and reactions.

*   *   *   *

Outside the country club, in the dusk, I looked down at Tori. Even though I was an angel, I loved my human. She was gorgeous today. I wished I could break angel rules and kiss her.

I felt my forehead wrinkle in a frown. She looked nervous. Her lips parted and she bit her bottom lip. She had only been doing that since I had revealed myself to her.

"People think you are my boyfriend," she said as she stroked the grass with her sandal. Tori stared at the ground. "You're an angel... you're a lot of fun, but we can't marry. I want to marry someone, but when you're around no men come near me." She looked up at me. My human form heart was beating so hard that my chest hurt.

"What do you want?" I whispered. I'm not sure how I managed to speak, as I felt like I had lockjaw.

"I need you to stop showing yourself to me," she murmured, staring at the grass. The blood in my human body arrested and my chest felt heavy and sore from panic. No! I couldn't stop our friendship. Right now, I wanted a demon to slice me up with his cutlass and murder all my strong emotions for Tori, but no one could get rid of those feelings except God. The Creator had once agreed to grant me one wish, anything, but I wasn't going to use it to forget about this human.

Suddenly I saw Odium and Pernicious off in the distance. Anger flushed through me and I knew my eyes were going to turn golden. The supernatural creatures writhed in laughter. Tori noticed my eyes, sensing my energy change, and then looked behind her. She placed her

143

small hands on her hips, her elbows bent, and stared at the creatures. Surprisingly, they vanished.

Tori's hands fell and she gazed up at me sadly. "I'm sorry, Vincent," she murmured.

*   *   *   *

Vincent was upset, but I didn't realize why. We were friends and he would miss my brothers. He probably mourned his new place in my family, but I couldn't stand loving someone who was unable to have human feelings for me. And even if he did love me, humans and angels couldn't marry. He looked agonized and I perceived the pain in his glowing blue eyes. His eyes then became golden. At first, I thought he was angry at me, but then the hairs on my body rose. I knew it had to be demons.

I whirled and my hands rose to my hips. Pernicious and Odium stood in front of the hydrangea bushes, giggling. I glared at them. Suddenly they disappeared and I trembled. Vincent's fingers touched my arm softly. When he caressed my skin, comfort and pleasure made me wish that he could continue appearing to me.

"Tori, are you okay?"

"No," I whispered, looking up at him. His eyes were blue again. I inhaled, then Vincent escorted me to the foyer doors.

"Do you want to go home or inside?" he asked softly. His right hand stroked my upper arm. I heard the music beating inside the country club. I was a fool, I realized. No other being could be like Vincent. No other human could compete.

Swiftly, a man and woman who had obviously drunk too much slammed through the doors outside. The foyer door almost crushed my face, but Vincent pulled me away just in time. His massive chest collided with me. He smelled so good, and he looked like a Greek statue.

The couple stumbled and slunk over to a cement bench where they commenced passionately exploring each other. I realized I had changed my mind about my Guardian.

"Vincent, please keep showing your human form," I pleaded, watching him.

He smiled, his eyes were golden, and there was intense joy on his face. Even though Vincent was in human form, he was an angel—and yet I wondered if he loved me like a human could. Maybe because he was a spirit, his love was stronger.

Vincent grabbed my hand and we walked back into the country club, where we sat down at our cleared table. After a moment, Vincent moved close beside me as we watched the other couples dancing.

"That talk outside... do you want to dance?" he whispered and I closed my eyes for a moment.

"Of course."

His large hand gently lifted mine. I knew my Guardian Angel was always aware that he could hurt my human body. Leisurely, we glided onto the tiled floor. His eyes glowed as he held my hand and ran his muscular arm around my waist. I wanted to breathe, but his expression was so intense that I was unable to think of anything else.

CHAPTER EIGHTEEN

THE DAY AFTER the wedding, I woke up early. Someone had left the central air on the night before, so the air was cold. I snuggled into my covers, closing my eyes again and remembering a beautiful wedding dress I had seen once in Smithington. Then I imagined standing beside Vincent in front of a preacher who was going to marry us. A beautiful arch covered with white roses and doves stood behind the clergyman. As I gazed up at my angel, his blue eyes were golden and I knew he really cared about me. He grasped my hand and we looked at the preacher. When Vincent was to put the ring on my finger, I gazed up at him and screamed because his eyes were black—like Odium's.

"What's wrong?"

I opened my eyes to see Vincent squatting by my bed. As I trembled, his supernatural heat comforted me. I stared at his glowing eyes and worried about demons being in my room; it was cold, after all, and usually it was warm around angels. While anxiety swept through my body, I gazed around my bedroom. I didn't see any demons. Then I gazed at Vincent again and bit my lip.

"I let a day dream get out of control."

* * * *

When I got out of bed and dressed, I studied the invitation to Janessa's party. I wanted to get something else on my mind besides marrying Vincent. I shivered, remembering Odium's dark eyes, which were scarier than his red demon form eyes.

I picked up the phone and called Janessa to RSVP to her costume party. She wondered what I was going to dress up as, so I promised to tell her if she came shopping with me the next day for supplies. She agreed.

When we finished talking, Kristen called. She wanted to do something this weekend because she had a new boyfriend and wanted me to meet him. As a result, I invited Kristen, our other college friends, and their boyfriends to come over on Friday for pizza and to watch DVDs.

* * * *

Janessa came over at ten o'clock the next morning and we drove to Smithington to buy supplies for our costumes. My cousin stared at me from the passenger seat and I grinned, knowing she was impatient to know what I was going to dress up as.

"So tell me, Tori, what are you going to be?"

"An angel," I replied as I drove.

"An angel, really? You always used to dress as a princess."

"Yeah, but I don't want to this year. Did I ever tell you that I saw an angel when I was fourteen?"

Her eyes widened. "Really?"

"It's true. I always kept it to myself because I thought people would think I was crazy."

She was obviously intrigued. "What did it look like?"

"He was—"

"He? How do you know it was a guy?"

"Trust me, Janessa. I went into Dad and Mom's room to check what time it was. He was pale and sitting on Dad. To be honest, I thought he was Dad, but when I reached out there was nothing there and I saw my dad was lying down."

"Wooo! That gives me the heebie-jeebies."

"He wasn't a demon!" I protested.

She trembled. "Still... a spirit, that's creepy."

*   *   *   *

When we got to the craft store in Smithington, I parked my car.

As we walked through the store, Janessa asked, "So how are you going to make your wings?"

"I'll use a wire frame... made of coat hangers, I think."

"You have to use feathers. Everyone does."

"Warrior Angels' wings are made of fire."

"Excuse me?"

I swallowed. I was giving away too much information. It was bad enough that I had confessed to seeing an angel when I was fourteen. I picked up a bottle of gold glitter and looked at her.

"Angels are spirits. Don't you think they might have wings of fire and not feathers? A Warrior is supposed to be scary. They have to fight demons. The only thing with feathers that would be scary would be a Gryphon, and I don't think those exist," I said, rambling.

Janessa shrugged, fingering marabou fur. "I guess... You're lucky, because most people have never seen an angel before. They have to use their imaginations."

"I guess I'll buy feathers. I don't know what to use for fire."

Her nose wrinkled. "You could use paint on the wings to make a fire design, or you could buy some red and orange tissue paper."

"Those are good ideas, but I'm going to stick with feathers."

*　*　*　*

On Thursday evening, Mom and I were completing our weekly house cleaning early in preparation for my friends coming over the following night. House cleaning was exercise, so we turned on our central air and wore shorts.

My mom was having trouble pushing the black vacuum, and I wondered why since she was still young. I was using our long-handled broom to clean cobwebs off our nine-foot ceilings.

"Mom, I'll switch with you," I offered.

Without warning, I noted two onyx imps around my mom. One gruesome creature was sitting on my Mom's t-shirt-covered back, grinning. Its sulphuric breath filled the air and its long yellow teeth pointed upward. The second demon perched on the vacuum but bent over the front with its dark claws and hands digging into the carpet. It was obviously trying to stop my mother from being able to push the vacuum. My mother's frustration made the demon hiss wickedly and laugh, causing its belly to writhe.

"Hey!" I yelled, glaring at the creatures.

"Whatcha gonna do, human?" the imp on the vacuum hissed, its large red eyes narrowing at me. The creature on my mom's back stuck out its grotesque, scaly green tongue. While the demon mocked me, I noticed Michael and Vincent appear. My mother's brown eyes were huge and her jaw dropped, so I realized she could see our Guardians.

"What's going on?" she asked.

"Just be still, Mom. It's okay."

Michael lifted his broadsword and spun it through the air of the family room. The blade sliced the atmosphere around the vacuum, but the imp jumped and grabbed my mother's neck. "Have a hack, Guardian!" it hissed. My mom shrieked and tried to pull the imp off her neck. I wasn't sure if she saw the demon or just felt it.

"Stop, human!" the imp groaned as Michael lifted his cutlass.

"Guardians aren't to kill their humans," the two-foot onyx creature cried. However, Michael nimbly stalked closer. My mom's brown eyes stared at the gigantic Guardian angel. When he looked at my mother, Michael's furious golden eyes stopped glowing and became compassionate.

"Marianne, it's okay," he spoke. When Michael gazed at the demon again, his golden eyes emitted radiance and his broadsword stuck into the imp. The scaly creature twisted and hissed. The other imp's hands mounted on its hips and it narrowed its red eyes. "I promise pain!" it screamed and vanished.

My mother quivered and her eyes closed. But she didn't fall. Michael sheathed his sword and lifted my mother, placing her in a blue reclining wing chair. I took a plaid blanket folded on the floor and draped it over her.

Her face was pale and her dark eyes stared at Michael. "Thank you, Michael," she whispered.

"No problem," he said softly, carefully gripping her hand. I knew Mom would relax if Michael continued to touch her skin.

When I knew Mom was safe, I looked at Vincent and noticed that he was watching me, so I walked over to him. "Can you help me clean the house? Mom can't."

"Okay, Tori." The blond angel smiled and shrunk to human form. His golden eyes, blade, and massive wings vanished. Even though the imps were gone, Michael remained in angel form.

As I picked up the large black vacuum, I felt a big shock. Cold, spirit power drove into my arms and I groaned as the demonic energy threw me onto the floor.

Vincent squatted beside me. "Tori?" he called.

As he spoke, I relaxed and my eyelids closed. Gently, Vincent put my head on his legs and I inhaled. *I'm safe.* I opened my eyelids as his supernatural warmth penetrated my head and shoulders.

"Vincent," I murmured, watching my golden angel.

His concerned eyes observed me. "The imp must have left that residual energy on the vacuum," he said.

I watched the worried, golden glow vanish from his irises and the blue return.

*　*　*　*

It was Friday evening, and Vincent and I were waiting for our guests. William and Stephen had decided to take Cassandra and Barbara out to a movie in Stephen's car, as Will's license was suspended for quite a while. Dad and Mom were planning to go out for a late supper with Katherine Windsor and her husband.

When Vincent and I heard the gravel crunching in our driveway and saw headlights through the kitchen windows, we hurried into the foyer to greet my friends. Amber and Jack were the first to arrive.

"Hi," I greeted, holding the screen door open for them.

"Hello, Tori. You remember my wild driver boyfriend, Jack."

"Nice to see you again Jack," I said. "You remember Vincent?"

While Vincent reached out to shake Jack's hand, Amber's blue eyes roamed over him. I rolled my eyes.

"Your name's Vincent, right?" she asked. Vincent smiled.

"Yes. Hello, Amber."

*　*　*　*

After the rest of our friends had arrived and sat in the family room, the screen door opened. I stared into Odium's black, human form eyes.

"Odium!" I gasped. Beside me I felt Vincent's supernatural heat intensify and out of the corner of my eye, I saw him move his hand to his side. I realized he was going to take angel form and was waiting for his sword to appear. I gripped Vincent's hand frantically and gazed up at him. "Don't take angel form."

"Back off, Guardian," Odium snarled. "I'm invited."

Anxiously, I gazed around the foyer, hoping my friends would stay in the family room and not see the angel form I was sure Vincent was going to take.

Michael stood glaring in the archway that led from the foyer into the rest of the house. He gripped the platinum hilt of his blade.

Just then, Kristen walked into the foyer.

"Lucas!" she exclaimed.

Odium smiled at her. "Hello, beautiful." Then he threw his arm around my petite friend's waist.

"Nice to meet you, Vincent and Tori," he smirked and then kissed Kristen. I trembled, clenching my fists while I tried to think of a way to make the Strong Man leave. My palms hurt. When I opened them, I realized I'd been clenching my hands too tightly; my palms were decorated with half-moon imprints.

* * * *

Vincent and I walked into the family room behind Kristen and Odium.

"Hey, this is my new friend Lucas," she announced to my other friends who greeted the Strong Man. Vincent and I sat on the love seat and I felt his intense warmth penetrating me. I knew he wanted to take angel form and defeat Odium, so I tried to distract him.

"Kristen, he's hot! How come you and Tori get the hottest guys?" Amber asked moodily. Jack shifted and narrowed his brown eyes at Amber.

"Maybe Lucas smelled my dad's money," Kristen said playfully as she and Odium sat on a couch.

Odium and wrapped his large arm around her waist. "No, I just like beautiful women."

All the hairs on my body stood on end and goose bumps appeared on my arms. *How are Vincent and I going to get through tonight?* I wondered. My eyes narrowed. I was astonished that Kristen could stand to sit so close to the Strong Man. Vincent encircled my shoulders with his muscular arm. As his heat penetrated my t-shirt, I leaned back and tried to enjoy being his girlfriend.

"Where do you work, Lucas?" Damien asked.

"I'm a salesperson for a large corporation."

"Door to door?"

"Yeah," Odium answered. He kept staring at me, his black eyes piercing me while Vincent tensed up.

Vincent had moved his arm away from my shoulders and his hand rested at his thigh. I knew he missed his broadsword. Gazing up at Vincent, I saw his teeth were clenched. The warm and cold supernatural energy in the room was palpable and I knew both beings wanted to take spirit form and fight.

"Tori, tell the boys how you met Vincent," Kristen said.

Quaking, I was grateful to look at Vincent again. His eyes were golden and glowing, so I desperately gripped his fingers, hopeful for his spirit energy to calm me. I also wished his eyes would stop glowing.

"Your eyes," I murmured, then gazed at my friends. I hoped no one would notice that his eyes were golden instead of blue. "I got out of work at Cedarwood and some man grabbed me, but Vincent was around and saved me. We became friends after that and he always tries to protect me."

"Good job, man," Damien stated and smiled at Vincent.

"He's a keeper," Cindy declared boldly.

* * * *

As I stood in the kitchen with Vincent getting the food ready, Michael and James appeared. The Guardians radiated light and I was terrified that my friends were going to see them.

"Please take human form. My friends might see you," I pleaded, reaching out to the spirits. The Guardians regarded me and swiftly took human form. However, their eyes remained golden.

"Marianne and Frederick are going out soon. Can you find a way to get rid of that demon before we leave?" Michael asked.

"I've tried to think of something, but Odium has a right to be here," Vincent said. "He was invited."

I noticed his hand slide to his thigh and clench as if he was trying to grasp his sword. He obviously missed the weapon. In giving up angel form to spend time with me, he lost so much.

"I could pretend to be sick," I suggested. All three Guardians stared at me seriously.

"You shouldn't lie," James said, but as I glanced up at his handsome brown face he didn't seem critical. I bit my lip. I didn't want to lie, but I wanted that demon to leave.

Vincent squeezed my hand. His human form hands were hot and I was reminded of who he really was—*an angel.*

"I'll stay with Tori and protect her. Odium knows we can't make him leave unless we take spirit form, and that would scare Tori's guests."

"Be careful," Michael warned. Then he and James vanished.

*　*　*　*

After Tori's friends had filled their plates with pizza and chips, she quickly stacked the empty pizza boxes to tidy up the kitchen. As Tori and I picked up our plates, Frederick and Marianne Davenport walked into the kitchen.

"We're going now," Frederick announced.

I saw both James and Michael in the doorway watching me seriously as Tori hugged her parents. My friends had to guard Tori's parents, but I knew they did not want to leave us with Odium in the house.

After her parents left, we walked into the family room and sat on the love seat. I tried to ignore the Strong Man who sat too close to Tori and I, but my spiritual senses were too heightened. His imps had killed Tori and I couldn't believe that we had once been friends. I wondered if Odium had come here just to torment me or to kill Tori. Even though I was in human form, I couldn't eat the pizza and set my plate on the floor.

*　　*　　*　　*

After my friends and I finished the pizza and one DVD, Kristen looked around and suggested we play hide and seek. My other friends liked the idea, but when I glanced up at Vincent his anxiety was obvious. My heart raced as I wondered if Odium would try to hurt me. I regretted not pretending to be sick. But if I hid with my Guardian, Odium wouldn't be able to harm me—besides, my friends' Guardians were in the house, too.

"We can hide together," I whispered. Panic filled me when I noticed that his eyes were glowing again. The last thing we needed was for my guests to see his supernatural eyes. "Your eyes are glowing again."

No one wanted to count, so we put our names in a fruit bowl and Kristen drew out Vincent's name! My Guardian and I glanced at each other. His fear for me was obvious. My pulse raced as I imagined Odium killing me while Vincent was occupied. There were disadvantages to my Guardian taking human form.

I tried not to look at Odium. The demon taunted and tried to scare me. Unfortunately, Vincent's tension was obvious. I caressed his hand to try to calm his stress, but when I gazed up at him, he was glowering at a smirking Odium. The demon winked at me.

Vincent squeezed my hand and muttered, "You're staying with me!"

CHAPTER NINETEEN

VINCENT COUNTED IN our foyer while I hid in the washroom nearby. As I was settling into my place, Kristen ran by and saw me. She looked into the washroom and frowned, her hands on her hips. "Excuse me? You're hiding place is too obvious!" she hissed. "Come with me."

I shook my head, placing a finger in front of my lips. "No."

"I know you don't want to leave Vincent, but come on!" She grabbed my hand and tried to pull me up the stairs, but I yanked back. "Tori Davenport! He's almost done counting!"

I wanted to appease Kristen, so I followed her upstairs, intending to come right back down. As soon as she darted into Will's room, a cold breeze drove through the hall.

Oh no! Is Odium up here?

I glanced around. I was going to run into Will's room when a cold hand covered my mouth and a muscular arm dragged me backward. *Odium!*

While I squirmed, the Strong Man hissed, "I have a proposition!" His breath made the side of my face cold and I yearned for Vincent's heat. My whole body shivered from the cold and I wondered how Kristen could stand to be around him. I wanted to bite Odium's hand so I could free my mouth to scream, but I didn't want a mouthful of demon blood.

Odium ushered me into my room, but he didn't remove his hand from my mouth. He hauled me over to my French doors. Then he touched them and they flung open violently. The glass in the doors shattered. He held me tight, then flew us to the roof and released me.

His black eyes watched me seriously as he slowly backed away from me. I was perched right on the edge of the widow's walk.

"Jump off the roof and I'll break up with Kristen."

I glared back at him. "No!"

He rolled his eyes. "Whatever," he muttered.

Suddenly, Pernicious appeared.

"Should I hold Tori for you?" she asked, raising her sharp claws and hissing at me.

"Go ahead," he uttered chillingly. As sulphur breath filled my nose, I coughed and backed away.

"Help!" I screamed. The imp jumped on me and I lost my balance, falling onto a steep area of the roof. As I slid down, Pernicious released me. I tried to grip the shingles so I could stop my slide, but nothing worked. Tumbling over the edge of the roof, I gripped the eaves trough and hung on. It creaked under my weight.

Where's Vincent?

When I screamed, Odium and Pernicious appeared at the edge of the roof, smirking. The Strong Man grinned, bent, and pried my hands off the metal. "You're not likely to die," he said, "but a broken neck is possible."

I stared up at him and wondered how a former Archangel could be so evil. Why had Odium chosen to rebel against God? I could feel his hate for me in those black eyes of his. His cold hands made my own feel numb and I wondered why Vincent hadn't come yet.

Without warning, Odium yanked my body up over the eaves trough so I stood in front of him again.

"What are you doing?" I gasped.

"You weren't going to fall far enough," he hissed. Odium smiled wickedly and then gave me a hard push.

*   *   *   *

After I finished counting, I heard glass shatter upstairs.

Tori didn't stay near me!

Anxiety filled me when I realized Odium was probably hurting her. I vanished and appeared on Tori's balcony in angel form. The French doors were decimated. Next, I emerged on the roof so I could see the whole yard. Odium and Pernicious were standing below me at the edge of the roof. Just as I was wondering what was going on, I noticed Tori frantically grasping the eaves trough. Horror overwhelmed me when Odium pried her hands off the metal.

I was about to leap to her rescue when Odium surprised me by hauling her back up onto the roof. Silently, I withdrew my broadsword.

Then, Odium gave Tori a shove.

"No!" I cried and hoped I was fast enough to catch her.

*   *   *   *

I felt warmth before my Guardian's hands caught me. My pulse slowed, but I felt nauseous and closed my eyes. As Vincent held me, I heard shoes running over the patio.

"Is she okay?" Amber asked, having come outside.

"Just barely," Vincent uttered angrily. I gazed up at my Guardian and noticed that he was in human form, but his blue eyes glowed.

"I saw Lucas throw her off the roof!" Jack exclaimed as he raced over.

I felt my pulse speed up again as I glanced over at Jack. I hoped he hadn't seen Pernicious, too. Trying to explain spirits to my friends would have been hard.

"What did you see?" I asked.

Jack looked at the ground and then at Amber. He shifted.

"I hid outside so no one would find me and I saw Lucas holding you on the roof. Then this weird black thing appeared and jumped on you and you fell. I thought Lucas was going to help you when he pulled you up, but then the freak pushed you. That's when Vincent ran out of the house and caught you." Jack frowned.

"What's wrong?" I asked, wondering what Jack would say about seeing Pernicious. It was really weird that he had been able to see her. Could he see spirits, too? Jack stared at me and then glanced back at Amber.

"Before Lucas threw you, I saw this brightness on the roof, but it went away as soon Lucas pushed you. Did you see that black thing that jumped on you? Am I crazy?" Jack thrust his hand threw his short brown hair. I knew he was horrified.

"You're not crazy, Jack, but it would be better if you don't tell our other friends," I answered.

Amber gasped. "Are you talking about ghosts?" Her blue eyes were wide. I groaned. I didn't want Amber to know about the spirit world because I was sure she would tell others, and most people would think I was insane.

I swallowed. "Amber, there's a world that most people can't see..." She gripped my arm, looking at me seriously. "Please don't tell anyone, Amber... about what Jack saw," I pleaded.

Amber shook her head. "I don't care what's going on. I'm calling the police!" Her hand trembled as she grabbed her cell phone from her pocket. "Hello? I need the police. My friend almost got murdered!"

I glanced down at my palms and saw cuts on the fingers. There was also a big bruise on my right thigh, as well as bruises on my arms. Elizabeth and Damien walked outside. "Did something break?" Elizabeth asked. "Damien and I heard noises, but we didn't want to leave our hiding place. Are you hurt, Tori?" She looked worried.

"I'm okay."

After a minute, I looked around for Odium. As the Strong Man, in human form, walked out into the yard next to Kristen, I heard sirens. Odium's eyes narrowed. Vincent kept holding me and I felt safe in his arms.

"What's wrong?" Kristen asked.

"Lucas tried to kill Tori!" Amber hissed.

"Excuse me?!" Kristen shrieked. She whirled and gave Lucas a hard shove. "What did you do?"

His black eyes narrowed at her. "Be careful," he growled, clenching his fists.

At that moment, car doors slammed at the front of our house and Lucas vanished.

* * * *

The following day, I wanted to clean up the glass in my room, but I was too sore. My family's kind Guardians had tried to clean up and they shocked me when they produced new French doors, which they were now installing.

As they went about their work, I climbed up onto the widow's walk. I wasn't afraid to come up here as long as Vincent was around. As I sat on the roof, I studied my bruises in the strong sunlight. Gazing down, I thought back on what had happened the previous night. A cold breeze swept around my body, reminding me of how cold I'd felt around Odium. His black eyes had been so horrifying and had conveyed all the hate in Hell. For a moment, I wished that I had never seen the spiritual world. I shivered and felt grateful that I hadn't been badly hurt.

In the distance, I could see Smithington, a few forests, and the sand hills.

Suddenly, Vincent's bare feet appeared beside me.

"Hello, Tori," he said warmly.

I gently caressed the skin on the bridge of his foot. Giving in to my mischievous mood, I then tickled his sole and he moved his foot away.

Grinning up at him, I asked, "You don't like to be tickled?"

"No one ever tickled me before. It felt strange," he answered seriously.

Giggling, I warned, "I might do it again."

His eyes sparkled. "You probably will."

Laughing, I patted the roof beside me. "Sit down," I said.

Vincent grinned at me and crossed his legs. Bright sunlight grazed his blue eyes, making them look like blue topaz stones. Then he gazed at the bruise and scratches on my thigh, and his eyes began to glow. He brushed his fingers against the bruise and tightened his jaw. I winced. I don't know how my Guardian noticed the expression on my face as he examined my skin, but when he gazed over at me, his intense eyes were filled with guilt.

"I'm sorry. We have to stay together, no matter what. You already died once." Vincent lifted his fingers and pushed some hair behind my ear. My breathing caught in my throat as I gazed at my angel. His eyes were glowing. "I can't believe you can actually stand to come up here," Vincent said, shifting nearer to me.

"I love looking out at Smithington. Being up here is the closest thing to flying with you."

He stared at me.

"Thank you for saving me. I'm also grateful to the other Guardians for cleaning up and fixing my doors," I declared, gripping his hand.

"We like helping you." He touched the bruise on my thigh again and glowered. "I'm not omnipotent, and I really hate it!"

"It was my fault. I shouldn't have gone upstairs."

Vincent put his arm around me. "I don't want you to die again!"

I sighed. *I don't want to die, either.*

We sat silently as I leaned against him. I enjoyed my Guardian holding me and I wished that he could hold me forever.

"Humans weren't created to die, you know," he murmured in my hair. His comment surprised me and I held my hand out, pinching it lightly.

"Our bodies age and die. I don't understand, how could we have been made to live forever?"

"Human body chemistry changed after Adam and Eve sinned."

"Why didn't God give me the chance to choose instead of cursing all of us?" I asked in frustration, pulling away from Vincent so I could see his face. He looked serious and I stared down at the roof, below us.

"I don't know, Tori. I wish he had." Vincent caressed my cheek. It felt nice, but I knew he just wanted to make me feel better.

"I realize God blessed me, though, by letting me be born in a peaceful country and giving me my parents."

"Yes," Vincent affirmed seriously.

"Adam and Eve could have chosen not to sin," I said. "Because of their sin, all humans have a strand of wickedness woven into their DNA. We age and it's a lot easier to sin because of them."

"Humans always had the choice not to sin, just like angels. The Creator never made anything that was forced to serve him."

"I wouldn't have sinned," I announced in frustration.

Suddenly, Michael emerged in human form, snickering and rolling his brown eyes. I stared at him, feeling confused. Why was he laughing?

"What is wrong with you? Rebellious human, you would sin right away," he announced righteously. I glared up at the dark-haired angel. Why did he have to be so mean? "You love to break rules."

As Michael spoke, Vincent sheltered me with his muscular arms and I felt his intense warmth through my t-shirt. I knew Vincent was going to take angel form.

"Stop, Michael!" he ordered.

Michael shook his head and glared at Vincent, his irises glowing. As quickly as he appeared, he vanished, his spirit heat dissipating.

* * * *

While at work on Thursday evening, I checked under Gertrude Hunter's bed; I had to do her bath as well as her laundry and she always left her clothes strewn across the private room.

I moaned while gazing under her bed. I could feel the pressure in my head from a cold coming on.

"Tori, stand up. I'll look under the bed for you," Vincent said softly.

When I stood up, Vincent lay on the floor and grabbed the clothing. Gratefulness filled me.

"Thank you. This is not your job, Vincent. I'm getting paid to do it."

He gazed at me seriously as he stood up. His forehead looked like a furrowed field. "You need to go home and go to bed."

"I can't."

"I know."

"You better disappear, or I'm going to get in trouble. I can't have a man in here with me on the job."

"No one else can see me, but if you don't want to look at me, I'll disappear," he announced.

Suddenly, I started to cough. The coughing didn't stop, and when I started to choke, I moved away from the doorway to a more secluded part of the room. Vincent followed me, but I couldn't pay attention to him. As panic filled me, I felt my Guardian's warmth penetrate my body. I visibly relaxed, even though I was still coughing. In a moment, the choking stopped and I felt him hug me.

"It worked... I hate when you choke," Vincent muttered near my ear. "I don't want you to die." I took numerous deep breaths and then smiled as he held me.

"But you might end up with a more interesting human to guard," I replied jokingly.

He snorted. "I don't want to guard anyone else."

"I know. I was just being silly."

My next bath was Dorothy Witzel, so I walked into her semi-private room.

"Hi, Dorothy. It's your bath night," I announced.

Petite Dorothy was disgruntled and stared up at me. "I already washed," she replied.

Immediately, her roommate clambered toward me and cupped her hand near my ear conspiratorially. "I was in the washroom and the washcloths are dry."

Furious, Dorothy's hands rose to her hips, her green eyes narrowed, and her white eyebrows lowered. "I didn't know there was a policeman in the building!" she saucily announced.

"Dorothy, I have to do your bath," I stated.

"I won't tell if you don't do it."

"It's my job, Dorothy, and I'm not going to say I did it if I didn't."

Dorothy responded by muttering to herself.

"I'll get your bath water started," I said and walked into the washroom. As I turned the chrome taps, water sprayed me from the shower head. The warm liquid trailed down my head and dropped off my nose. Someone had not turned the shower off.

When my body shivered, I gazed at the sink and saw a two-foot scaly imp mocking me. The creature laughed and jumped up and down on the vanity. Its thin arms and lengthy nails wrapped in front of its midsection.

"You're really pathetic. Do you expect me to start swearing?" I asked sarcastically. The creature hissed and garish yellow teeth rose up in its mouth. Then it vanished.

* * * *

Later, at three o'clock in the morning, Tori sat up and seized the comforter that had fallen on the floor. She coughed as she lay down and grabbed the other pillow on her bed to prop herself higher. I wanted to give her some water, but then the human fell asleep again. I closed my eyes and remembered Heaven, six thousand years ago...

I sat watching the diamond-eyed fish swimming in the clear lake when I sensed my Lord. I had been admiring their intricate scales and wished I shared my Master's ability to create. As soon as I sensed God, I turned and offered homage.

"Majesty," I uttered and kneeled.

My Lord was silent while I praised him. He always enjoyed the praise his angels gave him, but today I sensed his impatience. Curiosity filled me and I had to look up.

"Hurry, Vincent. Stand up," God beckoned.

"Are you finished, my Lord?" I asked, swiftly rising. I watched pride and excitement mix in his expression, his golden eyes glowing. The Creator had been restless until he'd started this new project, another planet.

When the Creator and I appeared together on his new planet, I simply stared at my surroundings. A large orange and black striped creature sedately glided by on four limbs beside a few palm trees. Its covering was smooth and I desired to touch the creature. A beautiful blue and green bird with a short but large curved beak chattered, "I am finished, I am finished." Then, two white creatures pranced from behind the trees, looking like the fiery horses that pulled my Lord's chariot, but these creatures possessed a single three-foot horn on their foreheads. A clump of hibiscus bushes rustled and I turned my head. Three furry, black and white animals chewing on leaves slowly crushed their way through the bushes.

"Those are pandas," the Creator announced warmly. A chattering cacophony that reminded me of a thousand talking angels in the palace erupted from the trees. Fuzzy brown and yellow animals climbed amidst the foliage. One yellow creature dropped and cried before its brown mother captured and comforted it.

All at once, giggling ensued. Two angel-like creatures strolled out of the forest and my eyebrows rose at the sight of them. They were shorter then angels, had olive skin, brown hair, and dark eyes. They didn't glow and they didn't have robes on.

Michael strolled out of the forest behind them. My dark-haired friend had been missing from Heaven for a few days and now I realized where he'd been. I turned my attention back to my Lord.

"These are humans, Vincent," God stated. "A man and a woman, my children. Michael is guarding the man and I need you to guard the woman. I need you to keep Eve safe from our enemies. Our rebellious enemies will try to kill them, so until I tell you to step back, guard her."

"Are you going back to Heaven?" I asked.

"Yes."

Frustration stormed through my stomach, because I loved Heaven and my Lord. Why did I have to stay here? I was my Lord's attendant. I sighed and straightened my posture. I would obey. I would still be able to sense God here, and I could always talk to my Master, but God's presence was more radiant in Heaven.

Staring at the green grass, I asked, "How long will I guard Eve?"

"A long time," God answered.

"All right, my Lord," I replied reluctantly. But I loyally submitted.

While my head was lowered, he announced quietly, "They have free will."

My head jerked up. "What is that?"

"They can choose to rebel, and you are not allowed to stop Adam or Eve from doing so. I have told the humans not to eat anything from that fruit tree, because they'll die if they do." The Creator gestured into the middle of the orchard. "They are immortal now, but if they disobey they will become mortal."

God's mention of disobedience made me think of the ancient war and I began to glow.

"There is one more thing. I want you to be invisible," God added. Then he appeared nearer the humans.

"Our Lord!" they exclaimed gleefully. Eve tried to curtsy, but her legs moved awkwardly. When God laughed warmly, envy chewed on my angel form because I had been a favoured angel for billions of years. What was so special about this man and woman? Why had he created them? Did he still love me?

"I'm a servant," I whispered, feeling resigned while I lowered my head.

Fourteen days later, fruit tree blossoms caressed Eve's shoulders as she stood in the orchard and stared at the forbidden tree.

"No," I whispered.

The beautiful human gazed around, looking for me. "Is that you, God?" she asked hopefully, but I didn't appear. When I didn't say anything, Eve glided away.

However, four days later, Eve came back to the orchard to stare once again at the forbidden tree. I couldn't understand why she found the fruit so tempting. As I felt my temperature rise like it had during the rebellion, I looked around for demons.

"Eve!" a hiss whispered. I scanned the garden and saw a snake curled around the forbidden tree. My eyes narrowed.

Eve's doe eyes widened when she looked at the snake. "Was that you, snake?" she asked.

"Yes, human... Gaze at that luscious fruit," it spoke, its forked tongue moving.

I pulled my blade, but the snake stopped me in my tracks, gloating, "Remember free will, Vincent." My eyes blasted angry light at the wicked creature. Eve hadn't noticed the snake speaking to me; she was mesmerized by the forbidden tree.

"No, Eve," I whispered.

"Human, it's so ripe," the snake hissed, seductively.

"No," she said and shook her head. Eve played with her knee-length tresses, pushing hair behind her small ears.

"God lies," it hissed. Its brown, scaled tail and rattler wrapped around the tree. Her mammoth eyes stared the creature. "God loves me. He wouldn't lie."

"Don't be stupid! The Creator eats that fruit every night when you and the man are asleep."

"God doesn't need to eat," Eve protested.

Garish, bloodshot, scaly-lidded eyes watched her. "God wants to stay wise. Do *you want to be wise?"* it hissed.

* * * *

Sunlight crept around the darkener blinds on my French doors and I woke up coughing. I had no more pillows to prop myself higher, so I sat up. Trying to breathe deeply didn't work and I kept coughing.

I need some water, I thought and pulled my covers off. As I stepped onto my carpet, Vincent appeared and stood in front of me with a cup of water.

I grinned. "Thank you." The water irritated my throat and I groaned. "I have a sore throat and my ears hurt." I felt a headache coming on, and I rubbed my temples.

Vincent held out pain medicine in front of my face. "Take these and lay down again," he said gently.

"Thanks," I whispered hoarsely. After I took the medicine, I laid down.

"Go to sleep again, human," he murmured, rubbing my hand.

"I want to talk to you," I protested, but my throat was hoarse.

"You can't talk, I'll talk to you. Here, have this." He handed me a popsicle.

"Thank you very much," I whispered and gripped his warm, powerful fingers.

He touched my forehead. "You have a fever, Tori. Why don't you just go back to sleep?"

"Your eyes are glowing," I whispered and coughed.

"I was going to talk to you so you would stay in your room, but—"

As he stared at me, I saw anxiety in his eyes. His forehead was furrowed. I lifted my fingers and brushed his forehead. "Don't worry. I was just sleeping."

"I need to take care of you," he murmured and grabbed my hand. My chest hurt as I watched him. There was so much emotion in his face. I think he cared about me even more then Dad and Mom did.

"Thank you so much. I couldn't survive without my Guardian." Vincent's eyes glowed brighter and I felt his body grow warmer.

"Talk about Heaven," I whispered hoarsely. His eyes turned golden now and glowed intensely.

I felt paralysed as his body started to radiate and I knew he was close to taking angel form. Magnificent wings emerged and I witnessed golden spirit energy ripple through them. Awe conquered me, but I wanted him to remain in human form. When Vincent took angel form, frustration hit me and I remembered that he was a spirit and couldn't marry me.

As soon as those golden eyes of his met mine, I pleaded, "I know you want to go to Heaven, but please take human form. It hurts me when..." I stopped talking. I had said too much.

His eyes pierced me inquisitively and I knew he really wanted to know what I had been planning to say. I didn't speak. Vincent's shoulders lifted in a sigh, then his wings and glow disappeared. He hoisted my pink wing chair and settled it beside the four-poster bed. He didn't grunt like William and Stephen did as they picked things up. Of course, his human form muscles were very striking, even when he wore long-sleeved t-shirts. Vincent sat on the velour upholstered chair and tickled my hand, his affectionate eyes regarding me.

"Beautiful music vibrates gently through my home, especially near the palace and the clear lake where glittering multi-coloured fish live," he spoke quietly. "When the fish come to the surface, their eyes look like jewels. The fishes' scales are so intricate. I have wished many times that I possessed God's ability to create. The Creator awes me, Tori. I can't describe what I see up there..."

My Guardian stared upward as I started to feel tired again. After a few moments, he watched me again with glowing eyes and I tried to stay awake.

"Joy and laughter. There are spirits walking on the gold streets with crowns filled with stars and precious stones. The sky is the same as on earth, with a few artistic clouds, and when I see them I realize my Master is having fun. But there is no night. Children play in the fields, climb trees, and walk across the clear lake. We praise God all the time and families visit with biblical and historical figures. When you sit on the ground, love birds and butterflies land on your fingers. Healthy roses, hibiscuses, and lilies grow..."

While Vincent spoke, I fell asleep.

CHAPTER TWENTY

THE NIGHT OF Janessa and Karen's costume party had arrived. Even though it was late August, I had made my costume with long sleeves. Gold tinsel adorned the ends of my sleeves, my neckline, and hem. I also fashioned a short piece of tinsel into a halo shape. White and gold tulle made an overskirt over my white dress, and the feathered wings had gold and silver sparkles on the rounded edges of the feathers. My golden mask had glitter around the edges.

"Vincent!" I called when I was ready. At once, the handsome being stood in my room, attired in World War Two army fatigues. I gasped at the sight of him. "Wow! You look amazing." He smiled back at me but didn't speak. "You didn't tell me what you were going to wear."

"I wanted to surprise you," he answered. His intense eyes observed me. "You're beautiful, Tori."

I grinned at him. "Thanks."

Do you really think I'm beautiful? I had hoped he would like my costume, even though he already knew what it looked like. He had appeared and watched me while I made the wings. Vincent had been so fascinated while I brushed the glitter onto the feathers that I had laughed at him quietly. It was so much fun to have a friend like him. My wings were not magnificent like his were, but I had done my best.

"When I was two, I was in a Christmas play and I was an angel—"

"What kind?" he asked mischievously.

I swatted his arm lightly. "You remember!"

"Yes, but tell me."

"Messenger... most likely. Apparently I was swaying to and fro to the music and everyone found me amusing."

Vincent laughed. "I remember. I wished you were my child," he disclosed.

"But—"

"You were cute." He hesitated. "But Tori, I certainly don't want to be your dad anymore."

"Good."

Someone banged on my door. "Tori!" William called.

I opened the door and gazed at my brothers and their girlfriends' costumes. Stephen was a doctor, in a white lab coat and scrubs. He wore my stethoscope around his neck. It looked good on a tall man, fitting his torso. Barbara was a movie star with a knee-length, sequined dress and red boa. Cassandra was a southern belle in a hoop dress and wide-brimmed hat. My younger brother William was obviously a hunter. He wore a lightweight camouflage jacket and pants, and carried a rifle bag.

"Will, tell me that rifle bag's empty," I said.

"Of course," he answered.

"Vincent, where in the world did you find that World War Two uniform?" Stephen asked.

Vincent grinned. "From a great friend."

We slowly walked down the stairs and sauntered to our cars. I noticed Will glance at his car, which he had recently been able to get out of impoundment. It hadn't been fixed yet; there wasn't much point since he still couldn't drive it. I perceived the pain in his face and felt sorry for him.

I turned my attention to Vincent as we walked up to my car. My angel surprised me when he opened the passenger door and gestured for me to sit in the Mustang. Wow, he was going to drive!

When I rang the doorbell, Janessa and Karen ran to the entrance. Karen looked like a butterfly and her creative wings sparkled. It looked like she had made her wings from wire and panty hose which she had painted bright shapes on. Janessa was wearing a lab coat and pink scrubs. Her petit dachshund barked at Vincent but then quick-ly walked up to him and lifted its small paws up onto his leg. Warm brown, dachshund eyes adoringly gazed at my Guardian Angel. When its thin, short-haired tail thrashed, I whispered, "She loves you, angel." As I stared up at him, serious, glowing eyes sliced into mine. My heart started to beat against my chest walls and I couldn't breathe.

Vincent's voice was low. "What about—"

Without warning, a blond woman with blue eyes bumped my side roughly and I fell into Vincent. "Ohh," I gasped. Vincent's muscular arm grabbed my body firmly so that I didn't fall at his feet.

Janessa glared at the blond woman, who glided into the house without so much as an apology. "Karen, who's that?" she asked, her large brown eyes staring at her sister. "Is that one of your college friends?"

"No," Karen answered.

When other guests arrived, and my cousins were distracted, Vin-cent bent down. "I would think the woman who pushed you was a demon if her eyes were black," he whispered. "But they're blue. Never-theless, she must be one of the prince's followers."

"Prince?" I asked softly.

"The devil," he answered as his irises glowed. I shivered and goose bumps appeared on my arms.

Later, Vincent and I danced. While the Guardian held me, spirit energy danced through my central nervous system, gyrating along my nerves as the handsome spirit gazed at me. Golden specks glittered in his eyes, and I was awed.

"Your hair matches your eyes," I whispered.

"I know," he murmured.

Abruptly, my body shivered. When the bridge of my nose wrinkled, I declared, "Vincent, that blond woman *is* a demon."

"I know," he answered. Panic kicked me when I saw golden sparks amassing in his eyes.

I clasped his forearm. "Don't let your eyes glow."

"Fortunately, my mask will disguise my eyes."

"Is she a Strong Man?"

"No. She doesn't have that much energy."

My skin rose in goose bumps. "Is she going to hurt me?"

Vincent hugged me and his warm supernatural energy calmed me down. "There's plenty of Guardians here," he assured me.

"But I'm your responsibility," I reminded. "They have their own responsibilities."

*　*　*　*

Later, I whispered to my Guardian, "I'm going upstairs."

He looked at me questioningly, then the angel realized why. "It's okay, Tori, but be careful... there are demons."

I sauntered through a pair of open French doors that led to the hallway and suddenly felt sharp nails digging into my arm. Before I knew what was happening, I was hauled outside behind some bushes which were beyond the patio. As soon as we were out of sight, the nails retracted and I was thrown onto the ground.

"Odium, why do you think a powerful Guardian Angel wants her?" a woman sneered, which made me gaze up darkly. The woman who had pushed me before the party stood beside a familiar demon. "She's not blond, she has no spiritual powers, and she's weak and ugly."

Odium, in human form, snorted as I rose. Naturally, I shivered. All the hairs on my body stood up and my heart began to beat faster. I had two powerful demons standing in front of me! Hissing, the woman walked toward me. She was pretending to be a beautiful human, but her hatred made her ugly.

"Nice try, human," she hissed and ripped at my wings. "Humans only make imitations."

Pain tingled and pinched through my arms as she pulled on my costume. Finally, the elastic straps broke as they wrenched my tender skin. I struggled to keep my face from betraying me and clenched my teeth so that I didn't moan.

"I hurt you, human, didn't I?" she grinned wickedly. "Pathetic."

She slapped me across the face. It hurt and I wanted to cry, but I bit my lip instead. Tears collected around my eyes as her sulphur breath oozed into my nostrils.

"You can't break her!" Odium said.

The evil woman glared back at him. "You can't break her either, Odium." She cursed, and he hissed at her.

I tried to escape, but the woman hit me, snatched my hair, and yanked hard. "Oww," I whimpered.

"Let go of her!" Odium's dark voice commanded.

The blond woman laughed and tossed me on the ground again. Pain coursed up my tailbone, jarring my back. My head felt hot where she had pulled on my hair. Defiant tears ran from my eyes and I stared at the grass.

"Go kill Vincent, Athaliah!" Odium hissed, apparently talking to the female demon.

"No!" I screamed, but both demons ignored me.

"Oh, and be a demon and take out your contacts!" he ordered. The woman's pale hands pulled blue contacts out of onyx eyes. Her black eyes glared at the Strong Man.

"If I kill Vincent, I will outrank you," she said. "But I need the contacts." She slid the contacts back in, then gestured to me. "Enjoy this pathetic creature on your own, then."

I suddenly felt Odium's sulphur exhalations near my face. "Stand up!"

I realized he was talking to me, so I tried to stand, my angel costume getting in the way.

"Why did you stop Athaliah?" I asked him once I was on my feet.

"I hate her!" Odium hissed. "Athaliah was a pathetic six-foot angel in Heaven. She's garbage. I was twelve-feet tall and now I'm a Strong Man. She can't outrank me. When you die, Tori, you get to go to Heaven... but I have to look like a demon forever. You know, there's no such thing as human form in Hell." He sounded bitter.

"Lucas," I said softly, remembering the name he had gone by when he was Kristen's date.

He grabbed my arm and pulled me toward my Mustang. "Go home," he growled. "As soon as Athaliah assassinates your Guardian Angel, she will come back to kill you." I just glowered at him. "With that expression on your face, I'd think you were a Guardian."

Rebelliousness devoured me and I faced him. "Pathetic imps, sergeants, or commanders can't murder a Guardian, and you know it," I said defiantly. At that moment, I realized that Vincent would think Odium had killed me. If so, he might *let* Athaliah murder him.

I twisted my arm in a quick rotation and got away from the creature.

*　*　*　*

I watched the humans dance. The blond demon who had pushed Tori was now sitting on a couch regarding me. I felt the hate lunging at me from her blue eyes. Humans didn't possess that much evil in their eyes; not even serial killers. Where was Tori? Was the blond demon distracting me so that Odium could have her for himself? Consumed with worry, my chest hurt and my eyes glowed. I fled the recreation room and ran upstairs to the washroom, but the door was open and it was dark inside.

"Tori!" I called. I didn't feel hate up here, so I ran back down the stairs and gazed around the large recreation room. My heart was galloping.

Just then, I felt demonic hatred! I was about to go outside when I saw the blond demon glaring at me from the French doors. My hand moved to my thigh before I remembered I was in human form; I had no sword. My eyes glowed as I stalked toward the creature. Glowering, I almost gripped her arm and threw her outside, but I restrained myself, both because of my human's life and the fact that I wanted to take human form to spend time with Tori.

"Outside!" I growled.

We stalked outside and I took angel form so that nobody at the party would detect the light I was starting to emit.

The woman spun and hissed, "Odium killed Tori."

Anguish overwhelmed me, but I tried to tell myself that the demon was lying. If Tori was dead, I could let this pathetic demon kill me. I couldn't stand to see Tori dead, once again.

The demon tossed her blue contacts and took spirit form. A robust, six-foot commander with four amethyst bracelets glowered up at me. The platinum handle of my five-foot blade was firm and I drew the metal. Her scaly, onyx arm withdrew her own three-foot blade and she exhaled a yellow sulphur cloud at me, but the odour didn't make me look away.

*　　*　　*　　*

I ran fast and saw the cruel blond demon standing in front of Vincent.

"Odium killed Tori," she cackled and then took demon form. I was about to show myself to Vincent when Odium seized me and slapped his palm over my lips.

"I wanted you to go home," he growled in my ear. I fought against the creature, trying to kick his groin. "Human, behave! Do you want to be unconscious?" His sulphur odour swept around me.

"You reek, Odium!"

*   *   *   *

The grotesque spirit tried to stab my abdomen with her blade, but I swiped my sword on an angle and her dark arm and blade flew. Then I beheaded her.

A pair of narrow red eyes smouldered at me from her decapitated head. Demon slime spilled out onto the grass and I forced my blade into the ground and pulled it out to clean the metal. The last thing I wanted was to get black demon gore on me.

"Ridiculous!" I heard Odium laugh from the shadows as he grappled with a squirming Tori. My heart leapt to see that Tori was still alive. Before I could say anything, though, the Strong Man let go of Tori and departed.

*   *   *   *

As I woke the next morning, my arms hurt from Athaliah yanking on my wings. While I rubbed my tender skin, I noticed something sparkling on top of my couch. Sitting up, I saw that it was a piece of my costume's wings. The sunlight was making the gold and silver glitter on the feathers sparkle. Athaliah had thrown the wings and I realized that Vincent must have found them behind the bushes. Gratefulness filled me and I smiled at the thought of him.

"Good morning, Tori," Vincent said as he appeared in my chair. He was gorgeous in a white t-shirt and jeans. I grinned. "Thank you for bringing my wings," I said quietly.

I pushed my covers off so I could stand up. Vincent's eyes stared at me and I sauntered over and kissed his cheek. When his intense eyes started to glow, I felt concerned. Studying his face, I didn't see anger but instead human desire. Confusion filled me and I shook my head.

"I have to get dressed," I announced, backing away.

Vincent vanished as I walked into my walk-in closet for a t-shirt and jeans of my own.

CHAPTER TWENTY-ONE

AROUND LUNCHTIME, THE rest of my family left the house to gather more information on the police training course William had applied to get into.

At one o'clock, I was playing the piano and singing in our living room. Vincent was listening and watching, sitting in the walnut rocking chair. As I opened the piano bench to search for more sheet music, I sensed another spirit in the room with us. Tension swept through the room, but the energy I felt wasn't cold. Vincent and another angel were talking and I closed the piano bench to watch them.

It was Michael, and he was in human form. I was filled with worry, fearing that Michael knew I had kissed Vincent's cheek.

"Did I do something wrong?" I asked and walked over to the angels. Michael's glowing eyes shifted to me. A mixture of anguish, panic, and compassion radiated from his eyes.

"I'm sorry, Tori," he whispered and vanished. Confusion and panic filled me at the emotions I had seen in his eyes. I jerked my head to look at Vincent. His blue eyes glowed and I felt compassion from him as well.

"What's going on?"

All at once, the doorbell buzzed and I walked to the foyer. Two thin police officers looked back at me. One was an African American man and the other a brunette woman.

"Are you Victoria Davenport?" the man asked.

"Yes," I responded seriously. What was going on?

"Your parents and brothers were hurt in a vehicular accident," he stated.

"Excuse me!" My chest tightened and I felt dizzy. "Are they dead?"

Supernatural energy penetrated my back and Vincent took my hand. I was grateful for my Guardian Angel or I would have fallen. The male officer looked up, and then back at me. *Vincent must be in human form*, I thought.

"They're alive," he said.

The tightness started to leave my chest. "Thank God! How severe are their injuries?"

"They're in critical condition. A truck hit the right side of the van," he answered solemnly.

"Are they at Smithington Memorial?"

"Yes."

"Are you okay?" the woman asked.

"No," I whispered and closed my eyes. *Why doesn't the dizziness go away?*

"We will take you to the hospital," the male officer said and took my other hand.

"Thank you, but I want my friend to drive me."

The officer released me and said, "If you need anything else..." Then he passed me a business card, which I barely held.

When the police officers left, I almost fell over. I could feel my heart pumping furiously and I was breathing fast. Vincent put his arms around me and I tried to calm down. I knew that he would always take care of me; he was an angel, after all. Fighting to calm myself, I leaned back against his muscular chest.

"Help me," I whispered. Then I remembered how I had healed Agnes in the retirement home. When I felt calmer, I turned so I could look at him. "I can heal... my family... Vincent." I put my hands on his chest. Grave, glowing eyes looked down at me. "Remember Agnes?"

"Yes, Tori," he answered hoarsely. My knees felt heavy and my legs were flaccid.

"I'm weak," I groaned.

"Let's go outside," Vincent said, holding me up.

We got in the car and drove to the hospital.

*　*　*　*

Stepping into my mother's curtained area, I started panicking. My chest was tight and I felt lightheaded.

They are going to die!

My family appeared worse than I had imagined. I needed to heal them.

Calm down, Tori. Do what you have to do! Breathing deeply, my fingers caressed my mother's hand and I started to pray, but as I did so Pernicious jumped onto the bedrail opposite me and snarled. My eyes widened anxiously, goose bumps appeared on my arms, and all the hairs on my body stood on end. My mother shivered. She could smell the sulphur and sense the imp.

"Go away!" I whispered.

"You're pathetic, Tori. You're a human. Human beings can't heal anything," she hissed. I closed my eyes, but the demon raced around the bed and I sensed her cold spirit energy in front of me. I trembled. When I opened my eyes again, I almost shrieked; her huge red eyes and large yellow teeth were three inches from my face. "I'm glad you weren't in the van. This way I can torment you better. They will die."

Abruptly, I noticed someone standing outside the bed curtain. A nurse might think I was crazy if she heard me seeming to talk to myself. Anxious, I hesitantly gaped out the edge of the curtain and saw Vincent in human form. When I looked back, Pernicious had disappeared.

"Thank God," I murmured.

My vision became fuzzy and I sat down, putting my head between my legs. Warm palms rubbed my shoulders to comfort me.

"Vincent," I whispered.

* * * *

After, Vincent drove me home, I stalked to the backyard.

I can't heal them, I thought. *I healed Agnes, but...*

Frantic coolness coursed through me. It was spirit energy. Despair overwhelmed me and I felt hated for spirits—all spirits. As I made my hand into a fist, Vincent touched my arm and tried to hug me.

"Vincent, go away!" I yelled, backing away. Vincent cared for me too much. His eyes emitted compassion. I was angry at God. Vincent couldn't understand human emotions and injustices. The only creatures who could understand what I was feeling were demons—and they would only try to destroy me by making those foul emotions worse. "It's your fault, Vincent! Why didn't you stop the truck?!"

His glowing eyes regarded me. "It's not my fault. I'm *your* Guardian."

"Then it's the other Guardians' fault!" I yelled, thrusting out my fists.

"Guardians aren't God, Tori," Vincent said calmly.

"Guardians have so much power. Vincent, you can do whatever you want! You can kill demons. You don't have to listen to God; it's your choice!"

His eyes turned golden. "I'll become a demon if I don't listen to God."

"You have a choice, Vincent!" I exclaimed.

"Yes, Tori, but if I disobey our God—" He raised his hands in the air. "—I won't be your Guardian. I'll be like Odium!"

"My family's going to die. I tried to heal them, but God wouldn't let me," I whimpered.

Vincent gently grabbed my upper arms and his calm energy passed into my limbs. His hands were so warm that I gazed down at them. He always comforted me and I loved when he touched me.

How can I be mad at him?

"Tori," he whispered and I couldn't help but look up at him. The compassion in his glowing eyes was the strongest I had ever felt.

My panic abated while I stared up at him, but without warning my body trembled and my skin rose in goose bumps. I heard Pernicious laughing at me as she hopped across the lawn.

"We overwhelmed the Guardians," she crowed. "The Creator didn't stop us."

Her yellow fangs were visible and sulphur overpowered my nose. I started to sneeze and cough.

"You're by yourself, human. No more Davenport family!" she shrieked.

Vincent started to glow.

"No," I told him. Don't take angel form. I want a human to hold me!" I cried, having captured his arms.

He hugged me and whispered, "She's going to tease you."

"She will get bored," I murmured. Vincent kept holding me. I closed my eyes and tried to relax.

The black imp continued to jump. "No more Davenports! Dead! Dead!"

Just then, I sensed another source of energy heating the yard near me. When I looked up, I saw Michael in angel form with his five-foot blade drawn.

"Guardian!" Pernicious hissed, furiously. Then she vanished.

Michael's glowing golden eyes studied Vincent and me. "I'm sorry, Tori," Michael said softly. He glanced at Vincent. "The human needs to go to bed."

Slowly I shook my head. "No."

"She can't sleep in the hospital, but she won't want to stay here," Vincent answered.

Michael's eyebrows arched over golden eyes. "What do you mean, she can't sleep in the hospital?"

"Tori needs quiet and low light to sleep, but she's not going to let go of me and we can't lie in her bed," Vincent answered.

Michael snorted and shook his head. "I have to watch Marianne," he announced and disappeared.

When we were alone again, Vincent tilted my chin up. "Do you want to stay here or go to the hospital?" Even though I was worried about my family, I was reminded of my love for him. The golden rays from his eyes mesmerized me and my breath caught. "Tori?" Vincent prompted as he moved his fingers to my cheek.

I breathed in. "I will go to the hospital."

*　　*　　*　　*

When a nurse showed us the waiting room, I walked over to the couch and watched over my human. "Rest, Tori," I said softly.

She gazed up at me, gripped my hand, and pleaded, "Sit down, Vincent."

When I complied, Tori perched on my lap. Her weight didn't bother me; it only reminded me how much I desired to be human.

"I can't sleep if you don't hold me," she murmured.

"You can't sleep when you are sitting up."

Tori leaned on my shoulder. Her brown and blond hair coursed down my t-shirt and teased my skin. I encircled my arms around her slim body and inhaled the essence from her long, perfumed hair.

When Tori criticized God, I didn't enjoy it. I loved God and my human. My Guardian spirit form was devoted to the Creator and my human form—and part of my spirit form—loved Tori. I knew so much... I had lived with my Lord for nearly twenty billion years. My Master loved all his creations, except the demons. Evil things occurred because humans gave demons permission to live on earth with them, which was made possible by Adam and Eve's disobedience. God was saddened when Tori was hurt, I knew.

As I reflected, Tori's breathing became slower and more relaxed.

* * * *

The next afternoon, when I got home, I realized that I wanted to pray again for my family to be healed. I came to the realization that it was God's energy that could heal. I was a human being, not the Creator. My body trembled and I noticed Odium in human form standing on my lawn in the backyard.

"Vincent!" I called, wanting his blade. As soon as the Guardian appeared, I hugged the angel and took his sword, which was hot in my hands.

"Tori," he protested, but I ran toward the backyard. Needless to say, Odium watched me approaching.

"You hurt my family!" I yelled.

"Actually—"

I held the broadsword with two hands at his human form chest.

"Human—"

"You want to blame Pernicious?" I asked.

"Yes. She is responsible, along with some imps and sergeants."

"You could have stopped them!" I shouted.

"I'm a Strong Man, human!" he vehemently reminded.

My hazel eyes narrowed. "I hate you, Odium!" I rammed the supernatural blade at him and it cut into his chest. Black gore issued from the wound. Odium's eyes were huge and his body started to give off sparks.

"Go jump in the abyss!" I shouted. "You belong there. And stop appearing to me in human form!" I cut him again.

He hissed as the yellow cloud emitting from him overcame the grass. Odium took demon form, but I glowered at him defiantly.

"This means war, human!" he yelled drawing his sword.

Vincent grabbed back his sword and Odium vanished.

*   *   *   *

A half-hour after I stabbed Odium, I stood in my mother's hospital room. Vincent took angel form and he pulled a vinyl chair near the bed so I could sit down. Michael gazed at us seriously as he gripped the platinum handle of his blade.

"I hope you can do this, Tori," Michael spoke.

"Not me, God," I answered and gazed over at his glowing eyes. The intensity in his eyes showed me his desire to protect my mother. Michael drew his broadsword and anticipated demons while Vincent stood behind me to help me concentrate. I turned away from the angels, touched my mother's, arm and prayed. When I lifted my head, my mother's brown eyes were open and gazing at me. I stared, openmouthed.

"Tori," Mom murmured.

"Wow," I heard Michael whisper.

At that moment, a young nurse hurried over to the monitors. "Marianne, how are you?" the nurse asked.

"Okay," my mom answered, then frowned. "I'm confused, honestly."

"Tell me your name and your family's names," the nurse directed.

"Marianne Davenport, Frederick Davenport, Stephen, Victoria, and William Davenport."

"Very good," the woman responded.

The nurse and I smiled at each other. Then I stood and walked across the hall into Stephen's room, where I touched my unconscious brother's fingers. I noticed his left temple was bruised and I hoped he wouldn't have a brain injury.

"Stephen," I whispered near his ear while a vigilant Huan-Yue watched me. "Did he open his eyes, Huan-Yue?"

"No," she mouthed.

I pulled a nearby chair close to the bed. Michael drew his blade again and Vincent stood behind me.

"Have you seen imps?" Michael asked, turning his attention to my brother's Guardian.

"No," Huan-Yue said. The pretty angel kept her blade raised and stood near one wall.

After I sank into the chair, I started to pray. When I was finished talking to the Creator, I let my eyes open again.

Stephen's brown eyes were looking at me and he slowly seized my fingers. "Tori, I'm glad you stayed at the house. These tiny black demons jumped on the van from the sidewalk, and it was as if there was a war occurring. Suddenly, this black truck was racing toward the side of the van with these winged-creatures sitting on the roof." His voice quivered.

While my brother spoke, I felt a breeze. I turned my head and saw a statuesque African American nurse walk in to look at the monitor and check on Stephen. I rose and Stephen stared at me.

"I have to see Dad and William," I explained, but frowned because I couldn't see the bruise on his temple anymore.

My older brother's brown eyes regarded me. "You're... special," he murmured.

I clasped his fingers. "Thanks."

I smiled at the nurse and quickly walked into Dad's room. Of course, I looked out into the hall to see if any hospital staff were approaching. Vincent followed me, but Michael walked back into Mom's room. While I sauntered to my dad's bed, James grinned at me.

"The human angel is here," he said proudly.

"James, if I am proud..." I took a breath. "It is God who does the healing. I'm only human."

James gazed at Vincent. "You're watching her, right? I'll keep an eye out for demons." He drew his blade. The sound of the metal was reassuring to me.

Once again, Vincent stood behind me while I prayed. When I stopped praying, my father's warm eyes were open and exploring the room.

"Daddy!" I cried joyfully and hugged him.

"Tori?"

"Do you remember what happened, Dad?"

Right away, my sensitive father's eyes widened in horror. "There were so many demons, I forgot I was living for a minute..."

"Mom and Stephen are awake, but I want to see William," I announced.

A petite blond-haired doctor sauntered into the room and looked at the monitor, her lab coat swirling behind her. I recognized her. It was Barbara!

"Hi, Barbara."

The woman whirled when I spoke.

"Tori!" she exclaimed. "I'm glad you're okay."

"Stephen, Dad, and Mom are awake," I said.

"Good. I was worried about them."

My dad turned his head at the sound of her voice. "Barbara?" he asked.

"Dad!" she exclaimed and my brother's gorgeous fiancée walked over to him.

While they spoke, I rose and walked into William's room. Frowning, Gabriella was sitting beside my brother. She let her angel hands play with his brown hair.

She obviously loves him, I thought.

"Hi, Gabriella," I greeted

The striking spirit gazed at me. "Did you heal the others?" she asked hopefully.

"They're awake, but it was God who did it."

"Yes," she stated, gazing at the tile floor.

Vincent pulled a wooden chair to the side of the bed and I sat down. He stood behind me once again, but Gabriella stared at William and me.

"Gabriella, you have to watch for imps," Vincent reminded her.

Reluctantly, she stood up and drew her blade, walking toward the opposite wall. She turned her head, her glowing eyes piercing me. "Can you make that deep cut on his cheek disappear?" she asked.

My attention turned to William and I saw the cut. "I have no idea," I whispered.

I closed my eyelids and prayed. When I finished praying, William shifted and I opened my eyes. His grey-blue pools were looking at me.

"William!" I cried and then gazed up his Guardian, who giggled. "William, are you sore?" Scanning his face, I saw that the gash was still there.

"Not much, Tori," he answered.

I sensed impatient spirit energy and gazed up at Gabriella. "Tori, I want to talk to you," Gabriella said. William didn't look at her, so I knew he hadn't heard his Guardian.

"William... Dad, Mom, and Stephen are awake. I'm going to come back to see you in a few minutes, but first I have to talk to your Guardian."

I grasped my brother's hand. Warm supernatural energy hovered on my left side. When I didn't come right away, Gabriella grabbed my arm.

"Human, come outside," she pleaded, then looked toward Vincent "Watch William. I will protect Tori."

Vincent's serious eyes stared at me. "Odium declared war on you, Tori." I knew Vincent wanted me to stay with him, especially when we weren't at home.

"It's okay, Vincent. There are so many Guardians here," I reassured him, touching his warm hand.

He squeezed my fingers. "You're not their responsibility." While his eyes glowed, he turned to Gabriella. "Guard Tori," he warned gravely.

"I know how you feel, Vincent," she answered seriously.

As soon as she took human form, we walked down the hallway to the end of the wing. When we reached the elevators, I pressed the upside-down triangle button next to the elevator and slowly the doors opened.

"Thank you for healing William," she said as we stepped into the elevator car.

"I can't heal, Gabriella. God put energy in my hands, but when I pray, I connect with him."

"I love William," she declared and I felt compassion overwhelming me.

This angel was like me. Pain and tightness sprouted in my chest.

"I'm sorry, Gabriella. I know," I whispered.

"You're a person! If you see, the Creator will know!"

I gripped her hand. "But William has never seen you. He doesn't know you love him. You never kissed him. Gabriella, you're okay."

"You're a special human. I wish you were an angel," she declared. "But Vincent wants you to be human."

"Why?"

Without warning, my body shivered and I felt hate assault my senses. The elevator stopped at the second floor and three humans entered, blocking the door. I frowned, realizing that they all had black irises.

Demons!

I tried to be still and hoped they had another errand that had nothing to do with me. The female pressed the fourth floor button.

They'll have a long wait, since we're going down, I thought.

However, instead of continuing down, the elevator starting moving up. My eyes widened. My body trembled and I anxiously looked at Gabriella. The Guardian put her finger over her lips and mouthed, "I'll get Vincent." Then she vanished.

She promised to protect me! I hope she finds Vincent before these demons kill me!

I pushed my hands back against the rear wall of the elevator while staring at the demons' backs. Then I looked at the ceiling and wished I could fly, or at least have a blade.

Couldn't Gabriella have defeated these demons herself?

As I worried, one creature turned and his onyx eyes looked at me with scorn. "Human, your Guardian is obviously afraid of us."

I glared at the demon and commanded, "Go back to the abyss!"

"Amusing," another of the spirits laughed.

They all spun, and now all three sets of eyes were staring at me.

"When you take demon form, watch your dagger," the female warned the others. "This human will grab it." She shoved her black hair away from her shoulders.

One of the males' eyes shot brutal hate at me. "No, she's a pathetic human."

The female grinned wickedly at him and hissed, "She stabbed Odium with a Guardian's broadsword. Like I said, watch your dagger."

"Odium's a pitiful excuse for a Strong Man if a human can stab him so easily."

As I stared at the demons, sulphur clouds began to drift around the bottom of the elevator. The demons facing me gazed around the small space and I noticed fear in their eyes. Then a monstrous demon emerged, cracking the ceiling tiles.

Odium!

I trembled as the Strong Man gazed at all of us. Fragments of the tiles fell and I wanted to close my eyes. The elevator was so cold. I shivered and my teeth started to chatter. His red eyes narrowed and he seized the male who had just spoken. As the Strong Man grasped the demon's collar, he hissed, "You think I'm pitiful, do you, Sergeant? Take demon form and show me who's pitiful."

Odium drew his blade and beheaded the demon. The others shrieked while I jumped back from the spilled demon blood. I couldn't let it touch me; I couldn't bear the thought of becoming as hateful as a demon.

"Get out of here, trash," Odium hissed, leaning in toward the lower ranking demons. The spirits quaked and took demon form, bashing me into the back wall of the elevator in their terror. Then they vanished.

Odium's heinous red eyes turned toward me. "Hello, Healer. It's too bad human flesh doesn't heal like demon flesh." His eyes narrowed as he stalked forward and grabbed me. His black claws pierced the skin of my arms. I winced and trembled, even though I tried not to. His sulphur breath swept around me while he spoke. "It doesn't feel good to get stabbed!" Then he restrained me against his cold body and drew his dagger. When I saw the metal, I writhed and tried to get away.

"Help!"

Unexpectedly, I felt the elevator halting and I gazed at the door, hoping a Guardian would save me. Hissing, Odium stabbed me. I froze. No one had saved me! Pain overwhelmed me and I gasped, pushing on my stomach, where the blade had entered.

"Heal yourself!" he whispered into my ear.

CHAPTER TWENTY-TWO

MICHAEL AND I appeared in angel form, outside the elevator as it opened. I roared as I saw Tori lying on the floor while red and black blood mixed. Her t-shirt and jacket were bloody. I raced to her, tramping through demonic gore to pick her up, but Michael restrained me.

"No!" he hissed. Anger lunged from my eyes at him.

"Leave me alone!" I growled, throwing him aside. Guilt filled me as he landed outside the elevator.

A security guard then tore into the elevator and grasped his radio when he saw Tori. "There's a stabbing victim on the fourth floor in elevator three. Get doctors and the police!"

I watched him move, not wanting to wait for humans to fix Tori, but there was nothing I could do. I glanced again at Michael, who approached me. He wasn't angry. In fact, I saw his compassion for me.

"We have to clean up this demon blood before anyone else gets here. We can't have any humans becoming hateful like demons," he spoke.

*   *   *   *

I stood in Tori's room, pacing after her operation. No family could be in here, because they were still being observed after the accident. I kneeled on the tiled floor and caressed her hand.

"I'm sorry," I said. "I was selfish. I shouldn't have tried to be your friend. I made too many enemies during the rebellion and now they're your enemies, but you're only human and I just can't keep you safe. I love you so much." I lifted my hand and stroked her hair. Tori's face was pale and I hoped the blood transfusion was going to help. Then I felt warm energy behind me.

"Maybe if you don't appear to her anymore, Odium will leave her alone," Michael spoke. I gazed at the dark-haired Guardian as panic swept through me. My jaw fell and I wanted to protest, even though Michael's suggestion was good. "I don't think Odium wanted to kill her,"

My eyes glowed more intensely and I felt my body heat up. "Yeah right," I said sarcastically.

"He's a Strong Man, Vincent. He stabbed her because she stabbed him. I think he likes tormenting you two. If she dies, he'll have less fun."

I clenched my fists and breathed deeply. "I won't appear anymore."

*   *   *   *

Five days later, I walked up to my room with Will's hand under my arm and winched with pain when I sat on my bed. My brother put my medicine on the nightstand.

"Take some medicine, Tori," he said compassionately. In a minute, he brought me a bottle of water and set it on the nightstand, too. When he left, I climbed into my bed, lay on my side, and covered my head. My stomach hurt, but I didn't take the pain medicine. I was too lonely for Vincent.

A voice said, "Take your medicine."

I lifted the cover off my head, turned on my back, and gazed around the room—but there was nothing there, so I curled up again.

I thought back to five days ago. When I had woken up after my operation, I'd gazed around my hospital room. Odium hadn't killed me! When I felt spirit heat on the side of my face, I called, "Vincent! Vincent, where are you?"

He didn't appear at any point when I was in the hospital, and I wished Odium had hit a major artery. Why did he have to miss? I had been so lonely and I couldn't bear it. My chest tightened and I cried.

Pulling the sheets off my head, I looked around my bedroom "Please, Vincent, come here. Please..." I let out a mournful cry.

Spirit warmth increased near me and the tears evaporated from my cheeks, but I couldn't see anyone. "Why are you doing this? We're friends," I uttered. When I trembled, I felt someone hug me, but I couldn't see anyone. I couldn't stand this anymore!

"Go away!" I muttered hoarsely.

But the supernatural heat didn't leave.

"I mean it. If you're not going to show yourself, go away!"

*   *   *   *

Our neighbour, Mr. Roberts, had been paid by the government to create a corn maze. It was the end of September and the corn leaves were starting to turn brown. Many youth groups and school age children took outings to his farm every year, but Mr. Roberts always let my brothers and I go into the maze for free.

Today, Stephen, William, and I wanted to go through the maze before we ate dinner, so we pushed aside the green stalks that barricaded our back gate and sauntered into the cornfield. There were four rows of corn to walk through before we found ourselves in the maze. The corn rose high all around us. Stephen and William were taller than six feet, but the corn stalks were eight or nine feet high.

"If Vincent was here, I could stand on his shoulders and we could get out of here fast," William said mischievously.

I turned away from my brothers. They didn't know that I hadn't seen Vincent for four weeks and that I was just trying to survive. Demons hadn't bothered me in that period of time, either, which made me very happy. I took a deep breath and then turned to face my brothers. "You have Guardian Angels. You could ask them, but it's more fun this way fun. We don't want angel help," I said flippantly.

William gazed at his waterproof watch. When Stephen laughed at him, my eyes narrowed and I gestured at the watch.

"Why is he staring at that?" I asked, irritated.

Stephen looked at me wickedly. "He's going out with Cassandra at seven o' clock."

I put my hands on my hips and frowned. "Why did you make a date? We were going to spend time together this weekend before Stephen gets too busy with University."

"Cass is home this weekend from university," William said softly. "She's in school in the States and won't be home every weekend."

I took a deep breath, guilt biting me. "Fine. Go back, Will."

"Tori, let's come back to the maze tonight, in the dark," William suggested. His grey-blue eyes sparkled. "Let's come back around 11:30."

I grinned. "Yeah!"

Our eyes turned toward our older brother, who rolled his eyes. "Sure," Stephen agreed.

"Hey, you could bring Cassandra," I said, looking at William. Then I turned to gaze excitedly at Stephen. "Barbara might want to come, too." Both my brothers grinned.

"Vincent will come, I think," Will declared.

"No, he won't," I mumbled.

I stomped through the corn stalks to get back to our property. I knew I was going to cry.

"Tori, what's wrong?" Will asked as he caught up to me.

My chest tightened and I stared up at Will. "I haven't seen Vincent for four weeks."

Stephen gasped. "Excuse me?"

I started to cry, even though I didn't want to. "I keep calling him, but he doesn't appear," I wept. I noticed their jaws stiffen and then my brothers hugged me.

"I thought you were depressed because of your wound. Why didn't you tell us?" Stephen asked.

*   *   *   *

At 11:30, the sky was glowing from the full moon and stars. William, Stephen, Cassandra, Barbara, and I sauntered through the four rows of dark green stalks into the maze.

"Wow, I'm like half the height of these stalks," Cassandra murmured. She looked over at Barbara. "You are, too. How did we pick such tall boys?"

Barbara smiled at Stephen and grasped his hand. "They're handsome and Stephen's smart."

"Hey!" William protested, indignantly.

Barbara grinned proudly up at William. "I heard that in Grade Five, all the kids stayed inside from recess to hear you recite your twelve times tables. No one in your school could do that."

"William *is* smart," I said, "but he only applies himself to study subjects he really loves."

William smiled wickedly, lifted Cassandra up about a foot and a half, and kissed her passionately.

The sound of coyotes yowling in the distance made Cassandra jump. Barbara trembled.

"Don't be afraid," William said to her. "I have a knife."

"Excuse me!" Barbara and Cassandra exclaimed, taken aback.

Will was strange sometimes. It wouldn't have surprised me if he had even brought one of his handguns. I laughed softly, shook my head, and ran down the hill through the cornrow. I loved running to feel the wind pulling my hair back. Unfortunately, my abdomen still hurt from the wound, so I had to stop.

After I reached the bottom, I looked back at my brothers and their girlfriends. They were slowly walking down toward me, holding hands. I was glad Barbara and Cassandra still wanted to stay, despite the coyotes.

Watching the couples, I felt a pang of regret over my relationship with Vincent. I should never have fallen in love with an angel. Why had I been so stupid to spend so much time with him? Now I was alone.

When my brothers and their girlfriends caught up with me, Pernicious appeared in our path and we screamed.

"What is that black thing?" Cassandra squealed.

The imp hissed and drew a rusty dagger. Cassandra and Barbara took off running back to where they were sure our house was, and William and Stephen followed them.

I remained rooted to the spot, glaring at Pernicious. All at once, I heard Barbara and Cassandra screech and I started to run back to see what was upsetting my friends, but a sergeant and a commander blocked my path. I balled up my hands into fists.

"Get out of here!" I commanded.

Their horns oozed sulphuric smoke and their bodies emitted red and orange sparks. Unfortunately, they were taller than me and the sergeant had muscles like Stephen. The commander was even bigger; he was monstrous.

Supernatural heat began to warm me up, and I knew Vincent was here. He would take care of these demons.

Where is Pernicious? I wondered as fear bit me.

While I was thinking, ten more imps appeared beside the sergeant and commander. When I noticed light beside me, I struggled not to look over at Vincent and confront him as to why I hadn't seen him for four weeks. Instead of speaking to the angel, I fled down the path.

"Tori," Pernicious hissed from somewhere inside the maze.

Why can't she leave me alone! Vincent and I aren't friends anymore...

I careened down a cornrow at my left and then quickly turned left again, but three imps with rusty daggers suddenly appeared in front of me. I screamed. Turning around, I sped into the stalks at the end of the path. The corn leaves scratched my face, neck, and arms with their sharp edges. I grimaced as I ran through them. The thin cuts in my skin burned and itched.

Demons hissed and screeched at me from within the maze. They could appear right beside me if they wanted to, but they didn't. I knew the creatures were up to something, but I had no idea what it was. There was no need stay within the maze; I could walk through the stalks and out of this field, since I was good at directions. Anger filled me and I started to stalk through the rows toward the road. All at once, a gigantic Strong Man appeared in front of me. His cutlass sparkled under the full moon. I didn't scream; instead, I glowered.

"Go away!" I ordered.

"Nice try, Tori," he hissed.

I tried another direction as fear accumulated inside my body. I shivered and all the hairs on my body stood up. My heart banged in my chest and I tried to take deep breaths. As I ran, I was shaking, irritated at my body's fear response. I tried to turn and take a different path, but the creature caught up with me and laughed.

I turned, moving in yet another direction through the maze. Ahead of me there was a long straight section of path with some brown stalks, so I thought the creatures had changed the paths by raising some stalks Mr. Roberts had ploughed down.

Escaping the maze, I ran into a nearby cemetery. It was an open graveyard built on a hill with a grove of cedar trees presiding in the middle. A wooden post fence enclosed the graveyard on all sides except for a narrow gated opening. The lettering on the old marble tombstones was covered with fungus and damaged from the passage of time. There were a few granite stones that were over a hundred and fifty years old.

Without warning, I heard Pernicious laugh. Distracted, I tripped over a concealed, broken tombstone. The imp pranced near me and I wanted to grab her dagger. Before I could stand, Odium appeared in human form.

"Vincent will be done with the other demons soon," Odium said to Pernicious. His onyx-shaded trench coat moved slightly.

I didn't know why he picked human form when he was so terrifying in demon form. "Why are you in human form?" I asked, standing up.

Odium's eyes bore into me. "Because in demon form, I'm ugly. It must be pleasant to be attractive and have hazel eyes all the time, not unholy black ones. But one day you'll get old. Angels are more stunning than human beings anyway. Those blond streaks in your hair... my hair was that shade in Heaven, and my eyes were green. Vincent took my angel form away when he betrayed us!" Odium cursed and stomped his foot.

When he finished talking, I tried to run out of the graveyard onto the roadside, but I tripped and fell in a patch of sunken ground.

I groaned, my hand coming up to push against my tender abdomen. The healed area still hurt.

"I warned you!" Odium laughed as I tried to crawl out of the depression. "Keep digging, Tori. Maybe the ground will fall in. That way, no one will have to bury you."

It took me several seconds, but I finally clambered out of the depression. But when I tried to stand, I froze—Odium's cutlass was touching the hollow of my throat. He was grinning malevolently. His black eyes looked at me wickedly.

"You're a beautiful human. It's sad you're my only means of terminating Vincent."

My eyes narrowed and the supernatural metallic point pushed in further. "Kill me," I whispered. "Don't tease me."

"Submit to my prince and I won't torture you. If you do, it will be worse for Vincent. If you are in Heaven, he can still see you."

"No," I said boldly. My chest tightened. Odium was wrong about Vincent; he wouldn't care whether I was in Heaven or on earth.

Suddenly, the cemetery glowed. I saw Vincent stalking toward Odium.

So he doesn't mind showing himself to fight demons, I thought.

Vincent's broadsword was swathed in black goo. It must have been demon blood. The angel's eyes were golden and light radiated from his form. The Strong Man cursed and I quickly backed away, getting to my feet. Odium changed out of human form and became massive at eight feet. My body trembled as fear rose up in me.

The monstrous black demon and the massive Guardian Angel clashed broadswords. Odium dove at Vincent, but the angel blocked Odium with his sword and the demon flew to the side, growling. His thin red eyes glared at Vincent.

"One day, I will take your human," Odium hissed.

The onyx-hued creature leaped onto Vincent. The Guardian Angel sprawled into the depression I had just stumbled out of and grappled with the Strong Man. As a result, both unearthly beings lost their swords. But I kept tabs on both supernatural weapons, staring at Vincent's fallen broadsword. I knew I could help Vincent if I could get to it in time. Without warning, Pernicious jumped on me, pulling my hair.

"No, human!" she hissed.

Oh, she reeked of sulphur. I reached onto my shoulders and grabbed her rusty dagger. After she slapped my face, I stabbed at the imp on my shoulders. She shrieked and I felt her weight vanish. I looked around the cemetery afterward, but she was gone and the dagger's blade was covered with black gore.

Tossing the dagger aside, I saw that Vincent and Odium were still fencing. The two beings moved back and forth in circles. Odium jumped onto tombstones and tried to decapitate Vincent, his broadsword chopping the air as it sparked, but Vincent flew up in the air so the demon couldn't get at his head. I was fascinated.

Suddenly, Vincent stabbed Odium's left side. The demon's red eyes grew monstrous and black goo oozed from the wound. With a shriek, the Strong Man disappeared.

When the fight was over, Vincent's golden eyes stared at me. He took human form and started to walk in my direction. His golden radiance disappeared. He was so handsome and awe-inspiring. My pulse raced, but I put my hands on my hips and glared up at him.

"You finally decided to appear!" My voice leaked pain, and I hated that. I was almost crying.

His eyes glowed and were filled with anguish and compassion. He brought his hand up and caressed my cheek, but I backed away.

"You said you would keep appearing," I accused. "I needed you. Why did you disappear?" I started to cry.

Vincent walked in front of me and lifted my chin with warm fingers. His bright eyes were overflowing with compassion. "I found you bleeding in the elevator and I didn't want it to happen again. I thought if I stopped appearing that Odium would leave you alone." He pulled me against his muscular chest. His warmth and tight hold comforted me. "I'm so sorry. I won't disappear again."

CHAPTER TWENTY-THREE

A FEW HOURS after the graveyard attack, I paced as golden energy ricocheted into my wings.

"You protect Tori until God tells you to step back," Michael announced.

"I don't know if I could stand back," I said.

My friend frowned at me, his wings aglow. "You are in danger of becoming a demon if you love something more than God!" He was clearly outraged.

"I love Tori," I announced.

"She is a human being and she's going to die someday. Rebellious angels become demons. You remember what happened to God's favourite angel, don't you? He was your friend!"

"I want to be a human," I said darkly. I squeezed the platinum handle of my broadsword.

"I loved a human being once, Vincent."

I gasped, blown away. "Excuse me?"

"She was an Irish princess," Michael said. "She was gorgeous and I spent one hundred years in Israel fighting after she died. I was watching her beauty instead of noticing she was about to be destroyed by a rival kingdom."

"Why didn't you tell me?"

"I've always been critical of humans, but the truth is I disobeyed and I was ashamed."

I groaned. "One hundred years separated from Tori is a long time."

"You have to stop thinking like a human. One hundred years... a thousand years...it's nothing." Michael snapped his fingers. "We are billions of years old, Vincent."

"I want to be human," I replied in a low voice.

"It's impossible."

*　　*　　*　　*

I continued taking fencing lessons. In October, I scored a lot of points on Master Jovanovich. One night, James and Gabriella wanted to watch my lessons, so Michael and Huan-Yue stayed behind to protect my family.

During my match with the Master, I foolishly looked at the angels on the side wall. James grinned, lofted his sword, and pierced the air. "You go, human girl!"

Vincent grinned at me, but gestured at Master Jovanovich anxiously. I shuffled back, but the Master lunged at me and hit the right side of my chest.

"Halt!" Jovanovich exclaimed and removed his mask. I lowered the button on my foil. He was glowering and I removed my mask nervously.

"What possessed you to look at the side wall, Victoria?"

I bit my lip. "Sorry," I murmured.

"Don't say sorry. This is your education and I scored on you. Pay attention!" he scolded.

"Yes sir." I put my mask on.

"Come, Kristen," Jovanovich beckoned.

My friend obeyed and put her mask on. As soon as we saluted each other and Master Jovanovich, we took the *en garde* pose.

"*Êtes-vous prêt?*" he questioned.

"*Oui,*" we replied in unison.

"*Allez,* ladies!"

Kristen was very aggressive, but I forgot to parry and attacked.

"Halt!" he shrieked. We lowered the foils. "Remember right of way, Victoria!"

"Sorry," I said, frustration overwhelming me. I wanted to show these angels that I wasn't pathetic.

After our match restarted, Kristen attacked. I blocked, then lunged and scored on her right shoulder.

"Bravo!" our Master called.

As soon as I won our match and saluted, we removed the fencing garments.

Master Jovanovich announced, "Victoria, you blow me away." Then, he glanced at Kristen. "Was your friend born with a sword?"

Kristen grinned at me. "I'm not sure, but she has a lot of natural skill."

"Exorbitant amounts," he stated fondly, thrusting his fingers through thinning dark hair.

"Thanks," I murmured thankfully.

* * * *

On Tuesday, Vincent and I went to a bookstore in Smithington. I had ordered a new medical dictionary and a clerk had called on Monday to tell me the book was in. Unfortunately, I had left my old medical dictionary at the college or Smithington Memorial Hospital... I couldn't remember which.

When Vincent and I walked into the store, I strode to the checkout counter. After I had paid for the dictionary, I decided to look for a good novel. Halfway through the romance rack, I felt myself shiver. Hairs stiffened on the back of my neck and I could feel hate close by. Vincent stood near me. When I felt his warmth increase, I knew there was at least one demon in the store.

Vincent whispered, "We have to leave." He grabbed my right arm and turned around before I had much of a chance to think.

"Ow," I complained as he squeezed my flesh. *He's just too strong!*

His compassionate eyes studied me and he relaxed his grip. "I'm sorry," he said.

While we walked toward the door, I saw an onyx-clad female smirking at us near the large bay window at the front of the store.

Is she the demon Vincent sensed?

Her black eyes were devoid of all feeling but hate. She turned away from us, squatted down, and started to talk to a child.

That child needs help! I thought.

I tried to go over to them, but Vincent pulled me toward the door. I grappled with the powerful angel, but he dragged me out the front of the bookstore and around the corner to my Mustang.

"We have to stop her!" I cried.

"No. The child has a Guardian Angel. She will take care of it." Vincent opened the passenger door and gestured for me to get in.

"But I didn't see another angel," I protested, sitting down in the passenger seat.

Vincent got in and turned to look at me seriously. He gripped the steering wheel and I noticed his knuckles whiten.

"Please don't do things that get the other side to notice you. You don't need to make more enemies," he said. "That demon in the store didn't want to hurt you—at least, not right now. Only imps, sergeants, and commanders under Odium are gunning for you. The other demons are occupied. But if each and every demon finds out you can see them..."

I trembled and my teeth started to chatter, as they always did when my nerves were stressed. Vincent reached toward me and lifted my hand from the seat; as he held it, I relaxed.

"Tori, they don't like me because I'm the one who informed God of their rebellion."

"I know, but God knows everything. It's stupid for those demons to be so angry at you. God was going to punish them anyways."

Vincent took a deep breath. "I betrayed them. They will hurt you to grieve me."

"Why?" I asked.

"You are my human."

"Have they hurt your... humans before?"

"No."

"There have been humans for at least six thousand years," I said. "The war was billions of years ago. Why me? Why now?"

Vincent was silent and his jaw appeared very stiff. "We don't meddle in your realm very often. Most of us never show ourselves to humans. I never showed myself to any human before you."

Vincent started my car and drove to the river. As soon as we got there, he opened his door and stalked toward the clear water. I could feel his tension.

"Vincent!" I called, opening my door. I ran over to the water and stood beside him.

When I reached for him, Vincent grabbed my hand. "I care about you," he whispered.

Looking up at him, I said, "Good. You're my Guar—"

"Tori, I love you," he interrupted. He was gazing at me with glowing eyes.

My body trembled and I couldn't breathe. *Does Vincent care about me like a human boyfriend does for his girlfriend?* "Good," I whispered. "Angels are expected to love their humans."

"Tori, my feelings for you are more than that," he answered hoarsely.

I gasped, stepping back. "Oh, but I was not... is it possible? You aren't human."

Breathing deeply, I approached the Guardian. Slowly, I stood on my toes and kissed his cheek. He was frowning, probably extremely irritated by my bold actions.

"I'm sorry," I whispered. *Why is he angry? I've kissed his cheek before.*

His eyes turned golden and I didn't know what to do. All at once, he pulled me against his chest and held me tight with his muscular arms. I shivered, but I wasn't afraid of him. Then Vincent bent down and kissed my lips softly. My breath caught in my throat again and I started to feel dizzy. I kissed him back and the pressure from his lips became firmer as he kissed me more fervently. I had rarely touched his hair, but now my hands roamed through it. Suddenly I was engulfed in supernatural heat and I pulled back while we gazed at each other. His body was glowing and he looked close to taking angel form.

In a moment, Vincent stiffened and goose bumps appeared on my arms. We looked across the water and saw two human-looking creatures with black eyes and ebony clothes. My heart stirred and I almost passed out as I heard the beings mocking us.

*   *   *   *

After I drove Tori home, I searched out Michael and appeared near him. My friend watched me intuitively, but I didn't know how to tell him what I had done. I really didn't want to admit to having kissed Tori. I had given into my emotions as if I was human! Spirit energy ricocheted through my body and into my wings as I paced in front of him.

"Please guard Tori," I beseeched. Michael frowned at me, his eyes turning golden. "I'm going to Israel."

I vanished.

Two minutes later, I stood alone in the Garden of Gethsemane next to a three-thousand-year-old olive tree by the Church of the

Agony. Two thousand years ago, it had been a cool evening as the Creator's son sat against that same tree, his brown eyes observing the sky as small orange-red rivulets of human blood bled from his pores...

I stood watching Jesus, having abandoned Simon Peter, my responsibility, when I sensed a frenzy of spirit energy in the garden. The ten other disciples' Guardians were in the garden as well, so I knew my human was safe. Michael was standing by Jesus.

I moved closer to God's son and stood beside an old olive tree as a six-foot Messenger arrived, radiating golden light.

"You have to step back," the Messenger said to Michael, his golden eyes glowing with compassion.

"No!" Michael roared, drawing his angelic broadsword. I was going to emerge beside my friend; however, Jesus intervened.

"Peace Guardian," Jesus said firmly.

"But you're God!" Michael protested.

"I need to die."

"No! Don't die for humans."

But Michael knew what Jesus had to do. My friend vanished and appeared beside me. One of his hands swung and the broadsword struck the olive tree, felling it. I watched as the tree hit the ground.

Michael clenched his fists. "This isn't right!"

Later, when the Roman soldiers thrashed our Lord's back, I fought with Michael.

"We have to obey. We're servants, Michael," I said while the infuriated Guardian Angel tried to escape.

"Humans are pathetic! He's God!" Michael uttered, enraged.

The wicked soldiers forced several rings of thorns, twined together to make a crown, onto his head. My Lord grimaced but didn't cry out, even when the thorns pierced his scalp.

At once, I sensed tense spirit energy. Billions of furious Warrior Angels with wings of fire had drawn their blades, their platinum handles radiating light. If my Lord had gestured or called, those Warriors would have annihilated those despicable people.

My narrowed eyes turned golden and spirit energy raced into my wings. As the humans disgracefully displayed Jesus on the cross and pierced his kind, powerful hands with rusty nails, I screamed, "God, help me obey!"

*　*　*　*

Vincent had vanished as soon as we got home and I worried that I would never see him again. Shaking, I walked through the house to my bedroom, where Michael appeared in human form.

"What happened to Vincent?" he asked anxiously. I bit my lip and gazed at the floor. Michael always obeyed the rules, so he wasn't going to understand what had happened.

"Vincent said he loves me," I replied.

"What did you do?"

"I kissed his cheek," I answered. Michael looked at me incredulously. "Then Vincent kissed me."

"You broke him!" Michael exclaimed, clenching his fists.

"No!"

"You are a rebellious human!"

"Go jump into the abyss!" I yelled.

Immediately, his eyes glowed angrily and I stared at him, terrified. He grew large and his wings erupted, becoming luminous. Then he quickly whirled toward the window.

Before Michael decided to kill me, I grabbed my music player from my nightstand, ran out of the house, and down our laneway.

*　*　*　*

Guilt overwhelmed me. I had tempted a pure Guardian Angel and told Michael to jump into Hell. What was wrong with me? I had wanted my Guardian to kiss me for so long, but now our kiss seemed sinful. It was late afternoon and I didn't want to be out walking after dark, but

211

I had to get away from Michael. I put the music player's earphones into my ears and jogged down Kinkaid Road toward Smithington.

Eventually, I got tired and slowed to a walk. Wanting to get a treat by the time I arrived in Smithington, I walked across a parking lot to the same ice cream store my brothers and I had visited earlier in the summer. The sun was setting as I ate my frozen yogurt.

Chills shot down my back as I sat on a park bench to watch the swans. I looked behind me and saw a middle-aged woman jogging with her dog. I sighed. It was good to see another woman around. It made me feel safer. I couldn't feel Vincent's energy now. I wondered if I was alone—without a Guardian. When two children and their father walked over to the pond to feed the swans, I relaxed.

* * * *

The sun had almost set when I finished eating my frozen yogurt. When I got off the bench, I noticed a young, dark-haired man standing by a nearby tree, watching me. I wanted to ignore him, but his black eyes pierced me. I shivered.

No! Black eyes. He's a demon, and a high ranking one at that!

My pulse raced as he smirked at me and I jogged out of the park.

Do I have a Guardian watching me right now? Surely that demon would have shown some fear if I had someone watching out for me.

"Vincent!" I whispered. Why hadn't I brought my car?

I looked behind me and the man was gone, but I didn't relax. I knew demons played tricks. The sun had finished setting and I hadn't brought my cell phone

"Stupid girl," I muttered. My kiss with Vincent had unnerved me. As I walked through town, I noticed some scary looking guys coming out of a bar. I wanted to avoid them, so I turned into a well-lit alley between two buildings. Suddenly the lights above the alley burnt out.

"For pity's sake, go away!" I hissed, thinking demons were trying to harass me.

All at once, I noticed that there was a being behind me. A warm, dirty hand grabbed my arm. Was it a demon? My attacker didn't smell like sulphur; instead he smelt like he needed a bath. This being was not a spirit! I twisted my arm to get away and fled, but the man yanked my hair.

"Ow!" I screamed. "Help!"

I pulled the earphone buds from my ears, dropping the player on the ground so he couldn't easily use the cord to strangle me. Then I bit his arm and scratched his face, getting his dirty skin and blood under my nails. My assailant grabbed my arms and threw me onto the pavement, swearing. I screamed when I hit the asphalt, but he punched me in the neck. Pain ran through my throat and I clenched my teeth, not wanting to show him he had hurt me.

God, help! I yelled in my mind as the man held me on the ground. Streams of tears ran down my face, moistening the hair around my ears.

"Don't hurt me," I whispered as his fingers pushed me further into the pavement. Suddenly, the alley filled with light and the man vaulted off me and vanished. As I trembled, I stared up to see which Guardian had rescued me. A glowing, spiky haired Guardian walked toward me, grasping the hilt of his sword.

It's Michael! Where's Vincent? I wondered.

Michael's supernatural heat comforted me and I stopped trembling. When I stood, he swept me up into his arms and flew away.

*   *   *   *

When Michael landed on my balcony at home, he placed me in a chair and stood near me.

"Do you need to see a doctor?" he asked softly. His golden glow was starting to recede.

I was astounded that his brown eyes looked so compassionate. I glanced down at my dirty jeans. "No... I'm sorry."

"Why were you out walking when you knew it was going to get dark?"

"You unnerved me," I answered softly, watching the Guardian.

He took human form and sat on a chair, sighing. "Tori, I've been too hard on you. I'm sorry. I don't have a lot of patience with humans, but in truth I've made mistakes just like humans do... I loved a human once before." My jaw dropped. "Most angels aren't aware of my mistake. I told Vincent about it, though, after Odium attacked you in the graveyard." He looked up into the air. "She was a gorgeous redhead, an Irish princess with green eyes. She died a thousand years ago because I was looking at her and not protecting her from another kingdom. I was in Israel for a hundred years as punishment, caught in the middle of the heavy fighting. I don't want Vincent to go through the same thing... Tori, human beings are forbidden. There's no way he can marry you. You'll only end up hurting yourself."

Michael reached out and touched the top of my right hand.

"But I love Vincent... Michael, I don't want him to be exiled."

"Tori, if you truly love an angel, you won't be able to stop. We are perfect, better than humans. You will never be able to love another human again if you love an angel. Vincent will go to Israel and fight constantly, and you'll miss him and never marry."

"Michael, am I ever going to see Vincent again?" I asked softly.

Serious golden eyes stared back at me. "Yes. But try not to get him exiled. Don't let the next sixty years of your life be a living hell," he finished gravely.

CHAPTER TWENTY-FOUR

TWO DAYS LATER, I was reading when I heard my dad calling from downstairs. "Tori, get the phone."

I picked up the receiver. "Hello?"

"Hello, Tori. Can you work tonight?" It was the administrator from Cedarwood.

"Sure," I answered. I worked nights at Cedarwood Manor very infrequently, but it was good to get another shift.

When I arrived at Cedarwood that night, I walked down the north hallway, checking to make sure the doors were locked. Vincent was invisible, not wanting to be seen by the health care aide and housekeeper, but I sensed his supernatural energy.

All of a sudden, my body shivered and goose bumps rose on my arms. The hallway behind me seemed to darken. I whirled and noticed that a pot light in the ceiling had burnt out.

I should leave a note for the maintenance team to fix that, I thought.

When I turned around, the pot light in front of me burnt out as well. The hairs on my neck rose. I could feel butterflies in my stomach. As I turned and walked down the wide east hall, all the lights burnt out at once.

Fear bit me and a shriek fled my throat.

"Vincent!" I called.

Low light fizzled through the massive windows as I gazed around the hall. I was sure demons were burning out the lights. I would rather have dealt with them now then have the creatures torment me all night while I walked up and down the halls. All at once, Odium appeared next to me, and I slammed backward into the wall. His onyx eyes mocked me.

"Hello, Tori."

I shook my head and breathed deeply, trying to calm myself. Why did I have to be scared of him even when he appeared human?

"Thank you for burning out all the pot lights," I said, crossing my arms. "The maintenance team is going to wonder how all these lights died at one time."

"They'll think the light bulb company made duds," Odium replied, smirking.

"Vincent!" I cried.

Odium snickered. "Human, my sergeants and imps are entertaining the Guardian."

"What do you want?" I asked.

"You've been around that grumpy, brown-haired Guardian too long," he growled. "Frail, pathetic human creatures like you are scared of demons. Does our human form not scare you?"

"No."

"It's fun to ruin a Guardian when he loves something. I killed Princess Áine. Do you know who she was?" he asked.

My eyes narrowed. *Michael's Irish princess.*

"You?" I asked.

"I turned into a tiger and chased her so that she fled right to her enemies. My sergeants and imps incited an enemy kingdom and Michael couldn't do anything to stop it. Maybe I should turn into a tiger now. Would you be scared?"

Of course! I just stared at him, hoping the demon wouldn't change his form. In a flash, a magnificent tiger soared at me. I didn't know what to do. Would Odium actually eat me? My chest tightened as my pulse raced. I thought I was going to have a heart attack.

"Aren't I magnificent?" Odium landed and crouched before me. He stalked back and forth in front of me and I felt like I was going to faint.

When he bared his teeth, a warm hand touched my arm. I looked up in time to see Vincent's back emerge in front of me. I jerked my head toward his radiance and saw demon gore on his sword. Odium roared. Right now, I didn't care if the other Cedarwood staff heard the demon or now. I was scared and just wanted out of this spirit world.

Vincent smirked at the tiger. "Terrorized yet, Odium?"

Odium quickly took demon form as Vincent spun around. "Go finish the door check and start your medications," he said firmly. I wondered what was going to happen if the housekeeper or health care aide walked into the east hall and saw the two spirits sword fighting.

I ran to the front desk, where the housekeeper was waiting for me. She was dusting the resident's lounge. She looked up and smiled at me. "Hello, Tori."

"Hi, Anna." I waved at the pretty blond girl.

"Did you get any sleep?" she asked.

"Some." I kept walking. I couldn't stop thinking about Vincent and Odium.

When I passed under a cold air vent, I shivered and whirled around, looking for demons; there weren't any. I breathed in and tried to focus. I couldn't keep watching for demons.

Oh, how I wish I didn't know the spirit world existed.

I started toward the south hall and checked the entry and exit doors. A few of the residents worried about thieves getting into the manor.

Out of the blue, Vincent emerged in front of me. "Odium's gone," he announced.

"He's not dead?" I asked, concerned. My muscles shivered.

He shook his head. "He's smart, Tori. Now, I'm going to vanish so you don't lose your job." With that, he disappeared.

"You'll let me see you if he comes back, right?" I asked.

"Yes," his disembodied voice whispered. "Don't be afraid, Tori."

I suddenly heard a shriek in the east hallway. Without warning, my arms rose with goose bumps and all the hairs on my body stood up straight. As the shriek echoed through the lodge, I spun around, but my knees felt weak. I leaned against a wall, frustration consuming me from being so afraid. I detested my weakness and took a deep breath.

"Help me, God," I whispered. Suddenly, I felt warmth under my arms.

"Tori, there aren't any more demons," Vincent whispered. His warm energy relaxed me.

"Thanks," I murmured, resting against his massive chest. Now that I had been tossed into the spirit world, I didn't think I could live without him.

After he dissolved, I ran into the east hall. Anna was bending over and gazing at a black mass of demon gore on the carpet.

"Tori!" she exclaimed, totally relieved to see me. Her azure eyes were huge. "Did you see this when you were checking the doors?"

"No," I replied. Fearfully, I scanned her hands and didn't see black on them.

"It's so gross," she said. "I really don't know how to clean it up."

"Don't touch it," I said seriously. "In fact, just leave it for now."

I knew Vincent could take care of the blood and I didn't want Anna to become hateful from touching it. I heaved a sigh of relief when the younger girl left. Afterward, I sat on the couch in a nearby sitting area.

"Vincent," I whispered.

He appeared beside me on the couch.

"Can you get rid of that blood?"

"Yes," he said.

"Thank you so much."

His grave eyes looked at me. "I hope she didn't touch any."

"I didn't see any black on her hands."

"Thank goodness."

"Now, I need to get back to work."

As I rose, he captured my hand. "Stay longer. That way, you can say you took care of the blood," he suggested.

I bit my lip. "I don't want to lie."

"It's not a lie. You called me, so you took care of it."

When I leaned against him, he placed a strong arm around me and I caressed his powerful fingers. "I wish I could sleep," I whispered.

"I know," he answered. His supernatural peace made my eyelids close.

Suddenly, I heard a call bell ringing.

"Tori," Vincent whispered. Silky hairs tickled my ears when the angel spoke and I brought my hand up to brush my right ear. "Tori, wake up. The health care aide is coming."

I groaned loudly, then sat up, and hurried down the hall.

*   *   *   *

When my shift was over, I walked out to the Mustang. Vincent appeared again. For the first time, I noticed a long golden stain on his left arm. I frowned at it.

"Vincent, what's that gold stuff on your shirt?" I asked.

"Odium cut my arm, Tori."

I was shocked. Spirits were more human than I had thought.

Confusion overwhelmed me. "I didn't know he could hurt you like that. Why is your blood gold?" I had known angels and demons could kill each other, but bleeding was so physical—and spirits definitely weren't physical.

"Angelic blood is gold," he replied calmly.

I gestured at the passenger side. "Get in the car."

"No. You're exhausted. I want to drive you home."

"Rebellious angel, get in the car!" I ordered.

Smiling, I opened the driver's side door, but my Guardian walked behind me and I felt his spirit energy through my coat.

"You're tired," he insisted.

"Vincent, you're injured," I said quietly, with my back to him. *Why can't my Guardian listen? I just want to help him.* I spun and gazed defiantly at him, hoping he would give in and go over to the passenger side.

"Tori, please. Someone might be watching us," he pleaded.

My angel was so determined to care for me. I couldn't help but love Vincent. "I want to help you." I stared at his injured arm. My chest was tight as compassion for my Guardian overwhelmed me.

"Human, let me drive and you can do whatever you want to the arm."

I put the keys in his hand. "Okay, agreed." After I sat on the passenger side, I looked over at him. "Does the cut burn?"

"Yes. It feels like a human injury, I think."

I leaned the seat back. "I'll look after you at home, Vincent."

* * * *

While I was driving, my human fell asleep. Usually she took a half-hour to go into slumber, but today was different. Brilliant sunlight penetrated the car's windows and I thought of God. I loved the sun, as it was the only thing that was nearly as radiant as the Creator. I especially enjoyed its warmth when I was in human form.

The Mustang turned onto a busy street and I noticed a long trailer and truck sitting on the right side of the road. A frustrated man was trying to unload his trailer with a forklift, but he had to come out into our lane and no one was stopping for him. I thought this might be a new job for him, because he was young and exuding anxiety. The morning traffic was heavy.

Out of the blue, a golden SUV stopped in our lane just ahead and motioned for the man to come out into the street. The trucker grinned and started using the three-wheeled forklift to unload the truck. He came out three times into our lane and the SUV remained where it was. I heard a few honks. *Humans are so egotistic,* I thought, irritation ripping through me.

While the young man unloaded his long trailer, I realized it wasn't a human in the SUV. My lips pulled up and I almost laughed. The angel inside the SUV sensed me and lifted his hand. When I waved, I winced at the pain in my arm.

* * * *

The flannel pillowcase was soft under my head. I felt cold, so I pulled my comforter up higher. Patting my arms, I realized I was still in my uniform. Irritation tickled me. I had wanted to look at his injury, but Vincent had put me to bed instead. I huffed and wondered what time it was.

My stomach started to growl, so I moved the covers and sat up. My alarm clock showed it was four o'clock in the afternoon. I sighed and stalked into my walk-in closet to take my uniform off. I was still annoyed at Vincent. I cared about him and didn't think that getting my sleep was more important than taking care of his wound. After taking a shower, I went downstairs to the kitchen.

"Good afternoon, Tori," my mom greeted. "Did you sleep well?"

I was about to answer when Stephen sauntered into the kitchen.

"Did your legs fall asleep this morning?" my brother asked, amused.

"Vincent drove me home," I said. "I fell asleep in the car. I guess he carried me upstairs. Last night was really bad! Odium almost killed me at Cedarwood."

Both of them gasped. "Excuse me?"

"He burnt out some lights in a couple of the hallways, then turned into a tiger and flew at me."

Their jaws dropped.

"I don't want your life," Stephen spoke.

Mom rushed over to me and gave me a hug. "Oh, my goodness!" she exclaimed.

"It's okay, Mom. Last night was nothing... imps already killed me once." I wanted to reassure her, but I knew demons would try to kill me again. "Vincent takes care of me."

My stomach growled and I wanted to change the subject so she wouldn't worry anymore about me.

"I'm going to treat the family tonight," I said, trying to change the subject. "We can order some takeout for supper and I'll pay for it."

* * * *

When I walked up to my room, Vincent appeared.

"You didn't keep your word," I said, pointing at him. "I wanted to see your wound, but you didn't wake me up. You put me to bed!"

"Tori, you really needed to sleep."

"Thank you for being considerate, but I really wanted to help you with that wound," I declared, caressing his left hand.

"I know."

"So why did you ignore what I wanted?"

"Because you're human. You needed sleep so that you wouldn't get a sore throat or something," he answered. "I care about you. I'm twenty billion years old and I have been cut before. However—" He broke off and rolled up his gold-stained sleeve. The gold blood remained.

"Why didn't you clean it?" I asked, confusion filling me. "Dried blood is uncomfortable."

"So you could see it," he said.

My chest tightened and I almost cried. "I love you."

"I love you, too."

I was so confused. How could he do that? Why would he leave that crap on his arm? I hadn't sensed any impatient spirit energy while I was sleeping.

"Sit down on the wing chair," I said, walking into the bathroom to gather all the supplies I needed to care for Vincent's wounds. Once I had everything, I knelt down beside the wing chair. It was strange to clean blood off an angel.

"I didn't think spirits could bleed," I confessed.

"I wish I couldn't."

How could he have let himself suffer for me? That dried blood was terrible on his skin.

Suddenly, I cried. Warm, energy-filled hands lifted my chin and his golden eyes stared at me.

He wiped my face with a gentle tissue. "What's wrong?"

I stopped crying. "I can't believe you left that pinching gore just for me."

"I promised you could care for me. I'm not human. You have weaknesses and I have to care for them," he murmured.

"I feel ashamed."

His eyes were filled with compassion. "Why?"

"I think my admiration for you is more carnal. I'm worried that's the only reason that I love you," I said, looking down at his injured arm.

"That's not all," he assured me softly. He swept my hair behind my ears. "We're friends, Tori. Your compassion for others hooks me, but don't imagine that I'm not attracted to your beauty."

CHAPTER TWENTY-FIVE

THE NEXT EVENING, I planned to go bowling with Amber, Cindy, Kristen, and Elizabeth. Vincent and I usually talked when I drove my Mustang, and I was looking forward to his company. Shortly after six o'clock, I put on my jacket and walked downstairs. William and Stephen were playing video games at the computer in the family room while Mom and Dad watched television. I walked into the family room to say goodbye.

"Bye, boys," I announced.

"Bye, Tori," William and Stephen called.

Mom paused the DVD and gazed at me. "Where's Vincent?"

"I don't know. He'll probably appear in the car," I answered. Mom didn't have to worry about me because she could see my Guardian. That was a luxury only fifty or fewer women on earth had.

I waved goodbye, and headed outside.

Michael appeared and walked me to the front door. "Tori, be careful," he said. "The roads are icy."

I stared at him in surprise. "Thanks."

I looked back toward the family room, really wanting to ask the angels why Vincent hadn't shown himself. Instead, I walked out to my car and opened the door. Disappointment filled me when Vincent didn't appear.

I drove for five minutes and passed the municipal dump. An intersection was coming up. When I was about a hundred feet from the stop sign, I began to brake, but the car didn't stop and I slid past the sign. My heart slammed inside me. I was in a lethal area in the middle of the road. My breath quickened and I wondered where Vincent was. A car was coming, so I tried to accelerate, but my car skidded violently to the right. While the car was sliding, I smelt sulphur and my body trembled. Terror tore through me as I thought of demons and worried about getting hit.

"Are you scared now?" Odium's voice hissed. The demon had appeared beside me, and he was laughing. The wicked noise made me shriek.

"Vincent!" I yelled.

Suddenly the car whirled onto the shoulder and I was safe. My teeth were chattering and my body quaked, but Odium was gone. The interior of the car warmed and Vincent appeared, emitting a severe golden glow. I wanted to curse, so I didn't ask him where in the universe he had been earlier. He remained in angel form.

"Are you okay?" he asked, anxiety twisting across his face.

I wanted to respond to his concern, but he hadn't been with me and I'd been scared. I glared at him. I had grown used to having him around to protect me.

"Why weren't you in the car with me?" I asked.

"I was outside the car. I pushed it onto the shoulder."

"But why didn't you hang on so it didn't fly into the intersection?"

He clenched his exquisite teeth, "I wasn't allowed to."

I opened my mouth and was going to say something rude, but I bit my lip to stop myself. Then Vincent took human form and looked angry, his forehead furrowing.

"Does God want me to die?" I asked.

"No."

"So why did I have to be scared?"

"You're human, Tori. Sometimes scary things are going to happen."

"But you're my Guardian," I insisted as I turned to face him. "You always protect me."

"Just because you can see me and we are friends doesn't mean you won't be hurt or scared," he said calmly. He put his hands on my shoulders. "It's the consequence of being on earth. You're not greater than the other humans."

Annoyance consumed me and I lifted my shoulders to make him remove his hands. "Thank you for pushing my car onto the shoulder," I said.

"You're welcome," he replied softly. The wrinkles in his forehead disappeared.

"I don't need you now," I said quietly.

He tried to hug me, but I pulled away. "Do your heavenly mission. Michael always gets annoyed when we're friendly with each other. Go ahead and vanish. That way, you won't have to argue with the other Guardians."

His human form started to glow. "Tori, I didn't want you to be terrified. I love you, but I couldn't show myself. You would have known something was wrong. I was furious!"

I laughed. His golden eyes were stabbing into me. "I have to accept life and not believe I'm excluded from fear and pain," I said, turning away from Vincent. "Maybe if I can't see you, I'll stop expecting special protection."

"Tori," he whispered, caressing my hand.

"Go away," I said harshly.

The golden glow vanished. When I put my signal on, I pulled off the shoulder and back onto the road.

* * * *

In the Smithington bowling alley, Amber, Cindy, Elizabeth, and I lined up for rental shoes. Four Eastern European men in their twenties or thirties were watching us. After some time, the shortest one glided over to Amber.

"Hey, hottie," he said, staring at her shirt.

"God help us all," Cindy muttered near me.

"Maybe they belong to Kristen," I whispered.

Kristen had been sitting near our lane and walked over to the counter. "Roderick, can you hurry?" she asked the shoe attendant.

"Sure, Miss Petrovich," the thin attendant replied, stuttering. He turned to us. "Sizes, ladies?" A chunk of brown hair dropped like mud over his left eye. He didn't look at Kristen.

"Nine," I said, feeling one of the European men gazing at me. I shivered and took a deep breath, forcing myself not to look back.

When I picked up the size-nine pair, I sensed a foreboding presence behind me. As I tried walking to our lane, a man seized my arm. I turned to look at him and found the European man staring intently at me. It was the man who had just been staring at me. His dark brown eyes were watching me darkly, making my blood pump faster. Kristen stalked over and said something to the man in Russian. At once, he let go of me. My pulse slowed as Kristen took my arm.

"Do they belong to your dad?" I gasped.

"No, but I figured they knew Russian. They started staring at us when Roderick said my last name. They're probably scared of my dad. Either that or they're wannabies."

I didn't want to look at my assailant, but I hoped our other friends were okay so I gazed behind me at the other girls. The shortest man was harassing Amber.

"Isn't there somewhere else you should be right now?" Amber asked sarcastically.

"Boys, look at that red-lettered sign over the door. Obey it!" Cindy ordered and took Amber and Elizabeth by the arm, pulling them away.

My body trembled and I sat down on the bench behind our lane. We put our rental shoes on as Kristen pulled shoes with white, rhinestone-encrusted ribbons as laces from a bag. We stared at her.

"They're rhinestones," Kristen stated.

After my friends and I had put our shoes on, Amber stood up. "I want to go first. Let's go in alphabetical order." We all smiled at her as she typed our names into the computer. Then she stepped up to the lane and picked out a pink ball. Nine pins fell on her first shot.

*   *   *   *

After we finished four games, my friends and I got up and paid Roderick.

"I can't believe you got a perfect score, Tori," Amber said as we left.

"Roderick probably tilted the floor for her," Cindy spoke while grinning wickedly.

I shook my head. "Nah. He likes Kristen."

As my friends got into their cars, I walked slowly through the parking lot, thinking about Vincent. I really wished I hadn't told him to go away. I had been really stupid and spoiled. After all, my Guardian didn't want me to get hurt and he had seemed angry that I'd been scared. As I approached my car, the tall European man from inside the bowling alley appeared from beside a nearby car.

"Do you want to get a drink?" he asked, walking toward me. His accent was thick.

"No, thanks," I said. I took my car key from my wallet. Fear accumulated in my body.

"You're old enough for liquor, right?" he asked, pushing my hair away from my shoulder.

"Yes," I answered and backed away.

Why is he touching me?

I realized I wouldn't be able to get into my vehicle, so I pushed the key back into my wallet. Vincent wasn't going to appear, I knew—I had told him I didn't need him, and he had told me I wasn't greater than the other humans. I had trouble understanding why I had a Guardian at all. I wanted to go inside the bowling alley, but I didn't think I would be able to get there. We were all alone out here. Maybe if I was nice to this guy, I could get away.

"I'm sorry for what my Russian friend said," I announced, looking up at him. His eyes were too dark.

How can I distract him? Ideas shot through my head as I saw lust in his eyes. I knew he wasn't going to allow me to get into my car, so the best alternative was to go back into the bowling alley. "Do you want to bowl?"

"No," he answered darkly.

Stupid Guardian! I thought, biting my lip. This man wanted to hurt me. *Maybe I should get a drink with him. That way, at least I'll stay in public.*

Abruptly, he grabbed my arm and yanked me against himself. The blood in my body was racing.

"Help!" I shrieked.

He cursed. Squirming, I tried to attack his groin with my boots, but he threw me onto the asphalt. Dark, odious eyes pierced me, causing my body to shiver. I didn't want him to rape me! I crawled backward, hoping someone else would come outside and see me struggling. When I tried to stand, the stranger knocked me down and crouched over me, smirking. Panic and pain raced through me.

"Vincent, help me!" I yelled, but the man pushed his cold hand over my mouth. The icy, damp asphalt hurt my head as my attacker forced me against the ground.

"Don't," he hissed, shaking his head.

Trembling, I bit his hand and tried to shove him, but he pinned my mittens onto the icy ground, swearing at me. Hate for me lunged out of his eyes and I knew if Vincent didn't show up, I would be brutalized. Tears trailed past my temples and into my hair.

Radiance lit up the air around me, causing my attacker to look up. Vincent stood magnificently in angel form. His wings rose, unfurled and burning behind him as he gripped his sword. My attacker was shocked. Swearing, he fell over me, gaped at the golden spirit, and tried to stand. The man's legs wobbled, but when Vincent pointed his angelic broadsword at the evil man he turned and fled.

My Guardian's furious eyes turned to me and compassion began to fill them. Then he squatted and picked me up. His muscular arms cradled me while I sobbed uncontrollably.

Vincent quietly walked me back to my Mustang and unlocked the passenger door. Gripping his arm, I couldn't bear to let go of him.

"No," I murmured, shaking my head. As long as the angel held me, I was safe. His warmth was beginning to comfort me and I was grateful that he had come to my rescue.

"Poor girl," Vincent said hoarsely. I sniffled and stared at him.

"He was going to..." I started to speak, but then trailed off. I didn't really want to talk about the assault.

"I promise I won't allow anyone to hurt you like that," Vincent whispered huskily. Pleasure filled me when his warm hand rose and caressed my cheek. My eyelids were heavy and being so close to the angel made me want to sleep.

Vincent gently placed me on the passenger seat and closed the door. Then he appeared on the driver's side and took human form. Remembering my anger with Vincent earlier, I trembled. He had rescued me, but I didn't know how he felt about how I had acted earlier. Vincent started the car and squealed the tires as he left the lot.

"Are you okay?" he whispered.

Relief surged through me when I realized Vincent wasn't angry. I was consumed with guilt. "Yes... I'm sorry for everything. Please forgive me." I gripped his free hand. "You hurt me when you said I was no greater than any other human, but it's true. In my defence, I was terrified." He stroked the top of my hand. "Why did you help me get all those strikes?" I asked. I was sure the angel had helped me.

"I love you and I wanted you to succeed. I also wanted to give you something. It's not your fault that you expect me to care for you all the time. We're friends and I'm a spirit, so I have extra strength and abilities. None of this is your fault. Because you can see me, you can't help but expect me to protect you from everything. I broke the rules. Humans aren't supposed to have relationships with their Guardians. It's my fault."

Panic overwhelmed me yet again. "Are you going to vanish?" I asked with huge eyes. My breathing slowed as his intense eyes gazed at me with that golden glow.

"No," he said. "I would die."

CHAPTER TWENTY-SIX

FOUR DAYS LATER, I sensed demons while Vincent and I stepped out of a variety store in Smithington.

At that moment, a black pick-up truck passed us slowly and I shivered painfully as it went by. I looked up at Vincent. His eyes glowed fiercely and he gripped my waist with both hands.

"What's going on?" I asked, filling with panic.

"Demons," he uttered. His graveness stoked my anxiety.

"Vincent, you're glowing. You better stop," I declared.

Just then, I heard young men laughing nearby and the pressure and warmth of Vincent's hold on my waist grew stronger.

"Oww," I complained. He loosened his grip.

Fifty metres away, there was a menacing, mixed race group walking toward us wearing green bandanas. Sergeants were sitting on their shoulders, pointing at us. The sight of the demons terrified me.

"I'm going to fly you home," Vincent announced.

"No. Someone might see us," I said. I looked back at the gang again and then pulled Vincent along the sidewalk. "Come this way."

The eerie black pick-up drove beside us again, but I ignored it and ran down a side street. Squealing tires complained behind us, and without warning the dark pick-up swept onto the sidewalk in front of us. Odium laughed from the driver's seat.

Then the Strong Man vanished from the truck and took demon form right in front of us. His scaly, muscled body sparked. As I coughed, Odium drew his dangerous blade. I knew that Vincent could handle Odium, but I worried about the demons I had seen with the bandana-headed gang.

Fear raced through me as Vincent and the demon fenced each other. I realized that if the gang showed up, Vincent wouldn't be able to protect me. I heard laughing and I spun, seeing the gang on their way toward us. I trembled but tried to calm down.

"Hit her!" one sergeant encouraged, yellow saliva churning in its mouth. Suddenly, a masculine hand soared through the air and punched me in the face. Pain throbbed in my jaw and I dropped to the sidewalk, falling unconscious.

*   *   *   *

When I heard the sergeant yell, I whirled and was about to appear in front of Tori, but Odium's cutlass pierced my left arm. Roaring, I punched him and he flew down onto the sidewalk. Golden blood flowed from my wound. When I gazed at Tori, I saw she had already been assaulted. Her body was lying on the sidewalk.

"Entertain him!" Odium called to the sergeants as he rose from the cement. My enemy threw his shoulders back and smirked at me. Sounds of unearthly metal blades caught my attention and I saw that I was surrounded.

As the sergeants pulled demonic blades, Odium took human form and hoisted Tori up into his arms.

"No!" I yelled. Odium chuckled and strode back to the pickup truck. He dumped Tori onto the truck bed and climbed into the vehicle. Nausea encroached on me when her body dropped against the steel. As soon as Tori was in the truck, three imps—Enmity, Malice, and Pernicious—galloped after Odium and shot into the truck.

* * * *

I woke up and perceived that I was resting on dry cement. The grit on the floor scratched my wrists, neck, and hands. Cold raced into my body from the floor and I shivered.

Where am I?

My jaw burned and my head pounded. My body ached and my stomach began to growl. What was I doing on the floor, and why did my jaw hurt? While I lifted my left hand, it brushed my coat, which lay on top of me. Then I noticed my hand was dirty.

What's going on? I wondered in confusion and gazed around. *This looks like a basement.*

I remembered the demons.

Odium must have brought me here. I was unconscious and my body's really sore now. How long have I been here?

All the hairs on my body stood up and goose bumps appeared on my skin. There must have been demons nearby; this room was too cold otherwise. Anxiously, I looked around the room and noted three familiar imps playing with a handheld computer game at a steel-legged table. They were Pernicious, Enmity, and Malice!

The light pouring through three wide cellar windows helped me see. A breaker panel was on the wall across from me and there was a dirty broadsword lying on the cement five feet away. I clandestinely noted that Odium was not in the cellar.

Thank God! My pulse quickened and I started to breathe heavier. *I need that broadsword!*

I scanned the room again. If I could kill these imps, I could get away. After all, I had fought these imps once before when they appeared in my room and tried to throw me over my balcony. Taking a deep breath, I crawled to the broadsword and grasped it. The metal was so cold in my hands! I looked up at the imps to see if they noticed me—they hadn't.

I jumped up and stood, trying not to make noise. One of the imps looked at me out of the corner of his eye; the others were dedicated to the game. Immediately, I sped at the three imps and beheaded one of them—Malice, I thought. His handheld game careened onto the floor. The two remaining demons stared at me with huge red eyes and gruesome yellow fangs. They were shocked. Without warning, Odium emerged in front of me with his fists clenched. He lowered his eyes to Malice.

Then his head jerked up, and I saw him raise his fist. Then I felt the cement wall slam into me.

* * * *

As I had warred with the demons surrounding me, I thought of Tori. I had no idea what Odium was going to do with her. He had been trying to hurt her for too long, and now he had access to her—possibly for hours. Tori was supposed to have a Guardian Angel like all the other humans, but now she didn't. I knew it was my fault; there were reasons for God's rules. While panic overwhelmed me, I drew my blade and tried to kill the sergeants without hurting the humans amongst them.

Following the battle, black gore filled the alley and I knew some of the humans had fled with it on their shoes. But if I tried to hunt them down to fully clean up this mess, it would take days.

I flew for hours before sensing Odium and Tori inside a decrepit farmhouse which didn't even have a lane leading up to it. I wasn't sure where exactly Tori was, but I decided to search the basement first.

Sulphur filled my nose when I made my appearance in the basement room.

"Guardian! Guardian!"

Two imps were standing near a metal-legged table, shrieking. Their voices tortured me, like course sandpaper rubbing against skin.

I searched the cellar and found Tori splayed on the ground. There was an ugly bruise on the right side of her jaw and a huge red mark on her left temple. Her locks were dirty and spread around her head. I clenched my fists.

She's dead, I thought, squeezing the handle of my broadsword. I wanted to escape from my eternal body and this realm. *I hate earth and demons!*

While my wings ignited, I was overwhelmed with pain and anger. I roared. I swung my sword at Pernicious and Enmity, but then stopped in mid-swing when I heard Odium yell.

"Tori is not dead!"

I whirled and found the Strong Man in human form. What did he mean, she wasn't dead? My gaze passed malevolently back and forth from Odium to the imps as I raised my sword and walked over to Tori. The imps jumped into a corner and cowered. I kneeled and put my hand above Tori's face. Warm air fled from her nose, and I felt a wave of relief.

"I will allow Tori to go back the Smithington, alive of course, if you allow me to kill you," Odium declared.

Rising, I stared at him and swallowed. "Fine. When are you going to return Tori?"

The Strong Man smirked as he took demon form and grew to his full height. "Finally, I can pay you back for God turning me into a demon! Take human form, Guardian!"

I took a deep breath as fear filled me. I knew what it was like to be cut, but to die in human form... I had seen enough death to know it would be horrendous. Humans preferred to die in their sleep, but most people died painfully—whether it was a heart attack, car crash, or being murdered.

I stared over at Tori as her chest rose. "I love you," I whispered and felt tears in my eyes. No other angels knew we were in trouble. The Davenport Guardians wouldn't know that we needed help for a while yet. I glowered at Odium, my body radiating hot spirit energy.

"Wait until Tori wakes up. I want her to walk out of this basement."

Odium sneered. "You're weak and pathetic Guardian. I'm not going to wait to kill you until the other Guardians get here. Glancing at Pernicious, Odium growled, "Wake her!"

The small imp poked Tori's left arm with her dagger. I wanted to stop her, but when I reached out to halt the imp Odium commanded me to stop. Helpless, Tori groaned and opened her eyes. The Strong Man snickered.

"Tori's awake, Guardian."

Lifting my shoulders, I looked at my former friend and took human form.

* * * *

Hearing voices, I sat up and gazed at the spirits around me. Odium was towering over Vincent, who was in human form, and they were speaking to each other.

The pressure in my head was overwhelming as I tried to remember all that had happened. Odium had whacked me. How was I still alive? My left arm was sore, too. But why?

I watched as Odium raised his left arm, encrusted with amethyst jewellery, and brought it down hard on Vincent's head. My Guardian careened through the air into a cement wall.

"No!" I screamed, wanting to help Vincent. Why was he in human form?

Vincent got up gingerly and turned to Odium. I needed to help him, but I was only human. Thinking, I remembered the sword I had decapitated Malice with and I scanned the basement for it. The sword lay near the table where the imps had sat. I got up ran toward it, but I jumped back when I heard demon growls. The two remaining imps jumped on my back and clawed at my skin.

"Nice try, Tori!" Pernicious hissed.

I screamed as I fell to the cement floor. Pain filled me. *I'm only human. I can't stop these demons!* Fury at my human weakness consumed me and I grappled with the drooling, hissing imps.

Across the room, Odium kicked Vincent's abdomen and chest. Vincent groaned, but let the beating go on. I couldn't believe Vincent was allowing that!

"Stop!" I yelled.

The Strong Man smirked over at me and laughed. Grimacing, Vincent turned his head toward me. I saw despair in his blue eyes.

"What are you doing?" I screamed, clenching my fists.

"You said she could leave!" Vincent accused, lying flat on the floor.

Odium grinned wickedly at Vincent, then gazed at me. "You're right. By all means, Tori go." The Strong Man bowed.

Vincent is allowing himself to be tortured so Odium will let me go! I realized. *I won't let him do it!*

Shortly thereafter, the huge demon gripped Vincent and threw him into the air. Horrified, I saw my Guardian's body hit the ceiling beams, splintering them. Vincent's body hit the cold floor. As he screamed, I scrambled for the sword again. Plucking it up, I ran at Odium full-tilt and plunged the blade into his back. The Strong Man whirled toward me and ripped the blade's handle out of my cold hand.

"Stupid human!" Odium roared.

I stared at the black demon blood dripping from the blade.

"I'm going to kill you, Tori!" he hissed.

I backed up, staring at the bloodied sword. Odium grabbed me and lifted me off the floor until we were at the same eye level. His red eyes pierced me and his nauseating breath filled my nostrils. I stared at the smirking monster, suppressing my need to cough. The demon smiled.

"Do you know what? I'm not going to kill you." My eyes widened but he lifted the sword with his black blood on it and held it near me. "You're going to hate forever, Tori, if this blood touches you. You're going to become like me."

I glared at him and tried not tremble, but I couldn't help it. I had always wanted to go to Heaven, but instead I would go to Hell. I wanted to plead for the demon to release me, but I knew he wouldn't.

CHAPTER TWENTY-SEVEN

SUDDENLY THE BASEMENT glowed. Odium dropped me and whirled to face the light. Michael, Huan-Yue, and James stood, forming a wall between the Strong Man and my fallen Guardian.

"Thank you, God!" I cried as their warm supernatural energy comforted me. Their radiant light stole some of Odium's wicked power.

"Foolish Guardians!" Odium screeched, sulphur twisting out of his mouth. The air was yellow and smelled like a chemistry lab.

Pernicious and Enmity growled cruelly at me and then scampered away. Odium swiped at Michael with his broadsword. As the supernatural beings skirmished, I hurried to my unconscious Guardian and looked down at his mangled human body. I lowered myself, kneeling in his blood.

"No, Vincent!" I murmured, pushing my hand under his back, feeling for his injuries. "Vincent, wake up!"

I cried and shook his shoulders. Grotesque bruises covered the left side of his face and blood had run out of his mouth, which I wiped off with my sweater sleeve. I touched the bruises gently and swiped his blond hair away from his face. I felt so helpless.

"Vincent!" I screamed in his ear.

He grimaced. "Tori..."

"Open your eyes please," I pleaded, my stomach pressed to the floor beside him. I rubbed his muscled shoulder.

"I'm sorry," I murmured.

"Why did you stay?" he croaked. He tried to open his eyes, but he couldn't.

"Your friends are here. They're going to kill Odium. Can you move?"

He didn't say anything. *What do I do?*

"Can you take angel form, Vincent?" Vincent's eyes remained closed. "Please don't die!" I hugged him tight, unconcerned about the blood that was getting all over me. "I love you..."

His body started getting hotter, but his eyes stayed closed.

"Vincent, are you better? Tell me you are," I pleaded, my head flat against his chest.

In a moment, he stirred and I raised my head. His golden eyes opened and stared right at me.

I gasped. "Do you have pain?"

"I'm tired, but I'll be okay," he spoke. He was glowing now, too. Slowly, he sat up and his wings emerged.

"Thank God!" I exclaimed.

Vincent came to his feet, holding onto the wall for support, and stared anxiously at the blood on my clothes.

"Are you all right, Tori?"

I pulled on my sweater. "Most of this blood is yours." Then I noticed a big rip in the left arm of my sweater, as well as all kinds of claw holes.

Once he was feeling better, he helped me up. "I'm all right, but you need help."

He swept me up into his arms and turned so we could see our friends.

James and Michael were in the heat of battle with Odium while Huan-Yue chased the two imps. Pernicious seized Huan-Yue's leg as I watched, piercing her spirit flesh and then started to bite her. Grimacing, Huan-Yue drew her angelic blade, but Enmity jumped onto her sword arm and mocked the angel.

I looked up at Vincent. "Help the other Guardians," I urged.

He reluctantly set me down, drew his iridescent broadsword, and joined the fray.

Huan-Yue shook Enmity off her arm and he fell. She swung at Pernicious next, and the irritating imp fell back as the Guardian sliced her right arm off. Cursing, she fled into a black corner of the basement. Enmity stuck around, but James left Odium and swung his sword low, decapitating the imp. Enmity's dark body evaporated.

Odium made a stab at Michael. Golden blood flowed from Michael's abdomen and he desperately pressed his hands against the wound. I saw pain in his face! His body began to glow brighter, and then he vanished entirely.

The Strong Man laughed, but Huan-Yue and James advanced to take the Archangel's place. Odium was about to launch himself at them when his eyes snapped wide and he stopped in place. Vincent stood behind him, his sword covered with black gore. Then Odium's head rolled free of his neck and bounced onto the floor. The demon's body evaporated.

Pernicious jumped out of the corner. "You can't guard Tori when you're in Israel, Vincent!" She shook her fists at the Guardians, then vanished.

The Guardian Angels turned and observed me with anxiety in their golden eyes. Vincent walked away from them and lifted me back up into his muscular arms.

"Is Michael going to be okay?" I asked anxiously.

Vincent's glowing eyes stared at me. "I think so."

"Where did he go?"

"To Heaven, where he's safe."

As Vincent carried me up the dark, rotten stairs, I looked into his tense face. Huan-Yue and James followed us. Upstairs, the house was bare but incredibly dusty. It reeked like mould and large spider webs hung from doorways, cupboards, and ceilings.

Vincent stepped outside onto the broken porch, then looked into my eyes. "You have to go to the hospital, Tori."

*   *   *   *

At Smithington Memorial Hospital, I rested my head against Vincent's firm shoulder. His warm energy seeped through my skin and calmed me. The other people in the waiting room stared at my bloodied face and shirt, which had holes in it from the imps' claws. I was sure I looked pitiful.

An older woman sat down next me. Her eyes widened and then she gave Vincent the evil eye. Embarrassed, I pushed my face into Vincent's jacket. I was glad that my hair was long enough to hide some of the holes in my shirt.

Twenty minutes later, two police officers walked into the emergency room and a tall, red-haired nurse in triage pointed them toward us. The policemen frowned and strode over.

"Victoria Davenport?" the stouter officer asked.

"Yes," I responded.

"I'm Constable Walker. You were kidnapped this morning?"

The other officer dragged a pad of paper out of his winter coat.

"Yes, sir," I answered.

The constable frowned and looked at Vincent. "We would like to examine the farmhouse. Why didn't you call an ambulance? She looks badly banged up."

"I don't have a cell phone," Vincent responded honestly.

"You did the right thing then. She definitely needs to be seen." The constable stretched his arms widely. "There are a lot of people in this waiting room today. I'm going to get a doctor to see you faster, Miss Davenport."

"Thank you," I answered gratefully as both policemen strode to the nurses' station.

Before long, the red-headed nurse called my name.

I swallowed and stood, feeling uncomfortable being covered with blood and having to walk through this waiting room in front of all these people. I felt Vincent carefully take my hand. Smiling, I looked upward and saw his beautiful eyes. I realized my Guardian understood that I felt embarrassed.

"You're beautiful," he murmured and stroked my hand with his thumb.

When we walked to the desk, the red-haired nurse gasped.

"I know I look terrible, but I got hit in the jaw and thrown against a wall," I explained. I gestured at the claw holes in my shirt. "My kidnapper's... pets didn't like me."

The nurse breathed in. "Your health card."

My eyes widened. I didn't have my card and I opened my mouth to explain this.

"Your purse," Vincent whispered.

"Thank you." I smiled, taking the purse as I looked into his distressed eyes. "What's the matter—?"

I was worried there were more demons around, but that wasn't it. It was obviously because I looked so bad. Vincent had flown me to the hospital so quickly that I hadn't had the chance to see for myself what Odium and the gang had done to my body.

I lowered my head and searched for the health card which I gave to the nurse. "Dr. Manning is going to see you, Victoria," she said after she entered my information into the computer.

"Can Vincent come?" I asked.

"Of course."

She led the way toward one of the exam rooms.

*   *   *   *

"You're not going to stay up late," I said while we flew Tori back to the Davenport home.

"You're really hot," she whispered.

I closed my eyes, realizing that's where the excess heat was coming from. It was from anger. Every time I looked at her, all I could think about was what Odium had done to her. The Strong Man had never hurt her so visibly before.

Even though we weren't at the house yet, we descended toward the ground, Tori's long hair raced up and teased my face. We landed at the side of a gravel road and James and Huan-Yue emerged in angel form next to us.

"I'm burning her accidentally," I explained to James.

James gestured for me to hand her over. "I'll take her the rest of the way. Come here, human," he said, picking her up. Her legs and hair draped over his brown arms. Irrationally, I felt a stab of jealousy at the sight of him holding her. My gorgeous human belonged to me!

The two Guardians took off into the air and I followed behind.

Five minutes later, we landed on the wooden balcony of the Davenport house and I opened Tori's French doors. James placed Tori on the couch.

"Get better, Tori," he said, his golden eyes glowing compassionately. Then James vanished.

"Check her over to see if I burned her," I ordered Huan-Yue, my spirit form vibrating. I was having a difficult time controlling myself. But if I took human form, I would have no self-control. I didn't trust myself to take the risk.

"Don't look, Vincent," Huan-Yue said softly, beckoning to Tori. My human followed her as she glided into the walk-in closet and closed the door behind them.

Time seemed to stretch on and on as I waited for them to come back out. Because I was twenty billion years old, earth hours were meaningless, but the more I took human form the more I felt the passage of time.

"Huan-Yue!" I called, the impatience of waiting just thirty seconds overwhelming me.

"Oh no," I heard the angel say.

Shame and fear raced through my energy-throbbing form faster than blood pumped through the human heart.

"Be still," Huan-Yue ordered and I heard Tori let out a painful groan.

"Hey!" I shouted. "What are you doing, Huan-Yue?"

"She needs ointment, Vincent. Her skin's burned on her shoulders, arms, back, and also under her knees."

Salty tears issued around my eyes and I squeezed the platinum hilt of my blade. I was consumed with guilt.

*   *   *   *

Later, after Tori brushed her teeth, Huan-Yue vanished. My fingers fisted when I stared at my human's bruised jaw.

"I'm sorry," I murmured hoarsely.

"Vincent, your strong empathy made you burn me. It was an accident. It's not your fault."

"It was anger, Tori. I'm so human. Before I showed myself to you, I had so much self-control. Even when the Roman soldiers pushed the crown of thorns onto the Lord's head, I stopped Michael from killing them because God had made his decision."

"But if you never showed yourself, I would have died on the cement floor in that old farmhouse," Tori said softly. "No one would have found me."

"Odium wouldn't have kidnapped you if you weren't friends with me," I replied tersely. Tori sunk onto the edge of her mattress and wept. I hugged her. "I'm sorry... I'm your Guardian Angel, but I love you so much. When I thought the Strong Man had murdered you, I was overwhelmed with grief and anger."

Tori squeezed me strongly. "I love you, too."

"Lay down," I said. "I want you to go to sleep."

She obeyed. "Please don't go over to my chair. Will you stay here tonight, and take human form?"

Once again, I felt my self-control diminish.

"Can I see the burn behind your knees?" I asked, rubbing her hand.

She nodded, then pulled her flannel pants up over her supple calves.

"I'm so sorry," I whispered when she turned onto her side and I saw the damaged skin. I clenched my fists, wanting to touch her but knowing I could hurt her if I did. Swiftly, Tori rolled over and kissed me.

"Stay away from me. I might burn you."

*　　*　　*　　*

I didn't enjoy thinking about the thousands of years I had spent being a Guardian Angel. There were too many memories and I was getting too old. But that night, in the darkness of Tori's bedroom, thinking about my failure in the Garden of Eden was better than facing my present ineptitude.

Pain and frustration had overwhelmed me after Eve disobeyed. It had hurt so badly not to be able to interfere in her choices. She had run and talked to Adam, to offer him the fruit she had tasted. There had been nothing Michael could do to stop Adam, and I knew my friend was furious.

When the sun set that evening, I hid in the forest even though I was the Creator's favourite. God beckoned his creations that night. I watched from afar, trembling terribly. I was favoured, but I had failed. The humans had to leave Eden...

After the Creator evicted Adam and Eve from the garden, Michael and I bowed low. My face was two inches from the ground. The Creator's robe rustled as it caressed the grass. When I stood up, God's fiery form was crying. My chest was tight and I felt weak.

"I'm sorry. I failed," I murmured, looking down at the grass. I could feel Michael's outrage beside me, so I glanced at my friend. His golden energy raced through his body and into his wings.

"We didn't fail!" Michael hissed, drawing his sword. "Those new creatures made a choice!"

"Michael, you have to control your anger!" my Lord exclaimed, his eyes wide and shooting bright light. Then he became pensive. "I have plans."

Michael shook his head and swiped his sword. "They're no better than fallen angels!"

"Guardian!" God bellowed. Golden spirit vapour lifted from his iridescent robe while his eyes and hands blew petrifying, fiery energy. Our Lord was furious with Michael's rebellious attitude. Quaking, my dark-haired friend fell to his knees, dropping his sword.

"Forgive me, Holy God."

The Creator stared down at Michael seriously and then smiled. "Guardians, I want you to shield Adam and Eve until they die. After they die, you will guard other humans. One day, you will both be grateful for humans. I promise."

CHAPTER TWENTY-EIGHT

WHEN HE APPEARED in Hell, Odium stared at his thin black arms, incredulously. *Where are my muscles? Oh no, I've been demoted!*

"I'm an imp!" he shrieked. He started to pace. "How is it that I was demoted so far for simply dying?"

Reaching behind his back, he stroked his crumpled wings. A curse bubbled from his mouth and he drooled. Yellow saliva evaporated as soon as it hit the hot ledge he stood on. Then he raised his hands to inspect his horns.

"Nooo!" he whined mournfully. His horns were barely horns at all. They were insignificant and only an inch high. He quivered while the sounds of screaming souls pierced his onyx ears. He needed to speak to his prince.

The former Strong Man rubbed his hands together and walked toward a massive rift. Below, seas of tormented souls were being flayed. He used to terrify the lost souls by just appearing in front of them. A cacophony of screams rang out below him and he cursed again. Higher-ranking demons could try to rip his skin off and cut him now that he was only an imp.

He clambered up rocks and then tried to fly. As wrinkly as his wings were, they worked. He soared up through sulphuric clouds, swerving away from ledges until he came to an arch where black fog billowed. He tiptoed through the arch and into the dark room beyond. Losing his footing, he stumbled forward and sprawled to the ground in front of a huge demon. His heart beat hard.

"Get away from me, Odium!" a roar issued and Odium flew back into a hot wall.

Pain and heat pierced his back. Odium knew now that the huge demon was his prince. None of the other demons would have known yet about his loss of rank. Blood oozed from Odium's back, but he struggled to keep quiet. He didn't want to display weakness. Trembling and consumed with rage, Odium stood on his own feet, but the wall had already burned his open flesh. Grimacing, he strode to his prince's throne and bowed low.

"My liege."

The great demon snarled.

"I am unworthy to request anything, but you will benefit... Master... from my proposition more than I will."

"What do you want, pathetic imp?" the prince roared.

Odium shivered. "Vincent is close to sinning. He lusts for Tori."

"What of it?"

"Make me a Strong Man again and I will make sure Vincent sins and becomes a demon. Then you, my prince, can have revenge on him for betraying you in Heaven."

The great demon blew sulphuric vapours at Odium. His red eyes narrowed as he clenched his fists.

"Vincent," the prince hissed, looking off into the cave. "You're pathetic, Odium. How many times did your imps try to kill the girl?" He pointed a scaly finger at Odium. "Vincent was only ever eight feet tall! How does a former Archangel like you get bested by an eight-foot Guardian?"

The prince folded his arms angrily and Odium cringed back, afraid of what he might do next.

"I used to be the most handsome angel in Heaven," the prince continued. "I do want to be able to kick that perfect angel. Fine, Odium. I will give you one more chance."

Immediately, Odium felt supernatural energy pouring into him. He grew, more than tripling in size.

"Yes!" he roared and vanished from Hell.

*   *   *   *

That evening, when I was in the family room, Vincent emerged in a snowsuit with black and white checks on the shoulders.

"Let's go tobogganing, Tori," Vincent said, grinning.

"Sure," I said and rose.

"Hey, Tori and Vincent!" William called.

I spun. "Vincent and I are going to Grandpa and Grandma's hill."

"Can Cassandra and I come?" he asked. "She's home this weekend from university."

I felt a slice of disappointment, because I wanted to be alone with Vincent.

As we talked, Stephen ambled into the family room and placed an expensive engineering textbook on the seat of a wing chair.

"We're all going tobogganing," I told him.

He smiled. "In that case, I'm coming!"

After picking up Cassandra and Barbara, all six of us drove to my grandparents' farm. We stopped the van on the gravel lane beside the barn. I jumped out and ran over to the house. My grandpa unlocked the screen door and grinned. His eyes danced.

"May we go tobogganing on your hill, Grandpa?"

"Of course," he said. "Good to see you, Vincent."

"Hello, sir," Vincent replied. He placed his muscular arm around my waist and I grinned up at him. After that, I turned and watched my brothers and their girlfriends as they walked toward the house.

"I'm making dumplings and soup for supper," my grandmother said, gracefully strolling up to the screen door. "Please come in after you're done out there."

We waved goodbye, then walked toward the hill.

"Last year, after we had freezing rain, the snow got really hard and I sliced my arm when I fell off the toboggan," I announced.

The girls' eyebrows rose.

"On the cornstalks?" Cassandra questioned. Even with this much snow, we had to be careful not to hurt ourselves on the leftover cornstalks sticking up out of the snow cover.

"No," I answered. "On some wicked ice."

* * * *

"Can we ride together?" Tori asked when we got to the top of the hill and looked down the slope.

I drew her close to me and grinned. "Sure. Now it's my turn to hold you."

Her eyes shone with excitement as I took the toboggan. "I used to have sleigh riding parties in high school," she said. "Were you there?"

"Of course. I had to put up with other guys wrapping their arms around you."

"That bothered you?" she asked.

"The first time I wanted to talk to you, you were seventeen. But I noticed how pretty you were. Are you disgusted by that?" I asked, afraid she would turn against me.

"No," she whispered. She removed my glove and caressed my hand. Her touch calmed me and I relished the affection.

* * * *

When we were done tobogganing, we all walked back to my grand-parents' house. My brothers and their girlfriends opened the kitchen door and the warm air flushed over me. After removing my boots, I massaged my frigid toes. Vincent crouched near me.

"I'll help," he offered. He cupped my feet in his hands and I felt them warm quickly.

"I love you," he whispered.

His blue eyes turned golden and I could tell he wanted to kiss me. The thought caused my heart to pound.

Suddenly, William appeared. "Come on, guys!" he beckoned.

Vincent and I walked into the warm kitchen where my grand-mother was working with the girls. Grandpa and my brothers sat in the small sitting room adjacent the kitchen.

"Mrs. MacKay, can I assist you?" Vincent questioned. Grandma glanced at him.

"Sit with the men," I said softly, looking up at him. He hesitated. "You are the Creator's servant and I wish to pamper you."

I kissed his cheek.

Then, placing my hands on his shoulders, I murmured in his ear, "Angel, I'll have to kiss you if you don't sit down. I can't help Grandma if I can't think."

Vincent grinned and walked over to a recliner.

* * * *

It was the end of November and I really wanted to put the Christmas lights up. I hadn't known Vincent was my Guardian the year before, but this year I had him to help me. My brothers and I usually put up the lights, but William was working too many hours and Stephen was in his final year in university. I didn't want to wait until a free weekend.

"Vincent," I called.

Suddenly, the being I was in love with stood in front of me and smiled warmly.

"I want to put up the outside lights and I need your help," I said.

"Sure, I wanted to carry the boxes for you," he said. "I was about to take human form."

William and Stephen usually brought out the ladder for the star on the pole light and for the lights on the blue spruce trees, but I was capable of hanging the rest. We had metres and metres of coloured outdoor lights to hang around the spirea hedge. I had wound the lights around large pieces of cardboard to keep them from getting tangled, but we still had a few knots to work out.

The two of us started to sing Christmas carols. His voice was beautiful, but I knew he was being thoughtful not to drown out my pathetic human voice. Except for God's laugh, all sounds were weak compared to an angel's singing voice.

"Kristen is having a Christmas party," I reported, "but she asked Amber to be Nikolai's escort this time."

Vincent laughed, then stared at me gravely. "If I have to be exiled, please don't date possessed men."

"Did God say you have to go to Israel?" I asked, panicking. My pulse sped up.

"No, but Michael warns me about it a lot. I love you. Angels can't love humans."

"You didn't even try to love me," I said with frustration.

"It was okay for me to help you in the parking lot, but I shouldn't have deliberately allowed you to see me in human form again after that. I didn't try to love you, but... if I get exiled, I can't protect you." I noticed that his eyes and skin weren't glowing. Most of the time, there was a brightness around the edge of his body—even in human form.

"How could a Guardian Angel love me, Vincent?" I asked.

"I love you because you are so compassionate. I've watched you since you were conceived. I have always been proud of you. I see you give extra attention to your patients. You treat them like family... giving some water even when they don't ask, for instance. I see you hug them and comfort them. You give of yourself to make their world better. I'm proud when difficult patients respond to you and not to others. You're beautiful. You can heal through God. You're brave and stand up to demons. You tease, you laugh, you're not proud, and Tori, you love the Creator and me."

"Wow," I murmured, feeling tears spring from my eyes. "Can we imagine that you're not going to get exiled?"

He put his hands around my waist.

"This is my favourite holiday," I whispered.

"Sure, Tori." The angel's voice cracked.

*   *   *   *

At seven o'clock the next evening, I was leaning against the medication cart at work when the room suddenly felt warmer. I heard quiet thudding nearby; it was the sound of the outside doors closing. I thought the pharmacy driver had arrived.

A thin blond tress fell against my ear, teasing it. As I checked the residents' medications, I sensed someone coming. I expected the pharmacy driver to ask me for a signature, so I turned. Abruptly, I found myself facing a fat man with a brown stocking over his face and a black toque. Fear ripped through me like a race car.

"I want your drugs," he said grimly.

Naturally, I scanned the man for firearms. Seeing none, I said, "You should try a pharmacy."

"All nursing homes have narcotics."

I felt furious and I clenched my hands, forcing my fingernails into my palms.

"These drugs aren't worth stealing!" I exclaimed. His eyebrows descended over light eyes and a squashed nose. "A pharmacy would be better."

Suddenly, the man body-checked me. I managed to keep myself upright, but I jolted into the side of the medication cart.

"I want the drugs," he hissed, leaning over me. My heart beat fiercely inside my chest and I couldn't breathe. Trembling, I forced my fingers into my uniform pocket and seized the nurses' keys. I was sweating slightly and wasn't able to find the narcotics key.

"Are you stupid?" he growled.

"No!" I snapped.

I hated when people hollered at me. I could feel Vincent behind me and wondered why the spirit didn't show his angel form to make this stranger leave.

All at once, Carla, a health care aide, walked by. She stared at the man, her eyes widening. Her brown hands landed on her hips.

"What do you want?" she asked, infuriated.

The stocking-shrouded face turned to regard her. "Sit down!" he commanded, pointing at the front desk.

"If you don't go, I'm calling the police," Carla said, lifting her chin. When she spoke, the man pulled a large gun from his cargo pants. Then he grasped my upper arm, his nails digging into my flesh. I grimaced.

"Sit down or this girl is going to hospital—or Hell!" He swung my body while Carla watched. The squashed-nosed face looked at me and growled, "Give me what I asked for!"

"I'm not going to Hell," I hissed defiantly. I shivered, all the hairs on my body standing up. Anxiety consumed me. The gun was against my temple.

"Please, let go of me." When I spoke, the maniac forced the chilly barrel even harder against my head. "Help me," I whispered.

CHAPTER TWENTY-NINE

FRANTICALLY, I LOOKED for the Death Angel. I put my hand between Tori's temple and the barrel, wishing she didn't have to feel the cold metal against her skin. I glared at the thief, feeling myself glow stronger. The steel narcotic drawer opened and Tori grasped a handful of pill cards. Some spilled onto the floor tiles. The stranger let out a curse.

Tori's teeth were chattering loudly. The Creator wouldn't let me show my angel form or my human form. Frustration consumed me because I was a Guardian Angel who obeyed, but I loved Tori. Killing demons was easy, but being powerless was not. This evening it was as if I was nothing more than a paralyzed human being. I couldn't even kick the intruder out of Cedarwood. My fists clenched. The broadsword irritated my right thigh and I felt the need to throw it, but I didn't; I needed this weapon.

Without warning, wide red eyes gaped at me; an onyx demon emerged behind the bandit. Its four-inch black claws penetrated the man's down-stuffed winter coat. It was Pernicious. She hissed at me, her red orbs glowing.

Pernicious leaned her head near the thief's ear and murmured, "Shoot the girl!"

Tori shivered and scanned the medication room; I knew she could sense Pernicious. I stared over at the gun against her temple, and then at the man who smiled as if he liked the imp's idea.

No one is going to shoot Tori!

I drew my broadsword, but the demon vanished. My eyes narrowed and I wanted nothing more than to leave the medication room and chase after her—but I was Tori's angel. I needed to get that gun away from her head.

I leaned over to the gunman and spoke, "Bud, take your drugs and get out of here. You don't want to hurt the girl."

His jaw dropped as he looked around, but the most important detail was that his gun veered away.

Tori raised her right leg and kicked the distracted intruder in the stomach. He fell on the hard floor and Carla picked up the gun. Shivering, Tori ran straight through me and called 911.

*　*　*　*

"Hello, I need the police," I said to the 911 switchboard operator. As the line transferred, it was quiet.

"Hello," a calm male voice spoke. "Police."

"I'm calling from Cedarwood Manor, 40 Hancock Street, Smithington. A huge man came in at 7:00 p.m. and demanded narcotics. He had a gun, but he's on the floor. My health care aide is pointing the pistol at him right now. Please hurry."

"Two officers are on their way. Don't shoot him," the officer instructed.

"Of course not," I answered and hung up the phone.

My body started trembling. At that moment, Vincent walked through the front doors in human form and I stared at him, feeling exhausted. He looked at me compassionately and put his muscular arms around me.

* * * *

When I looked down at the bandit on the carpet, I felt my eyes heat and become golden. I frowned at the man, then crouched near him and whispered, "Don't harm the nurse again or you'll roast in the abyss." As I spoke, I leaned on his shoulder.

"Your hand's hot!" he screamed. He ogled me when I removed my hand. He was mesmerized by my radiating eyes. "Are you a demon?"

I smirked. "I'm a Guardian Angel."

"Fine, I won't hurt the nurse," he vowed, his voice wavering.

Then I disappeared and reappeared, this time in the Cedarwood backyard. I fell on the ground and spoke to God.

"My Lord, forgive me... forgive me... I can't accept being Tori's Guardian. I love her... I want to slay every spirit or human who harms her." I thought of the thief again. Guilt hounded me like a cloud that followed me everywhere I went.

Angels don't sin, I told myself. *Unfortunately, I've spent so much time in human form that I'm too human now.*

* * * *

I was absolutely shocked when Vincent disappeared.

Where did he go? I still need him!

The thief watched me gravely from where he remained on the carpet. "Sorry," he murmured softly. His eyes looked guilty.

I frowned, not knowing why he had said that.

* * * *

At eleven o'clock that evening, I opened the doors and walked out into the night. As I stepped off the Cedarwood porch, I rubbed my boot on the hard mix of snow and ice on the sidewalk.

I looked up, hearing a vehicle approaching from the parking lot. I was shocked when my Mustang drove into the driveway and stopped beside me. My huge eyes returned to normal size when I saw that it was Vincent. I walked to the passenger side, feeling his blue eyes regarding me.

"I took your key ring," he explained.

I grinned at him. "Thanks. I'm so tired, Vincent."

* * * *

When I woke up, my flannel sheet and blankets were draped over me and light snuck around my room's darkener blinds. I gazed beside me and found Vincent's exquisite smile and blue eyes looking back at me. He was sitting on the floor peacefully.

"Why didn't you sit in my chair?" I asked.

"I really had to be close to you."

"You could sit on my bed," I teased.

"Too close," he murmured seriously. His eyes started to radiate while he regarded me. "I'm feeling less self-control."

"Oh... why didn't you help me at Cedarwood and scare the thief away?"

"I wasn't allowed to show any form."

"Why?"

His glowing eyes were consumed with compassion, regret, and love. I pushed the covers off and sat on the edge of my bed.

"What time is it?" I asked.

"Seven o'clock."

I climbed down on the floor beside him and pulled my knees up

"The Creator wants you to grow," Vincent said. "That's why I couldn't show myself today or the night when you went bowling with your friends. If I guard you from everything, you'll be too weak. You won't be able to make decisions or be able to stand up for others or yourself."

"Demons are the only beings who call me weak," I whispered softly, looking at the floor.

He seized my hand. "I was so angry when I wasn't allowed to stop that thief. I put my spirit hand against your temple as soon as he pointed his gun there. You just didn't feel it."

Vincent's eyes glowed at me and my breath caught. Fascination and awe filled me as they always did when his eyes became golden.

"I was looking for the Death Angel," he continued. "If I had seen him, I might have murdered the thief and vanished with you."

"You can't disobey!" I said, surprised. I caressed his shoulder.

His golden eyes smouldered. "I struggle with my commitment to the Creator," he whispered.

Once again, I was surprised. I touched his cheek with my fingers. When I stared at him, my fingers slipped down to the carpet. I was so enthralled with what he was saying that my sense of touch didn't register. I saw his eyes radiating golden light and my heart galloped.

I knew at once that Vincent wanted to kiss me. As soon as his lips touched my mouth, I felt his warmth spread across my face.

"Don't disobey the Creator," I whispered against his cheek.

CHAPTER THIRTY

LATER THAT NIGHT, I laid on my back with my head resting on my flannel pillowcase. My legs were covered with a green woollen blanket and I was reading a nursing book from college. When I felt peace in the room, I smiled to myself.

"Do you want to go skating, princess?"

It was Vincent again, standing beside the bed. I placed the book on my mattress, turned my head, and looked at him.

"The coyotes might be out," I said.

Vincent's perfect forehead wrinkled. "I'm a Guardian, Tori. I think I can handle it."

"I sometimes hear them in the middle of the night," I murmured. But I couldn't help but smile at his serious, intensely handsome face. "Guardians are only eight-feet tall. I think I need a Warrior or Archangel to protect me from wildlife."

He appeared taken aback and I felt guilty for teasing him.

"I'm sorry. I was just teasing," I said. I touched the t-shirt fabric on his muscled arm. "Vincent, I need you to be my Guardian Angel. You're the only angel I require." His smouldering blue eyes became golden and I became afraid. Was he angry with me? Goosebumps rose on my arms.

Without warning, he lifted me off the bed and kissed me hard and deep.

* * * *

It was nearly midnight when Vincent and I landed in the woods near my grandparents' house.

"No yelling," Vincent whispered mischievously.

The light of the full moon reflected off the snow, brightening the sky. Trees formed a dark barrier around us. My eyes fearfully scanned the snow at the edge of the bush. I didn't like to go skating or tobog-ganing when it was so dark.

All at once, I heard an eerie howl in the bush. Vincent smiled at me.

"None of God's creations frighten me," he said softly, and I knew he was reassuring me.

"Even when you take human form?" I asked.

"Human form has weaknesses," he admitted. Then he let out a sigh. "In human form, I feel human emotions. Sometimes fear bothers me, but I can take angel form very quickly. As a result, I'm not worried about my human form... just yours."

* * * *

Pernicious and Calamity stared at the fearful coyotes. The shivering animals growled as they hunched under ground cover and narrowed their yellow, glowing eyes. The two grotesque imps had used spirit energy to prevent the wild dogs from departing.

Pernicious let out a hiss and jabbed the coyotes with her blade. They started to howl and Calamity stuck her tongue out at the beasts. Pernicious gazed at her dagger and then plunged it into her own arm in an act of evil fascination. Demon flesh withered immediately when the rusty dagger cut into it. Then she rubbed the resulting gore on the coyotes.

"It's amazing what demon blood can do," she hissed.

* * * *

Vincent and I walked into the woods and I sat down near a frozen pond. I had decided to forget about the coyotes and just enjoy Vincent.

Once we had our skates on, Vincent held my hand as we glided onto the pond. We danced and I arched my back, enjoying the air skimming through my hair. I wished the Creator would let him continue to guard me forever.

Vincent spun me with one hand and I dreamed that I was a professional figure skater. When I finished twirling, we moved with our arms spread and my back to him. Vincent grasped my hands firmly.

"Thank you, Vincent," I told him. "This is amazing,"

His glowing blue eyes stared at me and my breath caught in my throat. My chest was tight and I felt lightheaded.

Suddenly, Vincent started to radiate golden light and he looked behind us. His blue eyes narrowed.

I frowned. "What's wrong?"

"There are imps in your grandparents' woods," he announced.

My heart started beating faster. Seeing how worried I was, Vincent picked me up and skated to the edge of the pond. His human form chest and arms were hard. When he put me down, my body trembled severely. He took angel form then, his spirit energy making me sweat.

Just then, a pack of coyotes launched themselves out of the trees, running toward us. Branches cracked and snow crunched under their weight. I stared at the wild dogs with eerie eyes, and I was terrified. They growled at me, but Vincent's golden energy kept them at bay.

Pernicious, Calamity, and a few sergeants appeared next to Vincent. The imps chewed violently at his spirit legs and the sergeants tried to stab him. The wicked imps pulled rusty daggers and slashed at Vincent's lower body while the sergeants targeted his chest and back.

But they hadn't gone after me, and I wondered why. Not for the first time, I wished I had a broadsword of my own!

While Vincent sliced and feinted, I regarded the coyotes and noticed the black gore on their fur.

No! It's demon blood!

If that demon blood got on me, I was going to hate forever and go to Hell when I died. Despite the ongoing attack, I stayed as close to Vincent as I could; his spirit energy almost seared me. The sergeants and imps swiped at me with their blades when they got close enough.

A flash of brilliance from Vincent made me take a backward step, and then another. Forgetting the coyotes, I ventured too far. When Vincent saw where I had gone, he whipped his head around and shouted a warning.

But it was too late. The coyotes had me surrounded.

Before they could attack, however, Calamity appeared and grabbed me by the arm. I gasped as her long black claws penetrated the nylon and polyester fabric of my coat. She threw me hard into the shadowed snow. I tried to jump up, but the wicked creature drove her rusty dagger at my face. I turned my head just in time and the blade whistled past me. Her feral growls filled me with terror.

I felt her back away then, just long enough for one of the coyotes to leap onto my stomach. I let out a scream!

"Bye, Tori," I heard Calamity hiss at me.

I stared up at the coyote's gigantic fangs. Demon blood dripped from the animal onto my coat. The thought of going to Hell was worse than being killed by a wild animal, and a part of me hoped they would just kill me and get it over with.

I tried turning my head to see how Vincent was faring, and saw three sergeants jump him. He lost his sword in the struggle, but I didn't have time to worry about him. If I could only get away from the coyotes long enough to get to Vincent's sword...

The coyote above me growled and bit my arm. Pain exploded through my body and I let out another scream. Calamity jumped up and down by my feet, mocking me, and I tried kicking her. One of those kicks finally connected, and Calamity's shriek ricocheted in the winter air. She suddenly vanished—

An extreme golden flash forced me to slam my eyes closed.

What was that? I wondered, still feeling the weight of the coyote on my chest. I worried about the demon blood again and cracked open an eyelid just long enough to see an iridescent blade lance through the animal's abdomen, killing it.

*   *   *   *

After Tori and I got back from the hospital, I held her and nestled my face against hers, the scent of her perfume sweeping all around me. I enjoyed the sensation of her smooth hair touching my face.

"Thank you for saving me," she murmured, leaning back.

My chest hurt, but I still wanted to hold her. "I'm glad I could. I love you so much."

She turned in my arms and looked at me seriously. "I love you, too. Are you going to be okay?"

"Yeah, but I hope I don't have to fight demons for awhile."

CHAPTER THIRTY-ONE

THE NEXT DAY, Vincent and I worked on Christmas cookies. When we were finished, I pulled him into the linen closet upstairs.

Vincent's eyes glowed. "What are you doing?" he asked.

I sensed the presence of another Guardian outside the closet door, and I was sure it was Michael. He had been glaring at Vincent and me all morning. I felt rebellious but hoped that the other Guardian wouldn't appear in the closet with us.

"He knows we're in here," Vincent whispered in my ear. His humid breath caressed my ear while I watched the doorknob nervously.

*   *   *   *

Pernicious and Odium appeared near the bedroom of Frederick and Marianne Davenport. The imp appeared a bit too close to the ceiling, and she fell to the hardwood floor. Strong Men were able to control exactly where they appeared, but not imps like her. She felt envious of him.

She bared her yellow teeth. Odium wouldn't let her murder Tori, because he wanted to make both her and Vincent go to Hell. Fury consumed her; she wanted to be a sergeant so that she could look human sometimes. Eighteen billion years ago, she had been a six-foot angel with a four-foot broadsword and blond locks that draped and curled to the back of her knees.

She shook her head and tried to forget her desires.

Without warning, she noticed Michael nearby. The righteous but flawed spike-haired Guardian turned golden and began to glow with radiant light. Pernicious pulled her rusty dagger and vanished, appearing on the north side of the hall, openly mocking the Guardian.

She screamed grotesquely as Michael caught her. His sword tore at her demon skin and black gore spread across her back. The smell of her own blood made her furious. She then vanished, leaving Odium to fight the Guardian Angel alone.

*　*　*　*

Odium growled and hissed at Michael.

"Catch me, Guardian," he taunted, his red eyes narrowing. As Michael sped toward him, Odium disappeared and re-emerged on the stairs. Michael vaulted magnificently after him over the railing.

Odium took a sharp turn into the kitchen, where Marianne Davenport was cutting out tree cookies. He pulled his blade and appeared directly behind her.

Marianne shivered, sniffing the air. Obviously, she sensed something. The wicked Strong Man held his blade to her neck and smirked at Michael when the Guardian flew into the room. The angel was livid.

*　*　*　*

Marianne frowned. She sensed the hate behind her and suddenly saw Michael's light in the air near the entrance of the kitchen. She tried to turn around, but a voice whispered, "Don't, woman!"

She froze, paralyzed with fear.

Unexpectedly, Michael allowed her to see him in all his splendour. It was a shock, but his appearance also brought her a deep sense of peace.

"Leave her alone!" Michael ordered.

Who is he talking to? Marianne wondered.

A voice behind her guffawed arrogantly. "Get a life, Guardian."

Still frozen, she stared at her Guardian. "Michael..." she murmured.

"It's okay," Michael said softly.

Abruptly, she felt a cool blade against the skin of her neck, accompanied by a burning sensation. She squirmed in pain as the smell of death overwhelmed her.

"God, help me!" she whispered.

* * * *

The night before, I had a dream that Vincent was exiled to Israel and I woke up overwhelmed with depression. I knew Vincent was going to be exiled and I rebelliously wanted to do something more passionate with him before he was gone for good.

Now, as we stood together in the closet, I realized my chance had come. Ignoring the guilt that tickled my stomach, I put Vincent's hands around my waist and started kissing him. I expected Vincent to walk out of the closet, but he didn't. His angelic lips swept over mine like a storm, almost causing his spirit energy to ignite. I had to stop briefly to catch a quick breath. His muscled body was hot and I pulled back slightly, but he didn't notice. Instead, his lips journeyed along my neck and a moan forced itself out of my mouth. When he pulled me closer again, my body felt weak and my heart pounded.

Why do you have to be an angel?

Vincent's hands sped up my back, and with that I knew he was serious. I had wondered why he didn't leave the closet, but understanding finally slammed into my brain that he desired me at least as much as I wanted him. He was a Guardian Angel, which meant I was going to suffer when I died. It was sinful to damn oneself, but it was unforgivable to damn an angel. If we went any further, my beloved would become a demon!

I frantically pushed his muscular chest away. "Stop!" I exclaimed.

His glowing eyes observed me. Our forms were too close. I could feel his body, but I was afraid of God.

"I'm sorry," I said, looking away. His eyes were too powerful.

"Tori," he whispered and lifted my face. "Don't forget, I have a choice."

"You *want* to be a demon?"

"No," he whispered and glanced down. Fear slid through me; he *never* looked down. "I have the same emotions you do, Tori. I love you."

I swallowed and reached my hand for the doorknob.

"Wait, Tori." His fingers gently took my arm. "I'm sorry."

"Don't believe I didn't want to be yours," I told him, tears in my eyes. "But I can't turn you into a demon, and I love the Creator."

His sad blue eyes stared at me. "I have spent so much time in human form that I've been consumed by human feelings."

*　*　*　*

Odium watched fiery-winged Michael in the kitchen doorway. Grabbing Marianne Davenport had only been intended to serve as a distraction to get Michael away from Tori and Vincent, but the longer the spike-haired Guardian challenged him, the more the Strong Man wanted to reawaken the angel's painful memories.

Humans and angels are both so weak and pathetic, Odium thought. His red eyes narrowed. He had pleaded with his prince to give him back his Strong Man body, so he couldn't fail now.

Odium bent down near Marianne's ear. "I'm sorry, human," he muttered.

With that, he slit her throat. Blood poured out onto the counter-top as Marianne collapsed, shock and confusion apparent in her eyes. Grinning, the demon turned to Michael.

"No!" Michael roared, igniting with golden light. He propelled himself at Odium, but before the two clashed, Odium smiled, released Marianne's limp body, and vanished.

A moment later, he arrived in Hell. He clenched his fists and hoped that he had indeed been successful in distracting Michael long enough for Vincent and Tori to commit a sin together.

He shook his head and roared.

*   *   *   *

As Tori and I emerged from the closet, her brother Stephen raced up the stairs noisily, yelling for her. Her brother, winded, stopped just long enough to seize her wrist, then pulled her in the direction of the stairs.

"Tori! Get down here... it's Mom! She's... dying... you can... help her," he gasped.

"What!?" Tori exclaimed as Stephen hauled her downstairs.

Gabriella hovered at the top of the stairs, tears rolling down her face. "Marianne's dead," she wept. "Odium cut her throat."

I felt supernatural energy race throughout my body as I took spirit form. My anger toward Odium caused my wings to ignite.

"No!"

I flew down the stairs after Tori, who was already kneeling on the floor of the kitchen, surrounded by a pool of blood. She squatted next to Marianne's body.

"Mama, mama. Open your eyes!" Tori cried. She shook her mother, but then I saw a being no Guardian Angel wanted to see—the Death Angel.

* * * *

Mom's throat was cut! She was bleeding so badly.

Who could have done this!? Everyone loves my mom!

"Call 911, Stephen!" I ordered. William sat on the floor, staring at Mom and me. "Will, I need a clean towel!"

My brother's blue-gray eyes stared at me as if I had spoken in Cantonese.

"Will! Get me a towel, please," I pleaded. Tears fell down my cheeks, landing on Mom and the kitchen floor, where they mingled with the growing pool of blood. Will handed me a towel and I applied pressure to her sliced throat with one hand, knowing it wasn't going to work.

Frantically, I tried to find a pulse, but I couldn't. I was too afraid to do CPR, worried that the compressions would only force more blood out of the severed arteries in her neck. Instead, I tilted her head and tried mouth-to-mouth, but her chest wouldn't rise and I realized that her wind pipe was probably severed, too. Moaning, I collapsed beside her and prayed. My prayers for God to heal my family worked before.

I sat up, then felt warm energy behind me and around my chest.

"Vincent," I sobbed. His energy had been absent when I came into the kitchen, but now he was embracing me. He was doing one of the tasks assigned to Guardians—comforting his human in times of grief.

Suddenly, I heard wheels sliding across our hardwood foyer. The paramedics had come.

"What happened?" a man asked.

"I don't know. I just found Mom's throat cut, ten minutes ago," Stephen said.

Ten minutes? Has it been that long?

I stared up at the paramedics, and then I saw an angel that I didn't know. I shivered as his golden eyes pierced me.

The Death Angel!

"Go away, please," I pleaded. "You can't have Mom." Even from several feet away, I felt his compassion; it was so strong. The Death Angel had his hand out.

Does he want me to go over there?

Then, I saw Mom's spirit rise. Her spirit lifted from her body and walked to him. I knew there was the nothing the paramedics could do. Nobody could save her. My mom was gone! Despair filled me. The pressure built in my chest and I felt dizzy.

"I couldn't save her," I muttered, and blacked out.

*   *   *   *

In angel form, I sat in Tori's pink wing chair, fidgeting. We were both restless. She had finally fallen asleep, hours after I'd flown her back from the hospital. The doctor had said Tori was in a state of shock. Just now, she groaned in her bed and changed positions.

I really wanted to go outside, so I vanished from her room and appeared on her balcony so I would still be close by. The snow was eight inches deep on the wooden balcony, but it had stopped snowing now.

Suddenly, the balcony glowed brighter and I looked beside me. Michael had appeared at my side.

"Are you okay?" I asked.

"No!" he snapped.

"Did you know Tori and I went into the closet?"

"Yeah, thanks. It's your fault that Marianne died. Your desire got a human killed. You're going to be exiled for this! There's a reason angels aren't supposed to love humans!"

"I'm sorry, Michael," I said. I was so ashamed.

At once, a Messenger emerged in angel form and I realized that God wanted to see me. I swallowed and clenched my fists, looking down. I deserved exile, but I didn't want to leave Tori. Breathing deeply, I glanced over at the Messenger. I had to accept the exile I knew was coming.

"Hello, John," I greeted him. John, the six-foot Messenger Angel, gazed up at me solemnly. "God wants to see me now?"

"Yes, my friend," John answered.

Panic and regret consumed me. I knew I might never see Tori again and I honestly didn't want to see how badly I had hurt the Creator.

When John disappeared, I jerked my head and tried to look through the French doors at Tori.

"One hundred years isn't so long, Vincent," Michael said. "Maybe God will come back to earth soon and your exile will be shortened."

I looked at my friend sadly. "Going to Israel doesn't bother me. But it might destroy me to be away from her, especially when she marries and eventually dies."

* * * *

A minute later, I was kneeling in front of the most powerful spirit in the universe—God Himself. Despite my conflicting fear of punishment and my joy to see God again, I breathed in deep.

Ahhh, Heaven, I thought fondly. The atmosphere was pure and clean... but the chatter of the angels who attended God was absent. His attendants had left and I was alone with my Master. God and I were close, but I had broken the rules. The Creator had always been clear that angels who disobeyed were subject to punishment. The battle in Israel was intense with demon strife.

"Angel, you broke a rule," God said softly.

My head was bent and I shifted my feet. "My Lord, I am sorry." I would never regret loving Tori, but I would always regret disobeying God. I had never wanted to hurt my Master.

"You were wilful and made a choice," God said firmly.

"Tori was so... it was so easy to be her friend, and then I fell in love with her."

"I am fond of that human myself."

I gazed up at Him, surprised. "You always made the right choices up here," the Creator stated.

"It wasn't hard to say no to trying to overthrow you, God."

"You didn't want more power," God said. "You always seemed content to serve me. But I know it was hard to lose a friendship."

"Yes, my Lord," I answered.

"Is there anything you want?" God asked.

"To not go to Israel."

"Think about the one wish I promised you, Vincent. Think about what you want while you are in Israel. You can come to Heaven whenever you decide what you want."

"Yes," I said softly.

"Vincent, I don't want to exile you, but there have to be consequences."

"Can I see Tori to say goodbye?" I asked.

"Yes, Vincent."

I looked up again. "How long is she going to live on earth?"

God frowned. "Angel, I don't talk about those things."

"I'm worried about her protection... and about her being lonely."

"Tori will be happy. Michael is going to guard her," God answered.

Concern flowed through me, because Michael and Tori clashed so much.

"Who is she going to marry?" I asked.

God frowned again and the glow around Him increased. His eyes emitted golden radiance.

I lowered my head once more and swallowed. "I'm sorry. I realize I can't know but..." Groaning, I shook my head. "I want to go to Israel, to get it over with."

"Goodbye, Vincent."

"Goodbye, my Lord."

*   *   *   *

A small angel stared at the Creator after Vincent disappeared.

"My Lord, why are you sad?" the small angel asked.

"Vincent does not realize that I gave him a powerful choice. I knew he would want to be with Tori. I gave him a wish so that he *could* be with her. In actuality, I formed that human specifically for him."

"But why didn't you make him human?"

"At the beginning, I needed him here."

The angel's glowing eyes were huge with incredulity. "You planned for him and Tori to love each other?"

"Yes," the immortal Creator answered softly. "But Vincent has to request that I make him human."

*   *   *   *

The morning after my mother died, I climbed up onto the widow's walk, crying. Michael had appeared in my wing chair that morning and immediately my chest hurt intensely, knowing what his presence meant. Vincent had been exiled. Michael's wings had blazed and I had been able to feel his rage, directed toward me. My new Guardian was frustrated with me more than ever, now that his friend had been sent to Israel.

I looked down at my hands, scowling. I had not been able to save Mom. Any supernatural power I possessed had been worthless to her. I was subject to the Creator's will, just like my exiled Guardian, who I was sure I wouldn't see again.

But I still had free will. If I jumped off this roof, I was sure Michael wouldn't stop me.

I wept as I walked to the steepest part of the roof. Both Mom and Vincent hadn't said goodbye. My chest was tight and I couldn't breathe. Stepping off the widow's walk, I clenched my fists, trying to work up the courage to jump.

Without warning, I lost my balance on the snowy roof and fell. Before I could go over the edge, I was roughly yanked backward into the arms of a warm being who picked me up and flew me gently down to the safety of my balcony.

I squirmed, not wanting to face Michael again. "Michael, let me—"

"It's me," a hoarse voice whispered into my ear. He was angry!

At once, I looked up into Vincent's golden eyes. He was glowering at me and his forehead was furrowed.

"I don't want to celebrate my Master's birthday by thinking about you lying in a hole!" he exclaimed.

"You know that souls don't stay in the ground!"

"No. But if you kill yourself, Odium and Pernicious will flay your skin in Hell forever," Vincent warned seriously. I trembled, but his frown disappeared and he caressed my cheek. Tears appeared in his eyes, which turned blue. I felt relieved, knowing that his temper had faded.

Vincent pulled me toward him and his lips kissed mine softly.

"I love you, Tori."

Coming Soon

EXILED

NEXT IN THE GUARDIANS SERIES